# DEMON'S REVENGE

## HIGH DEMON SERIES, BOOK FIVE

## CONNIE SUTTLE

Print Second Edition (2018)
Print ISBN: 1-63478-066-3
Print ISBN-13: 978-1-63478-066-7
eBook ISBN: 1-93975-908-0
eBook ISBN-13: 978-1-93975-908-5



Published by:
SubtleDemon Publishing, LLC
PO Box 95696
Oklahoma City, OK 73143

Cover art by Renee Barratt @ The Cover Counts

*To Walter, Joe, Larry, Lee, Dianne, Sarah and Mark.*
*Thank you.*

# ACKNOWLEDGMENTS

As always, this book is the result of collaboration. If it weren't for the support of my editor, my cover artist and my beta readers, it would be less than it is. All mistakes, as usual, are mine and no other's.

About the Author:
Connie Suttle lives in Oklahoma with her husband and a conglomerate of cats. They have finally banded together to make their demands, which has proven disconcerting to all humans involved.

You may find Connie in the following ways:
Facebook: Connie Suttle Author
Twitter: @subtledemon
Website and Blog: subtledemon.com

*Blood Destiny Series:*

Blood Wager

Blood Passage

Blood Sense

Blood Domination

Blood Royal

Blood Queen

Blood Rebellion

Blood War

Blood Redemption

Blood Reunion

Blood Destiny Series Boxed Set (Books 1-10)

Blood Recall

Blood Alliance*

*Legend of the Ir'Indicti Series:*

Bumble

Shadowed

Target

Vendetta

Destroyer

Legend of the Ir'Inditi Boxed Set

*High Demon Series:*

Demon Lost

Demon Revealed

Demon's King

Demon's Quest

Demon's Revenge

Demon's Dream

*God Wars Series:*

Blood Double

Blood Trouble

Blood Revolution

Blood Love

Blood Finale

*Saa Thalarr Series:*

Hope and Vengeance

Wyvern and Company

Observe and Protect*

*First Ordinance Series:*

Finder

Keeper

BlackWing

SpellBreaker

WhiteWing

~

*R-D Series:*

Cloud Dust

Cloud Invasion

Cloud Rebel

~

*Latter Day Demons Series:*

Hot Demon in the City

A Demon's Work is Never Done

A Demon's Due

~

*Seattle Elementals Series:*

Your Money's Worth

Worth Your While*

~

*BlackWing Pirates Series*

MindSighted

MindMage

MindRogue

MindMaster*

~

*Black Rose Sorceress Series*

The Rose Mark

Rose and Thorn

Black Rose Queen

Queen of Thorns and Roses

*Future Wars Series*

Buffer Zone

Black Zone*

*Other Titles from SubtleDemon Publishing:*

Malefactor

Transgressor

Underhanded*

by Joe Scholes

*Forthcoming

# CHAPTER 1

*O*6:22:5376—RA
      *Tory:*

*Today your twin daughters were born and they are beautiful. I was hoping you'd come to see them when they were new and innocent. Your father says you are busy and can't come. I am trying to understand that. King Jayd has already prepared a list of suitable mates, but Glinda and I have both demanded final approval. I have also asked your mother, Queen Lissa, to write to you as well, so you will likely receive correspondence from her. Vid-images enclosed. Hope you are well—Reah.*


*01:15:5377—RA*

      *Tory:*

*I was hoping to have heard from you by now. Your father, Gardevik, along with your uncle, King Jayd, and your aunt, Queen Glinda, are planning a trip to Surnath in two weeks. They have asked to take the girls with them. I have given permission. I hope you greet your daughters with the love and respect they deserve—Reah.*

      *07:07:5378—RA*

      *Torevik:*

*Today your second set of twin daughters were born. Lissa says she explained to you that Kifirin manipulated this pregnancy, taking your seed and fertilizing my egg while we both slept. Kifirin knows I am angry that he interfered in this way, but he has been curiously absent since then. Most likely not wishing to hear my thoughts on the matter. I was also hoping to hear from you at least for Tara and Raedah's birthday. I try to explain to them that they have a real father and that he is busy and lives elsewhere. Of course, they are too young to understand at this age, but they will question one day. What shall I tell them, Torevik? In the meantime, Lara and Kara, our newborns, are doing fine. Vid-images enclosed—Reah.*

*09:27:5380—RA*

*Torevik:*

*Our third set of twin daughters was born this morning after a difficult labor and birth. Karzac is waiting for me to finish this message to you before placing the healing sleep. Dara and Sara are doing well. Vid-images enclosed —Reah.*

*09:27:5380—RA*

*Tory, I am disappointed in you. Reah almost bled out delivering Dara and Sara. Karzac believes that it may have been similar to the situation Reah's mother faced when Reah was born, only Raedah's was worsened by the drug administered. I cannot understand why you refuse to respond to message after message your father and I have sent to you over the past day and a half. Somehow, you have transferred this unfounded hatred you have for Reah onto your daughters, and I find that unforgivable. I have threatened Kifirin and he has promised not to force another pregnancy on Reah without her consent. In the meantime, your firstborn are now four turns old, the second set two. You have only seen them at your father's insistence. Have you discarded all your family as well as your common sense? I hope Darletta is everything you ever hoped for and can make up for six little girls who don't recognize their father.*

*Your mother—Lissa*

*06:22:5396—RA*

*Torevik:*

*Today your eldest turned twenty and your youngest will be sixteen soon. Lissa and I have been arguing with your father and your uncle, King Jayd, asking that the claiming date for our eldest to be put off. I fear we are waging a losing battle in this matter. Philavik Weth and Rindavik Foth are impatient, it seems, and do not wish to postpone it. They keep promising that they will allow Raedah and Tara to finish their medical studies. Both are currently working with Karzac and will have their medical certification in five years if all goes as planned. Of course, I have difficulty believing anything a High Demon male promises. You should know why—Reah.*

*P.S. Vid-images enclosed.*


*08:29:5400—RA*

"Reah, its Dee."

"Dee, I can see your face on my comp-vid." I could; he was smiling at me. I wasn't smiling back. "What does the lord and master need this time?" I asked. Teeg never called to ask or tell me anything; he always told Dee to do it. Likely, it was some ball, banquet or state event that required a wife on his arm.

"Reah," Dee sighed.

"You know it's true. He can't seem to find five ticks to ask me himself. He tells you to do it. And I don't get to pick out my own dresses, shoes or anything. Those two floozies he calls assistants do it for him." My temper was rising and it wasn't Dee who deserved my wrath.

"They're not floozies. They work hard for both of us."

"I'm sure they do. Feel free to dress one or both of them up and send them off with Teeg San Gerxon. I'm sure everybody is gossiping about it anyway."

"You could live here if you wanted."

"When do I have time? I run the gishi fruit groves here on Kifirin, and Garde insists on sending me Crown employees injured or disabled elsewhere and then expects me to care for them or find work they can do in a limited capacity. I have to stretch every credit I get to cover expenses here, while all the profits go straight to the palace. And then I go to Desh's or Dee's twice a week to make sure everything is good and work over the menus and the financials with Radolf and Fes. That doesn't include the calls I get from my twenty-year-old twins; Garde insisted on sending them to that private college, yet I'm the one they complain to when they think they aren't kept well enough there."

"Perhaps you need some time to yourself," Dee suggested quietly. I realized he was trying to calm me, but that wasn't likely to happen.

"Teeg can't spare a few ticks to call me, but I can drop everything and fling on a dress and smile and say nothing to diplomats, Kings and rulers from across the Campiaan Alliance, just like the empty-headed twit they all think I am." I realized I should stop talking. Dee wasn't smiling any longer.

"Reah, the people who matter know better than that."

"I almost said what people who matter. I'll be honest with you, in case you haven't read the latest chapter in this book, all right? Teeg and Lendill are caught up in pirates and rebellions across both Alliances. Lok and Aurelius are too busy chasing after Ra'Ak spawn to even send mindspeech. Radolf went into a female cycle ten years ago and now he and Ilvan are together whenever Radolf isn't working at Dee's and Ilvan isn't cooking for Queen Lissa on Le-Ath Veronis. Farzi and Nenzi are knee-deep in keeping the farms and fields going on Campiaa, and Nefrigar shows up one night a month. For a woman who has eight mates, I spend most of my nights alone, Dee. Tell me why that is."

"Look, I see that things aren't going well for you at the moment. Teeg is holding the annual ball that marks the end of the conclave in three nights. If you'll be here around five bells, the hairdresser and maid will be available to help you."

"I'll be there," I grumbled, looking away. Yes, I was angry. About so many things. But mostly because I had mates who had no time for me unless they wanted sex or to keep up appearances. My daughters, all six of them, knew their father's name and little else. None had seen him in twenty-two years. The youngest had never seen him. They wrote his name on school forms when asked to do so, but that was the only purpose Torevik Rath served in their life. All of them had grown up treating Aurelius as their chosen father. He was the one they called Daddy and ran to, if he were home.

I never asked them to call him that, they'd decided on their own. Aurelius held them, dried their tears and treated the slightest of injuries as a legitimate reason to reassure and fuss. My eldest, Raedah and Tara, were less than a year from receiving their medical certifications. I was pleasantly surprised with Philavik and Rindavik—they'd allowed their wives to continue with their studies, even if they did show up in class from time to time, causing Karzac to grumble about High Demons underfoot.

Lara and Kara were nearly ready for their claiming night, although Lara begged Jayd and Garde to move hers up. Lara insisted that she and Eldevik Greth were ready and madly in love. Of course, she conveniently didn't remember how ill her older sisters had been when their claiming came. Raedah was feverish for days, while Philavik—Phil—worried and fretted the entire time. Tara had a slightly better time, but not much. Rin was just as fretful as Phil, wanting to hold Tara while she was ill. Karzac almost had to chase him away from her bedroom with a broom.

Cursing under my breath, I shut off the comp-vid and went back to walking through the southern grove of gishi trees. The fruit was almost ready, and insects would be waiting if I or another High Demon didn't walk through the groves as smaller Thifilathi or in my case, Thifilatha, to keep the tiny predators away. Yes, I'd answered Dee's call as Thifilatha and completely naked. It didn't matter; I think he was used to it by now.

~

"What is it, Garde?" I received Gardevik Rath's call the moment I stepped into the house several hours later. At least the groves were protected, now. Only the gishi fruit from Kifirin could claim that it was completely organic. Baetrah, the nearby volcano, had provided the Southern Continent on Kifirin with rich, black soil. The workers employed by the Crown tended and harvested for the most part, but I oversaw the crews, kept the records, helped the work crews out and made sure expenses were kept to a minimum. Pest control was just a sideline.

"We have everything ready at the palace for the claiming night," Garde informed me. I hoped he had everything ready. The dates he and Jayd had chosen coincided with the harvest. I would be hard pressed to divide my time during the next eight-day. Fes had called the day before, asking me to sit in on interviews with prospective assistant cooks for the new restaurant opening in Targis.

"Which healers are coming?" I asked, wearied from a full day of work. Night was falling and I was too tired to enjoy the beauty of it.

"Karzac and your father Edan are coming," Garde replied. "And they're bringing your two eldest, since they have firsthand experience with this."

"Of course," I sighed.

"And I sent word to Torevik."

"Why do you even bother?" I grumbled.

"He is still my son."

"I realize that. And still father to my daughters. Do you think he might notice them, one day?"

"Reah, I see I've caught you on a bad day. I realize the harvest is a concern right now. Next time, Jayd and I will take that into consideration."

"I'd like to say there won't be a next time, Gardevik Rath, but there will be, won't there?" There would be—he and Jayd had already selected husbands for my twenty-year-olds, with very little input from me.

"I sent another one down," Garde winced at my expression. When had it been decided that I was nursemaid to the Crown's injured?

"Who, when and how bad are they?" I snapped.

"A thirty-year-old man. Fell off the barracks roof when his crew was making repairs."

"And?"

"His back is still giving him problems."

"Of course it is. I'll try to find room. Good-bye, Garde. Unless there's other important news that just can't wait?"

"Reah, we owe you. We all acknowledge that," Garde muttered, his voice sounding less than grateful. "The gishi fruit groves are paying the bills and allowing us to repay loans. I realize we've shorted you, but that will change in a year or two. All the loans will be paid and we can redistribute the profits. Jayd is talking about dividing Tory's holdings and giving you half." I could tell Garde wasn't happy with that turn of events.

"Tell Jayd not to bother. Torevik doesn't have anything I want." I cut off the communication before Garde could say anything else.

∾

"She hung up on me." Garde slipped his comp-vid into a desk drawer and stared across the polished wood expanse at Jaydevik Rath, King of Kifirin.

"I heard." Jayd blew a cloud of smoke to show his displeasure. Not at Reah, but at the state of affairs that placed Reah in her current situation. He'd ordered Reah to oversee the gishi fruit groves. She'd suggested planting them in the first place as a potential money crop. The fruit had only been grown on one other planet before Reah experimented and grew the trees in volcanic soil from the Southern Continent. Jayd, thinking it was a foolish venture, placed Reah in charge twenty-five years earlier, while she was pregnant with her first set of twins. The trees had shot up quickly, bearing fruit within five years. Now, Kifirini gishi fruit was the biggest export the planet had. And the one that brought in the most money. Jayd saw those credit sheets himself. Loans that might have taken a century or more to pay off were now getting settled in one-fifth of that time. Everybody tightened their belts a little, but none more than Reah. She watched every credit spent on the gishi fruit groves while maintaining a fair wage for her employees.

When Garde suggested that they send some of their slightly injured state employees to Reah to sort fruit before crating and shipping, it had turned into a steady flow. Reah had been forced to ask Aurelius and some of the Saa Thalarr for help. A clinic and rows of single-story apartments now stood near Reah's small cottage. Reah depended upon assistance from Karzac, her father and two oldest daughters to treat the influx of injured over the years. Most recovered; some were permanently disabled and would never work at full capacity again. Reah found some way to stretch her budget to cover the expenses the Crown's monthly stipend couldn't afford.

"Child, I think Reah is nearly at the breaking point." Dee set a comp-vid in front of Gavril Montegue, known to the Campiaan Alliance as Teeg San Gerxon.

"These the figures for the defense budget?" Gavril ignored Dee's comment and scrolled through rows of figures instead.

"Yes."

"These pirates are killing us, Dee. Norian and Lendill are saying the same thing about the Reth Alliance. We haven't been able to track these thieves; they must have small bases on every asteroid and meteor between here and hell. And they can move in and out quickly, with lightning strikes that leave dead crews on empty ships while they get away with the cargo."

"Which they then sell to desperate buyers at ten times the price," Dee nodded.

"While we're trying to make Campiaa as self-sufficient as possible, other planets aren't moving so quickly. They think we're supposed to be the answer to all their problems," Teeg added.

"They think we can hire Karathian warlocks to track these miscreants and get rid of them."

"I wish it were that easy. Wylend says it's extremely difficult to track a moving target, especially if you don't have a name or an object in mind in order to track it. These filth are more slippery than a Darthinian eel."

"I agree. And they want to bankrupt us and send us back into martial law."

"What did you say about Reah?"

"Nothing, child."

"Daddy, he's just dead weight. We don't need him, and it will cause too much of a stir if we get rid of him the usual way. Let's just get him to sign the stupid agreement and get him out of here." Darletta paced inside her father's office.

"Have you taken care of the little problem, first?"

"I have. I'm not stupid, Daddy. I just can't figure out why he doesn't look any older than the day I married him." Darletta fumed silently for a moment. "Anyway, the documents are ready and he's going to sign as soon as I set the comp-vid in front of him. We'll send him back to mommy as a surprise."

Dantel Schuul watched his daughter. He knew she'd found a new candidate to be her lover. She'd found plenty of those while married to Tory; she'd held Torevik Rath as a plaything for twenty-five years and she'd tired of him. Dantel didn't care; he'd just force Darletta's future husbands to sign pre-marriage agreements. That would leave his daughter's wealth out of the contracts, should they divorce.

Dantel had given up his ambitions for a political career six turns earlier. His time and efforts were better spent watching over his manufacturing concerns. Meanwhile, Torevik Rath would soon be a bad memory.

Dantel had never been able to use Torevik as he'd liked. A man had come; black-haired, black-eyed and dressed in near darkness early on, threatening Dantel if he used Torevik's family or connections for political gain. Dantel normally didn't back down for anyone, but this one held a persuasion that Dantel couldn't explain or deny. Tory had remained married to Darletta, but just as she'd said, he was dead weight. Dantel thought several times over the years of killing him so Darletta could access Tory's holdings, but something always held him back. Dantel couldn't explain that, either.

"Get him to sign the agreement and put him on the first passenger ship out of here," Dantel huffed. He was done with this meeting.

"It'll be finished in less than a click," Darletta promised and oozed out of her father's office, her expensive heels clicking on wood floors that few could afford, nowadays.

～

"That's it. We're done," Darletta pulled the comp-vid away from Tory and transmitted the signed data to the state's records a short while later. "You're free. Shoo. Go away." Darletta made a dismissive motion with her hand. Torevik Rath sat and blinked at her for a moment or two.

"We're done? I'm free?"

"I said that." Something must have clicked in Tory's mind at Darletta's words. He stood, beginning to feel angry; that was something that hadn't happened in a while and he couldn't explain it. A stream of smoke curled from his nostrils. Darletta, who'd never seen that before, took a step backward. "Here's a ticket for passage to Le-Ath Veronis," She held out the small chip, her hand shaking. "Daddy wants you off the planet by the end of the day."

"I don't need a ticket," Tory snapped, disappearing right in front of Darletta Schuul.

～

"I swear I'm going after this scum myself." Lissa fumed at the dinner table. A shipment of oxberries and wine from Le-Ath Veronis had been hijacked by pirates on its way to Refizan.

"You could transport the shipments yourself," Roff suggested.

"I could. But we do a lot of shipping. Where would it end?"

"No idea. Toff sends his love and says Nissa, Yoff and Trik are well."

"Can't Glendes let go of those four so they can come home once in a while? Yoff is barely twenty, for Pete's sake."

"He says they stay busy."

"Well, busy isn't always good," Lissa pointed out as a servant placed the soup course in front of her.

"Mom, do you have a place for me? Darletta and I just got divorced." Tory stood at the entrance to Lissa's dining room.

"Tory?" Lissa rose and stared in shock at her son.

"Reah," Rylend Morphis dipped his head to me and offered his arm. As Teeg's ambassador, he'd escort me to Teeg, who was busy making small talk with this potentate or that. I'd seen Wylend off in a corner, talking with someone while Erland and Garek guarded him. Wylend had tried once, early on, to schedule a meeting between us. I'd refused. Ry had also refused a meeting with his great-grandfather. After Wyatt's death, Rylend had renounced his citizenship and went to work for his brother, Teeg. Teeg depended heavily on Ry to smooth ruffled feathers here and there among rulers and planets belonging to the Campiaan Alliance.

"Have you talked to Mom lately?" Ry asked as he led me toward Teeg.

"No. Should I?" I asked.

"Darletta and Tory are divorced. As of three days ago. Tory's on Le-Ath Veronis, now."

"I'm not surprised she didn't tell me," I said stiffly. Tory and I had nothing in common, except for six daughters and the claiming marks that still scarred the back of my neck.

"She says he wasn't feeling well when he showed up."

"I'm sorry to hear that."

"I haven't talked to him, yet. I may get some time in the next day or so to visit."

"Ry, don't ask me to go. His girls don't even know him. Whose fault is that?"

"There isn't a way to heal that hurt, is there?" Ry looked at me briefly before turning his eyes back to our path through visiting dignitaries.

"I don't think so." My answer made Rylend sigh. He was perhaps the handsomest man I'd ever seen, barring his father and Kifirin. Kifirin appeared handsome, then marred his image by doing some of the worst things imaginable. Twice I'd found him sitting on the side of my bed when I awoke. Both times it was to tell me he'd manipulated a pregnancy with Tory's seed. He'd disappeared, too, both times, before I could scream at him. I hadn't seen the Lord of the Dark Realm in twenty years. That was fine with me.

"Here's Reah, now." Teeg held out a hand as Ry handed me over. I felt like a bit of superfluous fluff, batted from one person to the next, having no real purpose in the posturing and presentation.

"Reah, this is President Drix of Avendor. Where the gishi fruit is grown." Teeg placed emphasis on gishi fruit, as if I didn't know where it was grown originally.

"I love gishi fruit," I enthused, taking President Drix's hand. It was the expected thing to do. Right then, I envied Dee because he set these things up and then refused to attend them.

I wore a black beaded gown that was nearly backless, boasting only a few narrow straps to hold the thing on; my hair was piled on my head and fastened with jeweled combs and my nails would make any wealthy woman proud. Yes, I looked like the wife of the Founder of the Campiaan Alliance, but I wished they could see me most days, wearing stained or torn trousers, flat-soled shoes and old shirts I scrounged from here and there. Why dress up when there wasn't money to buy fine clothes or shoes? Those poor souls that Garde insisted on sending to me were paid a little by the Crown, but where would the money come from if they needed clothing or supplies that couldn't be had on Kifirin? I subsidized those needs from my own pocket. Who cared what I looked like while I worked the groves? It was better knowing that the sick ones had necessities.

"I'll send you a crate of fruit," President Drix smiled.

"You're so kind," I thanked him. The rest of the night went exactly the same; meeting with this one and that while muttering inane conversation as I stood at Teeg's side. He didn't need a wife; he needed a robot that could spew the required phrases and smile tirelessly while they did it. My mind was on my middle daughters and their claiming the following week, in addition to the two trucks currently in the shop for repairs. I hoped the vehicles would be ready to haul crates of harvested fruit to the barns and that the shipping freighters would escape the pirates.

On top of that, the new one with the back injury would be coming to the groves. I had no idea where to put him. The infirmary and apartments were full and I hated to contact Adam, an Enforcer for the Saa Thalarr. He'd put up the buildings in the first place, with help from Martin Walters and a few of the others.

"Reah, it is a pleasure to meet you." The King of Gorshil was holding out his hand.

"How lovely to meet you," I dipped my head to him. Kings got a dip of the head. The gesture was respectful and often required. Then came the one I was dreading.

"King Wylend." Teeg greeted his great-grandfather. Ry had disappeared when Teeg forged his way toward Wylend.

"Teeg. Reah. So nice to see you both." Wylend nodded to both of us. Every time I saw Wylend, I wanted to weep and pound his chest. He was at the root of so much pain.

"Wylend," I dipped my head.

"Reah, have you spoken to Lissa?" Erland asked.

"Not personally, but I have heard the news." I wasn't about to drag it out here. It would only make me angry.

"I don't suppose a meeting might be arranged so Lissa and I can speak with you," Erland went on.

"I'm afraid I have no time for the next eight-day," I said. "You might contact me after that."

"Reah, don't be rude," Teeg admonished. "You may have some time with Reah tonight," he told Erland. "Reah will be here until morning."

I felt like kicking Teeg for doing this to me. What were they going to do? Try to talk me into seeing Tory? I had no desire to see him. Was he asking about his daughters, now? It was a little late for that, I think.

"We'll meet in your kitchen, perhaps?" Erland sounded hopeful.

"Contact Astralan. He'll get you in," Teeg agreed. "We'll be along as quickly as we can."

∼

"The least you could do is ask me first," I jerked my arm away from Teeg's hand later as he walked me through the tunnel connecting the San Gerxon Casino to his palace. Teeg had the tunnel built ten turns earlier. The underground passage was a safer way to get back and forth when he had to go.

"Reah, you need to hear what they have to say," Teeg growled.

"Maybe so. But do I get to make up my own mind once in a while?"

"Reah, don't."

"I could say the same to you, Teeg."

"It's half an hour of your time."

"Fine. I'm not spending the night. I have too much to do."

"You will spend the night."

"Teeg, you have guests. In your kitchen." Dee broke up the fight by appearing out of nowhere in the dimly lit tunnel.

"Thanks, Dee. I just have to convince my wife to come along."

"I see," Dee said dryly.

It wasn't just Erland and Lissa. Erland, Lissa, Garde and Wylend had come. I almost skipped away immediately. Teeg gripped my arm and growled. He knew what I was thinking.

"Sit," Teeg said. I sat. And glowered, my arms folded tightly across my chest.

"Reah, Tory is divorced from Darletta and is now home on Le-Ath Veronis," Lissa began.

"Ry told me," I muttered, refusing to look at any of them.

"Did he tell you that Tory isn't well?"

"He mentioned it."

"Torevik can't seem to remember much of the past twenty-five years," Garde said.

"That's convenient, isn't it?" I raised my head and looked Garde in the eye.

"Reah, we don't know what's causing this. He vaguely remembers Raedah and Tara, but he doesn't recall the others," Lissa said. Well, she could smell a lie. Maybe she was listening to Tory objectively. How would I know? It still made no difference to me. Tory had gone off and married Darletta because he was in a snit. Wylend had given him a half-truth, and Tory had retaliated.

"Look. It doesn't matter to me that he can't remember. It won't change things between us. I'm sorry if he's ill. If my daughters want to see him, that's their choice. They're all old enough to decide these things for themselves."

"He asked about you." Garde was blowing smoke.

"Gardevik Rath, I can blow smoke, too. Tory married Darletta. He never offered to marry me. Kifirin gave me four additional children with Tory and that was definitely not in my plans. Or Tory's. He's not obligated to them in any way."

"Reah, we know you got hurt." Erland was talking again. Hurt? That word didn't begin to describe what I was. Where was he when I was in labor, birthing three sets of twins? Of all my mates, only Nefrigar had been there all three times. I was particularly thankful he was there the last time. I'd bled. A lot. Nefrigar and Renegar managed to get it stopped. I was also thankful I hadn't gotten pregnant since then.

"I wrote to him. At the birth of all his children. Sent him vids and photographs. What happened to those? Has Karzac examined him? What does he say?" I stared across the wide kitchen island at Erland, Lissa, and Garde. I deliberately didn't include Wylend in my gaze.

"Karzac says there are unexplained gaps in Tory's memory," Lissa sighed.

"I don't believe this." I wiped my face with a shaking hand.

"He remembers what Wylend told him, and then getting back at you through Darletta afterward. But things are hazy after that," Garde said.

"He thinks all that was last week and not twenty-five years ago?" My voice was filled with sarcasm.

"He thinks only a couple of years have passed," Lissa nodded.

"Great. Perfect. Can Karzac or one of the Larentii fix it?"

"Connegar says it will be done gradually, so his Thifilathi doesn't go crazy. That's the other thing, Reah. He hasn't turned the whole time he's been married to Darletta. The Larentii told us that," Erland said.

"The full moon is two days away," Lissa said. "We wanted to warn you."

"Warn me about what?"

"That Tory's Thifilathi may come looking for you."

# CHAPTER 2

"You think he'll come looking for me?" I wanted to laugh. At all of them. Tory wouldn't come looking for me. Hadn't even before he married Darletta.

"Reah, the Thifilathi may take over when he turns, and if that happens, we think instinct will kick in. He hasn't seen his mate in more than two decades. The Thifilathi will try to rectify that." Garde was speaking again. The expert on everything High Demon—that was Gardevik Rath.

"Then I'll make arrangements to be elsewhere. He won't find me, I guarantee it."

"Reah, what if that's the worst thing that can happen? What if his Thifilathi becomes destructive if he can't find his mate?"

"Oh, that's perfect. Is this some sort of conspiracy? I assure you I don't find it amusing." I didn't. Only once before had I been in the grip of Tory's Thifilathi, and that had been for the claiming. It wasn't a pleasant experience.

"Reah, he won't hurt you, he just has to have his hands on you. Make sure you're safe."

"I am safe. And safer still, if I'm nowhere near him." I was ready to go. I had no desire to listen to any more of this.

"Reah, I know you're frightened. But it's only one night and it may help Tory in ways we can't imagine. I don't know what's at the bottom of this memory loss—Karzac says he's in perfect health otherwise," Lissa said.

"Sure. It's not you who Garde screwed over and then went off to marry somebody else, only to show up twenty-five years and six children later, with holes in his memory. Tell me you'd go willingly so he can snatch you up while in full Thifilathi, sniff you over, blow smoke and scare the crap out of you?" I was shaking, now.

"Reah, he won't harm you," Garde repeated.

"And what if he does? What then? Will you fight your son over what's left of me? Will you?"

"I've never known a male High Demon who harmed his mate," Garde blew more smoke.

"Have you heard of one having gaps in his memory?" I snapped.

"Reah, it's only one night, and only for reassurance. We can have Larentii nearby, in case it's necessary. I don't believe it will be."

"And what then?" I asked. "Let's say it all goes peachy fine. What then? I won't go back to him. It's impossible."

"Reah, Jayd can order you to do this." Garde played his trump card.

"Then Jayd can harvest the fruit next week. Jayd can see to the disabled that fill the infirmary. Jayd can pay for the medical supplies that I buy out of my own pocket. Jayd can balance the books and chase away insects and inspect the shipments and settle disputes between the workers. Jayd can see that the worker's children are getting a decent education." I stood up, ready to go.

"Reah, I didn't mean to open that can of worms," Garde said.

"And Jayd can live in a two-bedroom house and wear rags," I snapped and skipped away.

"Garde, could you fuck this up any better?" Lissa glared at her High Demon mate. "And what's this about buying medical supplies out of her pocket? Does she wear rags?"

"She never asks me for money," Teeg pointed out. "I'd give it to her if she asked."

"Her house is tiny," Dee said. "I've seen it. She goes to the workers' barracks twice a week and cooks for them. Probably pays for those meals as well."

"How do you know this?" Teeg stared at Dee.

"I went and asked questions, that's how I know. You didn't hear the conversation I had with her this afternoon. Shall I play it back for you? I recorded it on my comp-vid." Dee hauled out the comp-vid in question and ran the entire conversation for those present. Teeg cursed when Reah talked of eight mates and spending most of her nights alone.

"The harvest is next week, and Lara and Kara's claiming is scheduled right in the middle of it," Garde raked fingers through his hair.

"Let's go see if she went home or if we need to start looking for her," Teeg sighed. Lissa was the one to fold all of them to Kifirin.

~

"She was here earlier. She's out fixing a broken sprinkler line in the east grove," a man leaning on a crutch informed Garde when he asked about Reah. "She wore a fine dress when she came in. Never seen her in a dress before."

"Come on; let's go to the eastern grove." Since Garde was familiar with the area, he directed Lissa so she could fold everyone again. They found Reah, barefoot and clad in stained trousers and an old shirt, replacing a section of flexible pipe in the sprinkler. She was cursing while she did it.

~

"Reah, I can send someone to help with that," Teeg offered.

"Sure. One of the reptanoids? Or do you have farmers coming out of your ass?" I was angry and didn't care that I'd snapped at him. I got the part hooked up and went to turn on the water. Spray drenched everybody immediately. I wanted to laugh, but held it back.

"Are you ready to go back to the house?" Teeg asked. He was angry, too.

"Sure." He folded everyone to my tiny house. There wasn't enough seating for all of them—my kitchen had a small table and two chairs. No island. That lack made it difficult to cook, but then I didn't have much time for that anymore. The sitting area had a small sofa and one chair. The smallest bedroom held my office. The larger one, and it wasn't that much larger, held a bed and a dresser.

"Reah, I didn't know the house was so tiny," Garde said.

"Because I'm seldom here," I pointed out. "You've always come to the barns or out to the fields. The girls have stayed at the palace, at Jayd's insistence, once they were old enough to be educated. I had to visit them there after that. But they're family, aren't they, Garde? While I'm not."

"I told you she was nearing the breaking point," I heard Dee say.

"Get out of my house, all of you," I shouted. "Get out!"

"Raedah, we don't think your mother is doing very well right now." Lissa offered Reah's oldest daughter—by a matter of minutes only—a cup of tea. Lissa had taken everyone back to the palace on Le-Ath Veronis, leaving Reah behind.

"Mom's under a lot of stress." Raedah sighed as she slipped onto a stool at Lissa's kitchen island. "And yes, I heard that our real father came home. That can't be helping, now can it?"

"Does she really take it badly that you were raised at the palace while she lived in a small house on the plantation?" Garde asked. He was still a bit damp after the drenching in the gishi fruit grove.

"What do you think, Grampa? She came to see us every night, sometimes with dirt still under her fingernails. Our bedroom was larger than her whole house and we didn't want for anything, Aunt Glinda saw to that. Dara and Sara are making it hard for Mom now, because Mom can't send them money like the other parents do at their private school. They don't really need it, they just think they do. Everybody wants something from her, they just don't want to pay for it, or give her the care and support she deserves. If Mom had somebody like Philavik, she wouldn't be such a wreck."

"You think your mother's a wreck." Garde said it flatly.

"Yes. She worries about the groves. She worries about those people you keep sending to her to get them out of your sight. Tara, Karzac, Grampa Edan and I go once a month to check on them and do what we can. Mom has them the rest of the time. She brings family members if they ask. Goes looking for supplies or treats if they need or want them. She needs at least three assistants on that plantation. Karzac is a bear every time he comes away from there."

"Why hasn't he said anything to me?" Lissa wanted to know.

"It's not your problem, Gram. Karzac says that every time. He says he's waiting for Kifirin to pull its head out of its ass."

"Do you want to meet your father? When he's better able to handle a fully grown daughter?" Lissa asked.

"Maybe. Just to see what he's like. And I want to know why he ignored us all those years. Did he hate Mom that much?" Raedah sipped her tea. "I need to get back; I'm on call at the hospital." Raedah set her cup down.

"I'll take her back," Teeg offered. He and Raedah disappeared together.

"I need to go home," Wylend hadn't said a word until then. "Erland, if you wouldn't mind." Erland folded Wylend away.

"I don't think he hated Reah," Garde defended Tory.

"She and her daughters think otherwise," Lissa said. "What do you intend to do, Gardevik Rath? And how are we going to convince Reah to let Tory's Thifilathi approach her?"

"Teeg, I thought I told you to get out. Go back to your palace." I'd dumped a good portion of bourbon into my cup of tea. I'd need it to sleep. Teeg had appeared as I'd sat miserably in my tiny kitchen, going over the night's events. Everybody seemed so shocked that my house was tiny. That I had more of Kifirin's disabled than I could handle. That I did my own repairs to save money. I knew what was going on with them. Made it a point to do so. Were all of them so self-involved?

"Reah, all you have to do is ask if you need or want something," Teeg sat on the only extra kitchen chair I owned.

"Teeg, I don't like to ask. Should I have to? Jayd and Garde don't have to worry about where the money comes from for clothing and supplies. I do."

"I guess this isn't a good time." Lendill folded into the kitchen.

"Here. It has bourbon in it." I pushed my cup of tea toward him and rose from my seat to make another.

"Land and sky, Reah, this is strong." Lendill took a sip from my cup.

"Yeah. Sit down," I said. "What do you want?"

"Is that any way to treat a mate you haven't seen in months?"

"You only show up when you want something," I said. "So what is it?"

"Bel has disappeared," Lendill swallowed more tea, grimaced and then swallowed again.

"Wizard Bel?" I hadn't seen Bel for years, yet I knew he still worked for the ASD.

"Yes. I sent him to investigate a problem on Surnath, and he vanished. We can't find him."

"What kind of problem?" I asked, sitting down with my freshly poured and spiked tea. I didn't even ask Teeg if he wanted any. I was still pissed at him.

"A worker in an electronics factory went crazy and killed twenty of his coworkers after getting his hands on a laser pistol somehow. And then, two weeks later, a secretary at a legal firm killed six people there. The Governor of the Realm on Surnath asked us to investigate. We thought it was just a copy crime. Bel was in so he volunteered. Was there for three days before he came up missing."

"That's terrible," I said. "And you tried mindspeech and everything?"

"Yes. No answer. Bel isn't one to fall easily into a trap, so we're all concerned."

"Me, too," I nodded. I'd known Bel when I was a conscript in the Regular Alliance Army.

"Norian and I are willing to pay top credit if you'll work a special assignment on this."

"Lendill, I have the harvest next week and my middle daughters' claiming."

"We'll set you up afterward. There's no hurry since the trail is cold anyway. He's been missing for more than a month."

"Crap." I used one of Lissa's favorite phrases more and more as time went on. "Can you bring someone to watch over the disabled workers?" I asked.

"I think I can arrange something," Lendill nodded.

"Why do you want her to go?" Teeg was finally weighing in. I knew he wanted to—he'd been standing by, listening with a deep frown on his face. Teeg was handsome, no doubt about that. Lendill, once brown-haired and a bit plainer (I'd seen vid-photos) was now just as pleasing to the eye. He'd been changed by one of Lissa's Larentii after a criminal had his face remade to look exactly like Lendill's. Lendill liked the change and kept it.

"Because all our regular agents are out chasing pirates," Lendill answered Teeg's question. "I hear you're on the same boat, if you'll pardon the pun."

"We are," Teeg admitted, rubbing the back of his neck. He hadn't liked making that admission. I knew that gesture. It meant he was worried.

"Have we tried to find how they're getting shipping schedules?" I asked.

"What?" Teeg and Lendill chorused the word.

"I've been checking the hits on comp-vid during meal breaks," I said. "They're only hitting high-credit shipments. Have you noticed?

They let three ships go past outside Ooklarr, only to hit the fourth that carried expensive hovercraft."

"Reah, I'm getting a headache," Lendill said. "How did you come up with that?"

"My codes still work," I mumbled, thinking that now I'd called his attention to that bit of information, those codes would likely be shut down. "We have access to manifests after the fact, just not before. Isn't that right?" I looked at my half-Elf mate, who was also Vice-Director for the ASD.

"So you backtracked."

"Yes. And three other ships went through the same lane in less than fifteen ticks. Don't tell me the pirates conveniently showed up for the fourth ship to come through. Those others were carrying cotton bales and tea shipments."

"We thought they hacked into ship communications," Lendill said.

"Also a possibility. But how would they know to go there to begin with? All of those ships could be carrying raw cotton. They wouldn't know for sure until they got close enough to intercept the communications. And they've been hitting President Drix's gishi fruit shipments. Avendor's harvests run a month or two ahead of ours, but they also export data chips and medical supplies. None of those were hit, were they?" I turned to Teeg.

"We were assuming the same as Lendill and Norian. Ship communications," Teeg said. "All the ships now keep communications to a minimum, and they've always been scrambled, but we're still getting hit. Granted it's a bit more random, but still." Teeg knew just as well as I did that anything could be decoded nowadays, if you had the right equipment and sufficient determination.

"Somebody on the ground may be selling shipping information." Lendill whipped out his comp-vid, his fingers flying so fast over the digital keys even I had a hard time keeping up. He was sending a message to Norian Keef, Director of the ASD. Norian and I still didn't speak much. Not after my first daughter died. I still didn't like to think about that.

"I'll place compulsion myself, if it'll get me to the bottom of this," Teeg growled. Lendill got a message from Norian right away.

"Reah, I'll be in touch in a couple of eight-days, all right? Be ready to go, breah-mul." Ever since Lendill had awakened his Elvish ability, he folded almost everywhere. He was gone in a blink. His father, Kaldill Schaff, was King of the Elves and still I didn't think that Kaldill knew the full extent of Lendill's talents.

"I don't think it's going to be easy to get the information," I said, looking at Teeg.

"Why?" He came to put his arms around me.

"I just don't," I said.

"Baby, why didn't you tell me you needed money?" Teeg's lips were warm against my temple.

"Teeg, when do you have time to talk to me?"

"Baby, I was busy. If you'd sent a message, I'd have gotten back to you."

"Those floozies answer your messages."

"Reah, they're not floozies. They're qualified assistants. Let's not fight. I want to take you to bed and kiss that look off your face." That could take some work; I'm sure I was frowning deeply.

In twenty years, Teeg had never slept in my tiny bedroom. The room was neat, even if the walls needed paint and the furniture wasn't the best. I wasn't going to apologize for it. Teeg lived in a palace. Lendill had rooms in both Ildevar Wyyld's palace and Lissa's. I'd seen vid-photos of Dantel Schuul's home in vid-mags that certainly showed Tory and Darletta living in a palace, although Dantel Schuul employed false modesty and called it a house.

After being invited to join the Saa Thalarr as a Spawn Hunter, Lok had built a nice home near Aurelius' on the light side of Le-Ath Veronis. He'd brought wood in from Falchan and Adam helped put it together. Adam said he enjoyed the experience, having never put together what he termed an *Asian* construction project.

Radolf had taken over the house in Targis on Tulgalan, and Ilvan either lived in Lissa's palace or spent time on Tulgalan with Radolf as time allowed. Farzi and Nenzi had an expansive plantation house, something that Farzi had always wanted. Teeg built it for him and deeded much of Campiaa's farmland to the reptanoids. Farzi, Nenzi and the others were doing very well, but then they weren't expected to pay off Campiaa's debts, either.

The Crown owned the land I occupied on Kifirin. It had once belonged to the Croth and Drith, but when those two High Demon houses had thrown their lot in with the Ra'Ak nearly a century earlier, Jayd's first act as King had been to execute the traitors and confiscate their lands. Back then, the main crop had been sugar cane. Many worlds exported that product, and for a time, Kifirin competed against them.

Now, there was only Avendor in the Campiaan Alliance that also grew gishi fruit. Something about the volcanic soil on both Avendor and Kifirin supported the trees. Kifirin supplied the Reth Alliance with gishi fruit; Avendor supplied the Campiaan Alliance. Still, there was a larger demand than either of us could supply. I wondered what President Drix might have said earlier if he knew he was speaking with the one who oversaw the Kifirini groves.

"Where did you go?" Teeg slid into bed beside me.

"Just wondering what Drix would have said earlier if he knew I grew the gishi fruit on Kifirin."

"Reah, stop thinking business," Teeg pushed me back gently and kissed me. I didn't point out that business was exactly what he thought about, most of the time.

"But she never says anything." Jayd was angry. "She didn't tell us there wasn't enough money. And how many disabled does she have there, now?"

"I had to go back through the records," Garde shoved a comp-vid toward his brother, the King. Jayd's office was where they sat, this time. His desk was larger, the décor more opulent.

"Fifty-six? Where is she putting all of them?"

"Adam Chessman and Aurelius, with others from the Saa Thalarr, put up the infirmary and single-level apartments. They're both full, and some of those who live there are unable to work at all. Reah and the others take care of them."

"Why hasn't the Crown put something together like this?" Jayd enlarged the vid-photos of Reah's disabled quarters.

"Because it was easier to ship them off to Reah and let her deal with them. Wasn't it, Garde?" Queen Glinda walked into the room. "No wonder she always said she couldn't come shopping or go visiting. She didn't have the time."

"Glinda, most of the time I'm glad you were allowed to leave the Saa Thalarr. Now isn't one of those times." Jayd looked up at his wife.

"I would still need help. I know nothing about building. That isn't why I came to see you."

"Then why did you come to see me?"

"Because my brother Denevik retains his title of Prince," Glinda said. "Although he works as a liaison with the Reth and Campiaan Security Details, he keeps his status as a Prince of Kifirin."

"You don't want him to have it?" Jayd stared at Glinda. She loved her brother. He'd married the humanoid woman who'd birthed Reah's mother, following Bresca Loffus' divorce from her politician husband. Now they lived on Tulgalan. Denevik was hoping for another child with Bresca, but so far, his hope bore no fruit. Bresca was aging, too, and would be past childbearing in ten years.

"No. That isn't what I meant," Glinda huffed. "What I meant is that if things hadn't happened as they did, Denny's daughter and granddaughter would have the title of Princesses of the Realm. Through my father, the former King."

"And Reah's daughters as well." Jayd sighed.

"That would give all of them votes on the Council. I don't like it," Garde said.

"Once they reached maturity," Glinda agreed. "Dara and Sara aren't old enough."

"And certainly not mature enough." Garde blew a bit of smoke.

"It was just a suggestion," Glinda said. "I see that I'm outnumbered once again by High Demon males. How many female High Demons are there, husband?" Glinda glared at Jayd.

"Seventeen," Jayd unwillingly muttered.

"And six of those are Reah's daughters."

"Yes."

"And how have we been paying off our debts after Tarevik emptied the treasury and Rorevik had no idea how to build it up again?"

"With gishi fruit," Jayd said. "I'm planning to send four High Demon guards with the next shipments, in case pirates attack."

"Reah says that she's not releasing the date of the shipment for some reason," Garde said. "I asked her how she was going to book a ship. She said to let her worry about that."

"Garde, why don't you want Reah to have a vote on the Council? Tory is your son and a King's nephew. And he's the son of a Queen. His title is a matter of record here in the archives. Aren't his daughters entitled that way? Admit it, Garde. You have something against Reah. You think it was her fault that Tory went off like he did."

"Do you think that?" Garde stared at Glinda.

"Careful how you answer, Garde. Glinda and I are both Gulis. And Reah is as well, unless I miss my guess," Jayd said softly.

"I don't know. Do I have something against Reah?" Garde rose from his seat, confusion in his voice.

"Not intentionally," Kifirin appeared inside Jayd's office. "We have larger problems at the moment. Torevik will indeed come looking for Reah tomorrow night. I intend to give her to him. He will cause a great deal of damage otherwise."

"Lissa, he'll destroy the groves if we leave Reah where she is. He'll go through anything in front of him if he can't get his hands on her easily. Even if we force her, she'll fight him." Garde was trying to explain things to his mate while Kifirin silently stood by.

"Kifirin, if I could go back in time and kick your ass for making High Demons the way they are," Lissa glared at her most powerful mate. "Just how do you propose to get Reah within his reach, if she refuses to go willingly?"

"Healing sleep," Kifirin blew smoke with the answer.

"You're just going to dump her unconscious body in front of him? Is that what you plan to do? Like tossing a piece of meat to an angry dog?"

"Lissa, our son is not an angry dog," Garde was blowing smoke now.

"No? How angry do you think his Thifilathi will be, after not changing for twenty-five years? Connegar and Reemagar spent some time with him today. They say it could take a month or two, because they have to move slowly."

"What are they doing?" Garde asked.

"Slowly taking him through the passage of time."

"Reconstructing his memories?"

"No. Not that much. He doesn't want to recall Darletta. What he does remember of her makes him furious. I couldn't see for the cloud of smoke after Gavin mentioned her name. His appetite is good, though. Ilvan is feeding him anything he wants."

"I thought he looked a little thinner when he came home," Garde sighed.

"Mom?" Tory's voice came through to her office, where she'd met with Garde and Kifirin.

"We're in here, honey." Tory walked in. "Sit down," Lissa said. "Do you want something to drink? We're just discussing the full moon tonight."

"Where can I make the turn?" Tory asked. "I don't remember doing it the last time."

"Honey, don't worry about that, it'll come. Karzac says that things have been somewhat traumatic for you. We'll get you what you need. Where should he go?" Lissa quirked an eyebrow at Garde and Kifirin.

"The high fields on Kifirin," Garde said. Kifirin nodded silently. "I'll be here later to take you there. You can breathe the free air on Kifirin, son."

"All right, Dad. I missed you and Mom while I was gone." Tory rose and wandered out of the room.

"He's like that all the time," Lissa muttered, dropping her head into her hands. "Tell me you'll protect Reah if she needs protecting," Lissa lifted her gaze to Kifirin.

"I will be there," the god of the Dark Realm replied.

"The fruit will be ready in two days." Hifil, my crew supervisor, handed me a gishi fruit that he'd cut in half. I sniffed it, agreeing with him. "Are the repairs done on the trucks?" I asked.

"Tomorrow," Hifil nodded. He was as old as I—fifty-one. Only Hifil came from one of the shorter-lived races. His kind tended to live around ninety turns or so, and Hifil had gray in his hair. He thought I was young. I wasn't. At times, I felt as old as the ground beneath my feet.

"Reah." Kifirin was suddenly there before me, standing in the space between rows of gishi trees, their deep green, oval leaves sighing in the late afternoon breeze and fruit hanging heavy on their branches.

"Hifil, I'll handle this," I sent my supervisor on his way. No need to involve him in anything Kifirin wanted. "What do you want, Kifirin?" My arms were crossed tightly over my chest. "You said the last time that I wouldn't be pregnant again by Tory without my consent. I haven't consented."

"And you're not pregnant by Tory. This has nothing to do with pregnancy."

"Good. State your business and leave." I tossed out a hand. Who knew where Kifirin went when he disappeared? I didn't.

"Glinda wanted to give you the title you should have been born with. Gardevik disagreed."

"No surprise. Garde hates me. Don't try to deny it. Something in him dislikes me. I'm sure it has to do with Tory."

"It does." Kifirin stepped closer.

"What does he want from me? Garde, that is? I gave him six

grandchildren. All girls, so your precious race can be pulled back from the brink of extinction. And then I do this." I jerked my head toward the trees. "I hear Kifirin's debts may be paid off in a few turns. I don't see Garde out here harvesting or doing anything that might get the fruit to market. Yet he takes his due when the credits are transferred."

"I understand all those things," Kifirin moved closer, speaking softly.

"Of course you do. You just made me pregnant twice, without my knowledge or consent. Hauled Gavril into the past so he'd grow up and create the Campiaan Alliance. Sure, he says he loves me. When he wants sex." Kifirin was close enough to touch, now. I wanted to poke a finger in his chest as I made my point. I didn't. Kifirin poked a finger to my forehead instead, making the air around me dark. I'm sure I dropped to the ground, too. Kifirin wouldn't likely lift a hand to stop it.

∾

"Torevik isn't the only one who may be slighter." Reah's slender body rested in Kifirin's arms.

"I don't hate her." Garde denied Reah's statement. "I don't."

"She thinks you do. Often, perception is everything. You live in a palace. She lives in a hovel that doesn't leak because she repaired the roof herself."

"And suddenly you're kindness itself toward her?" Garde didn't appreciate Kifirin's jab.

"Come, this argument gains us nothing. Show me where you intend to bring Torevik, and I will leave Reah there."

∾

"Honey, be careful, all right?" Lissa gave Tory a hug while his father waited to take him to Kifirin.

"I'll be fine," Tory sighed. "I wish you'd all stop fussing over me."

"And we will. Soon." Lissa smiled up at her tallest son.

31

"Tory, let's go." Garde gripped his son's arm. Tory was three inches taller than his father. Garde could fold; something that most High Demons were incapable of doing. They skipped, and except for a very few, could only skip themselves. Garde folded his son to the high fields on Kifirin.

"Go ahead and change, son. I'll be nearby." Garde used his skipping ability to get away. High Demons didn't encroach on one another's changing grounds, unless there was a score to settle. It was too dangerous. Garde, however, didn't go far. Kifirin plucked him from the air and surrounded him with a shield.

"We will watch," Kifirin said, as Torevik Rath, who hadn't changed in two and a half decades, went to full Thifilathi with a roar and stomped through the fields.

"Where did you leave Reah?" Garde hissed. He felt exposed, although Kifirin had him well shielded. Garde would have to turn, too —sometime before the moon was down.

"Not far. We must watch carefully, Gardevik. If your child harms Reah or mistreats her in any way, then I will remove the claiming marks. That is why I came tonight. To see if his Thifilathi still recognizes her. If not," Kifirin shrugged.

Garde stared at the god in shock. "This is an experiment?"

"A test. Yes. If his Thifilathi does not know her, or chooses to harm, then the claiming marks will be removed. Perhaps a more suitable High Demon male may come to her." Kifirin glanced up at the moon, directly over their heads. It wouldn't be long, now.

"What?" Garde sputtered. Now that it came to it, he didn't want Reah to leave the family. Didn't want her away from his grasp. Out of his control.

"Now do you begin to see it?" Kifirin asked. "You control the fate of the High Demon race if you control Reah. How long have you been angry, Gardevik Rath? At your child? At Reah? Because some foolishness separated them. You keep her hidden away because you fear just what I said. That some High Demon male may come along and turn her head, taking control away from you. You chose to leave her in the groves instead of housing her at the palace, where she should have been. None have thought to question why Reah has no High Demons working with her on the plantation, either. But it's true, is it not? She depends upon humanoids for help. There are more than enough High Demon males lazing about who might assist her, but you, as Jayd's Prime Minister, will not send them. If I allow Reah to produce more daughters with another house, then that could endanger the ruling house. Isn't that right?"

"Fuck," Garde cursed and made to walk away.

"No, you will stay," Kifirin hauled Garde back with a hand covered in blackened scales. "You and I will watch." Garde stared up at Kifirin's smaller Thifilathi, the god blowing clouds of smoke. "We will see together if your son deserves a second chance."

# CHAPTER 3

Torevik Rath, in full Thifilathi, sniffed the air and roared. And then roared again. Leapt into the air and came down with a thump, shaking the ground around him. Beat his chest and shouted out his pleasure at being one with the planet he walked upon. Could feel the hum of life through his bare feet. This is what he'd missed and longed for. But for how long? He couldn't remember. He remembered a beautiful face that hid wickedness. Betrayal. Pain. How might he think he'd ever loved it? If he had her now, he would squeeze the life from her.

Tory ran over the open fields, a giant among tall grasses. Every animal in his path ran and hid from the largest predator they'd ever seen. But then he stopped. What was that? Something lying in the grass. Tossed carelessly in his path. He'd see about that. Nothing would stand against him or obstruct his course. Cautiously Tory sniffed the air. He wasn't close enough yet. Two large strides brought him in range. Suddenly, he knew that scent. How had it come here? Was it done purposely, so he'd find it? He cared not. It lay there, unmoving, waiting for him to do as he pleased with it.

Garde made to move forward; Kifirin held him back. Tory stood over Reah's body, examining it. As if he were deciding what to do. Now, all Garde could do was hold his breath. The fate of the High Demon race could rest on the next few moments. Tory blew smoke; Garde could see it clearly in the light of the full moon. Reah's body looked as if Kifirin had tossed it carelessly on the ground, uncaring as to how it landed. "Please," Garde whispered, begging his son to do what was right. What any normal High Demon male should do with his mate. Tory hesitated.

I ached for some reason, and my limbs were tangled. As if someone had—as if someone—*Kifirin*. He'd done this to me. Tossed me naked upon the cold ground, somewhere. Sturdy stems of tall grasses poked into bare skin, making me extremely uncomfortable. And I had a headache. How was that possible? The last thing I remembered was Kifirin's hand, shooting out quick as a snake, poking me in the forehead and laying a healing sleep. Only nobody woke from a healing sleep like this. I moaned as I untangled arms and legs, struggling to sit up. The full moon hung overhead, bathing the field surrounding me in light.

Somehow, a full moon didn't affect me or Glinda as it did the males. They had to turn, and the full moon called out stronger to them than any other time. Kifirin had done this. I almost wondered why when I remembered. Tory. He'd be somewhere nearby. That meant I needed to skip away before he found me. Before it was too late. I moaned and gathered my wits to skip. Nothing happened. Tried again. Still nothing.

That's when I heard the noise. A snort. I recognized it. Jumping to my feet I made to run, barefoot as I was, when the huge, black-scaled and clawed hand reached for me. Scooped me up, even as I screeched and flailed. Thick smoke poured from Tory's Thifilathi. Was I frightened? Nearly to death. Kifirin was behind this and keeping me from skipping away or turning Thifilatha. Would I never be free of him and his meddling? He was about to get me killed. My heart pounding in my chest, I beat on Tory's hands as he held me away from him, kicking with my feet, but I was too far away to hit anything and my attempts to do him harm were pitifully useless.

"Let. Me. Go," I hissed between clenched teeth. "Let me go," I shouted louder. As of that moment, I was done with High Demons. If I could get out of Tory's grip, I was going so far away none of them would find me. I was finished with Kifirin and the ones he'd created in his image. They had my daughters. Had High Demon males lined up to take them. I'd served my purpose and now, in a last attempt to torture me, Kifirin had tossed me on the ground for a half-crazed High Demon in full Thifilathi to find.

"Reah, your little fists are bloody. Stop beating them against my scales." I stared at Tory in shock. He'd spoken. High Demons seldom were able while Thifilathi, small or large.

"Put me down, Torevik Rath. Now."

"No, Reah. You belong to me."

"Tory, don't be delusional. Put me down." I stared at his face, black with a finer layer of scales than the rest of him. Curved, black horns grew away from his temples, the tips pointed upward. His eyes were black as well, with no white showing. A curl of smoke lifted from wide nostrils.

"Mine." I disagreed with Tory's declaration of ownership, attempting to pry his fingers from around my waist. His grip was tight and it hurt.

"Tory, you're squeezing me," I wheezed.

"You'll get away. Not my fault I have to hold you this hard."

"Tory, let me go. Put me down." I wanted to hyperventilate, but my lungs couldn't draw in the air. My fists were bloody, just as he'd said. A High Demon's scales while full Thifilathi could cut if you rubbed against them. Now, my entire body was at the mercy of those scales. "Tory, I can't breathe," I whimpered.

"Reah, I can't let you go. I know I'm hurting you, but I can't let you go."

"Tory." That was the last thing I remembered before things went black for the second time that day.

≈

Garde watched as his son threw back his head and keened mournfully. "Now we go, so stay behind me," Kifirin ordered, folding Garde and himself to a spot right in front of Tory.

"Here." Kifirin held out a blanket. Tory, even in his current state, recognized the god of the Dark Realm. Carefully he laid Reah's body on the blanket. All of them saw the blood and bruises around Reah's ribs, waist and hips, where her skin had come in contact with Tory's scaled and clawed hands.

"I want her back," Tory demanded, once Reah was folded in the blanket. His wings rustled impatiently while Kifirin wrapped Reah firmly so her arms and legs were secure.

"I'll allow it, but she'll need attention later," Kifirin handed Reah over.

"I can't let her get away," Tory sat on the grass, the small bundle cradled in his arms.

"Son, you'll have to convince her while you're in your other shape," Garde ventured to say.

"I'll say I'm sorry."

"We'll work on that. Later."

≈

"We'll make it right. We'll make it right," someone was crooning to me when I regained consciousness. I ached. Over most of my body. My ribs felt as if they'd been crushed.

"Who are you?" I opened my eyes and found a black-skinned male running his hands over my body. I'd never seen him before. Who'd let him in my house? I was in my house; I was staring at the same crack in the plaster ceiling that I'd been looking at for twenty years.

"I'm new to this side of things. I and one other have been assigned to assist Kifirin."

"You're Kifirin's assistant?" It hurt to talk.

"Yes."

"Get out."

"I understand how you might feel that way about him."

"Then get out." This one had a nice face. He might look even better if he smiled, but I didn't want him to stay until I saw it. If he were Kifirin's assistant, then he needed to get away from me. As soon as he could. A tiny curl of smoke came from my nostrils. Kifirin had knocked me out and dumped me in a field for Tory to find as full Thifilathi. That was unforgivable. Just another unforgivable thing in a long line of unforgivable things at the hands of the Dark god. He wasn't the Dark god for nothing.

"My name is Neeki," my attendant said, continuing his examination of my naked body as if he hadn't heard a word I'd said.

"That's nice," I said. "Get out."

"My associate is called Teeki, but he could not be here right now. He is busy elsewhere." Dark fingers ran down ribs so tender I almost cried out. "Ah, cracks. I will repair them." Light formed around his hands.

"Probably straightening out some of Kifirin's other mistakes," I drew in a painful breath. He'd hit a really sore spot. "Now, get out. I mean it."

"Ah, but you want to be able to work the harvest tomorrow."

"Sure I do. As soon as you get out of my way, I'm skipping out of here. Garde and his bone-crushing thug of a son can harvest the fruit. I'm done, here. Kifirin stepped across the line one time too many."

"He does not mean to harm."

"Don't try to make excuses for him. He does so mean to harm. Has done harm. Every single time."

"Our little one is very tired. And sore. Needs rest. Rest, Reah. Shall I ask someone to hold you after I heal your body?"

"I want you and everybody else to leave me alone. Where are they now? Why are you here instead of that pile of mates I have? And

Torevik Rath? If I see him again in Thifilathi, small or large, he'll have a fight on his hands. Kifirin prevented me from turning earlier. Where are all those lofty promises he made to the Dark races, long ago? That he wouldn't interfere with their decisions? He keeps interfering with mine."

"I was not his assistant when he made that statement."

"Yeah? Who decided he needed an assistant? Or two?"

"The one who made him. So he sent Teeki and me. To help."

"Great. More meddling gods." I raised up in bed, whimpering at the resulting pain.

"Don't move, I haven't finished, yet," Neeki informed me.

"You're finished." I slipped off the bed and moved stiffly toward my closet. Dawn was close. Tory had probably dumped me as quickly as possible and skipped right back to Mom and her palace, leaving Kifirin's newly appointed assistant behind to clean up his mess. I was leaving, just as soon as I could get dressed.

"You cannot leave; many depend upon you."

"Yeah? Watch me." I pulled a pair of pants from a hanger. A shirt came next. Nothing in my closet could be described as neat or new. Everything was old; some of it patched, ripped or threadbare. I found the best of it, pulled the nicest underwear I owned out of a drawer and slipped into it, my body aching the entire time. When I managed to pull the best shoes on that I could find, I still looked as if I were prepared to work the groves instead of leaving the planet.

"But what shall I do?" Neeki, much taller than I and somewhat thin, looked as if he were about to wring his hands.

"I don't care. Feel free to wait here and tell Garde when he shows up that he can oversee the harvest and care for the disabled and arrange for a ship to haul the fruit. I won't be back. Tell King Jayd that he can cancel my membership in the High Demon club. I don't have any use for it. Good-bye, Neeki. When you see your lord and master again, tell him he can kiss my ass." I skipped away, leaving Neeki behind, a look of shocked concern on his face.

~

"You were supposed to keep her here!" Kifirin shouted at poor Neeki, who cowered before the Dark god.

"I saw no way to do so; I am not allowed to restrain." Neeki gave the only excuse he had. Garde and Jayd both stood inside Reah's house while the work crews were scrambling to get out to the fields and harvest ripened gishi fruit.

"She said she wasn't coming back?" Jayd repeated what Neeki said.

"Yes. She said that. And left before the healing was complete."

"She wasn't supposed to wake. Either time." Kifirin was blowing smoke.

"I do not understand either. She woke while I was tending her, and then left. I tried to reassure her, but she kept telling me to get out."

"Reah is past listening to those promises." Nefrigar appeared. Kifirin had never seen an angry Larentii before.

"I know. But she is all I have." Kifirin hung his head.

"You don't have her now." Nefrigar's blue skin was glowing, he was so angry. "Make these lazy louts who call themselves High Demons do for themselves instead of piling it all on Reah's shoulders. If they become extinct, perhaps it is as it should be."

"Now wait a minute," smoke poured from Jayd's nostrils.

"Do not attempt to harm me, King Demon. I assure you I will separate your particles just as easily as any other creature's."

"He can," Neeki nodded at Nefrigar's statement.

"I piled it on Reah," Garde admitted. "Kifirin was correct last night. I kept her buried in work here so she wouldn't go looking for another High Demon to replace Torevik."

"Lissa told you, didn't she?" Kifirin stared at Garde.

"Told you what?" Jayd was staring at Garde as well. Garde was firstborn to the House of Rath, Jayd was third.

"That Tory's claiming marks wouldn't hold Reah, if she made another choice. Removing them would just be a formality."

"So you set about turning her against all High Demons." Neeki blinked at Garde.

"It wasn't intentional. Not like this."

"Where is she?" Teeg appeared, Farzi and Nenzi at his side. Teeg's warlock bodyguards, Astralan and Stellan, were with them.

"We don't know." Jayd sat heavily on a chair in Reah's kitchen. "Kifirin dumped her out in the field so Tory would find her last night. She was supposed to stay in a healing sleep so harm would be kept to a minimum. She woke and she wasn't supposed to. Kifirin kept her from turning or skipping away, but she still ended up bloodied and bruised when she attempted to fight Tory."

"Did he mean to hurt Reah?" Farzi was becoming angry.

"No. He kept saying he couldn't let her go. But a full Thifilathi's scales will harm, if someone comes in contact with them. Tory had to grip her hard to keep her from getting away. It wasn't intentional. Kifirin brought a blanket after she fainted, and Tory held her that way for quite a while. Wouldn't let anybody take her away from him until close to dawn. Kifirin convinced him to change and told this one to see to Reah while he took Tory home." Jayd explained as best he could the events of the night before.

"Fuck," Teeg rubbed the back of his neck. Farzi and Nenzi exchanged troubled glances.

"Where is she, Nefrigar? I know you can find her." Garde looked at the Larentii.

"Yes. I can find her. As can the god, here." Nefrigar nodded at Kifirin. "I will go to protect her. What will you offer when you go?" His gaze was hard on Kifirin.

"I was told she might slip away from me. I think I'm losing her."

"Losing her?" More smoke poured from Jayd's nostrils.

"To the other side," Neeki offered. "We were sent to attempt to keep her with the Dark Realm. But she may move to the Light Side."

"Do you mean to tell me that you won't have any control over Reah if that happens?" Jayd was incredulous.

"That is what it means," Neeki nodded. "Teeki and I will try to prevent, but we can only do so much. We were told to help, not interfere."

"She has no money," Teeg said. "She can't get far without it."

"You think to hold her back that way?" Nefrigar was now staring at

Teeg. "I am not without resources. I will see she has as much as she needs."

"Why are you assisting her now? I don't understand this." Teeg tossed up a hand in frustration.

"The question is, why aren't you assisting her now? She has a legitimate reason for leaving, don't you think?"

"Neeki?" Another black-skinned male appeared, who looked exactly like Neeki.

"Teeki, the little female has run away. I could not keep her in the healing sleep," Neeki sighed mournfully.

"I feared it could come to this." Teeki nodded at his twin.

"You can all stop worrying, I sent mindspeech. She's safe at the moment." Rylend Morphis folded in beside Gavril. He never called his brother Teeg unless they were in the presence of someone who didn't know already.

"Where is she?" Jayd demanded.

"I promised I wouldn't tell. She'll be back tomorrow night for the claiming, but she's leaving right after to work that special project for Lendill. I wanted to let you know, Gav, that I volunteered to work the investigation with her. You owe me vacation, after all."

"She answered your mindspeech?" Gavril stared at his brother.

"Yes. Did you try to contact her?"

"No. I didn't think she'd answer."

"Next time don't assume that, all right? She got back with me right away."

"But she's not pissed at you."

"True."

"Are you going to tell us where she is?" Jayd was angry.

"No. I promised. You'll have to haul in the harvest yourself."

"We're working on it," Garde grumbled. He was grumbling because some of the help he'd brought in had stacked the fruit too deeply in packing boxes, crushing the bottom layers. Half of what the new crews hauled in was ruined.

"My work is done, here," Ry held out his hands and disappeared.

~

"You're packing, Master Rylend?" Dee lifted an eyebrow at Ry, who was so handsome he hurt. Women fell over themselves, offering their charms and anything else in order to get Rylend Morphis to notice them. Ry treated them with polite coolness, much of the time. Ry, resembling his father greatly, had dark hair and eyes, sculpted lips that could make almost any woman swoon if they smiled even a little, a beautiful nose and well-shaped eyebrows that quirked a bit if something interested him. Nowadays, that wasn't much. He was also a strong and talented warlock, his power and ability only improving over the years. He still worked with his father at times, although he'd never stepped onto Karathian soil after renouncing his citizenship. Wylend knew of Ry's progress. Ry knew that Wylend knew and didn't care.

"Dee, I offered to help Reah track a missing agent for the ASD. Gav can do without me for a couple of weeks, don't you think? Nothing important is coming up in the near future. Nobody needs their nose wiped or their tears dried. Not that can't wait, anyway."

"You're equating some of the Campiaan Alliance leaders with children?"

"I sometimes offer them ice cream if they'll stop screaming and behave."

"You jest."

"Dee, do you know how many five-gallon drums of Niff's ice cream I've transported to this palace or that state house? Do you? I've even taken cakes that Reah's made along with the ice cream a time or two, although I hate asking Reah for that, she's so busy all the time."

"Am I wrong in assuming those days are over for our Reah?"

"I hope so." Ry closed his second bag with a sigh. "I thought they were going to drive her into the ground. And I have to tell you that if someone who was part of my family insisted that my children be raised apart from me, so, in their words, they could have a better life and a better education, I think I'd tell them where they could shove all that."

"I take it that King Jayd and Prime Minister Garde said that?" Dee offered dryly.

"They did. They almost twisted Reah's arm over the first set of twins, saying that no female High Demon was ever born or raised anywhere except Kifirin. They didn't take Reah's mother into account, either, since they didn't know about her. Then, they made Reah a citizen of Kifirin and promptly brought the royal arm on the neck to bear. I don't blame her for walking out on them. She should have done it long ago."

"You worry about her."

"Yes. I worry about her. Have worried about her. For a long time. I watch from the sidelines, Dee. I don't think Reah has forgotten anything that has been done to her over the years. I know I haven't." Ry used power to lift both bags off his bed. "I'll be at my chateau in the mountains until tomorrow evening. Feel free to contact me until then." Ry disappeared.

"Reah, I brought something for you." Nefrigar appeared inside my tiny hotel room. The room was the best I could afford, and I'd locked myself in after the desk clerk imagined that he recognized me. Most likely he'd seen vids or vid-photos of me on Teeg's arm for some function or other, and thought I looked similar, even dressed in an old shirt and pants, with worn shoes that showed mud stains.

"Hi, honey." I was dressed only in underwear when Nefrigar appeared; I hadn't taken any extra clothing with me from Kifirin.

"I brought this." My Larentii mate produced a tiny credit chip that he held out on a large, blue finger.

"Honey, you don't have to do that," I sighed, staring longingly at the credit chip. It meant better food, better hotel accommodations and clothing, perhaps.

"It is all those things," he nodded, taking my wrist and using only a tiny bit of the vast power any Larentii has, caused it to sink below the skin on my right wrist. "I also have this." He produced a round, metal ball, so tiny I almost couldn't see it on his finger.

"What's that?" I asked.

"Protection," he said. "I am allowed to protect my mate. I am doing so now."

"But what is it?" I repeated my question as I stared at his handsome, blue-skinned face. Nefrigar's eyes alone might drown me if I allowed it.

"It is future technology, therefore I cannot tell you. Just know that it carries my love with it."

"Are all Larentii so secretive?" I smiled at him as he pressed the tiny object against my collarbone. When he drew his finger away, it had disappeared. Another object carried on my person. I had no idea what it was meant to do.

"Of course," he smiled. "Would you like for me to love you in a conventional manner?"

Usually, Nefrigar offered energy sex, but upon occasion (mostly when Farzi and Nenzi weren't involved, they could have energy sex too, if Nefrigar included them) my Larentii mate loved me senseless with his body thrusting into mine. Those were good nights.

"Yes. Can you make the bed better?" I asked.

"Certainly."

"You said Mom was coming." Now that the claiming was at hand, Lara fretted. Grampa Garde was trying to reassure her, while Karzac stood by to place the healing sleep before Eldevik was allowed inside the bedroom. Lara's twin, Kara, was in the bedroom next door, waiting as well, but more sedately.

"That's what she said," Garde agreed, doing everything he could to keep smoke from pouring from his nostrils.

"I'm here, baby." I was in the room bare seconds before Lara flung herself into my arms. Taller than I, she could knock me over if I wasn't prepared. None of my girls had the white hair that Glinda, my mother and I had been born with. They all favored Tory, with dark brown hair and gray eyes.

"Mom, tell me it'll be all right."

"Honey, it will be. You'll just have to let Karzac and Grampa Edan take care of things afterward, all right?" I did my best to reassure my daughter, but there was pain lying ahead for her. Days of it.

"Are you ready, young one?" Karzac came forward.

"I guess." For a moment, she was four again to me, and needing comfort after a scraped knee or a disappointment of some kind. I leaned forward to kiss her forehead before Karzac placed the healing sleep. Garde carried her to the bed. I waited until both males were out of the room to remove the simple robe that wrapped her body as it lay on the bed. Eldevik would only rip her clothing away if he found her dressed. Smaller Thifilathi or no, in the heat of claiming they were beasts, plain and simple.

"She's ready," I walked out of the bedroom, finding Garde, Jayd and Karzac waiting outside with Eldevik, who was blowing curls of smoke from his nostrils. "Hurt her afterward," I poked a finger in his chest, "and I'll kill you myself." I flung away Jayd's hand and walked stiffly to the bedroom next door.

Kara was frightened but didn't say it. She'd always been more composed than Lara. You always think the older one might be calmer for some reason. Not so with my middle born. "Baby, Sheldevik will treat you well, I think." Sheldevik was one of only a few Croth that still lived. When he learned that he'd been selected as Kara's mate, he'd wept, never thinking that a female High Demon might come to him.

"Mom, how long will I feel bad?" Kara knew pain was coming. She'd talked with Glinda and me. Plus, she'd listened to her older sisters. She knew what to expect.

"For a few days. Baby, if you hurt, ask Karzac to take care of it, all right? Sleep through as much of it as you can."

"But Glinda told me you were leaving tonight."

"I know, honey. An old friend who works for your Uncle Lendill has come up missing. I need to find him if I can."

"But you won't come back here. Not to live."

"Honey, the other night I woke up and found myself staring at the same crack that's been in my bedroom ceiling for more than twenty years. I think it's a good bet that Garde doesn't have a crack in his bedroom ceiling. I'm tired of it. It's time for me to move on. Your younger sisters are away at school; you'll have a new husband and a new life. Mom doesn't have to be around that much, anymore."

"I love you, Mom."

"I love you too, honey." I kissed her forehead, too. Karzac, who'd stood by with Garde and Jayd this time, came forward and placed the healing sleep. Garde carried her to the bed. I removed the robe. Sheldevik was waiting outside the door, a worried look on his face.

"Treat her as carefully as you can, Shel," I said, and patted his arm. Jayd lifted an eyebrow at me but didn't say anything.

"It won't take long." Garde walked beside me as I headed toward the massive kitchen inside the palace to get something to drink. At that moment, straight bourbon sounded good. Garde was correct, it wouldn't take long before both Thifilathi would be roaring from the top of the palace or some other, similarly ridiculous place. As if they'd accomplished something. The females had accomplished something in my estimation, surviving the claiming.

"Reah, it seems I have a lot to apologize for," Garde began as I poured three glasses of bourbon. Jayd downed his right away.

"Garde, if you think I'll listen to apologies now, you are sadly mistaken," I said and gulped my glass of liquor.

"Tory asked about you."

"I don't care." I poured another helping of alcohol and drank that.

"Reah, you're still a citizen of Kifirin," Jayd said.

"If you think I'll ever bow my head to you again, you are just as mistaken as your brother," I snapped.

"That isn't what I meant," Jayd said. "I was letting my brother make the decisions where you were concerned, because I saw him as your kin. I see now that was a mistake. I should have stepped forward and protected a citizen of my realm. When you're done searching for your friend, come and see me. I will make sure that one of Kifirin's treasures is treated with proper respect and given what is due to her."

I laughed. He'd called me Kifirin's treasure. Even Kifirin didn't see me as that, although once he'd called me the daughter of his heart. He'd lied. Many times. "King Jayd," I said, still chuckling humorlessly, "If you can't see what's in front of your face until somebody points it out to you, then you aren't much of a King."

At that moment, we heard the first roar. Eldevik, unless I missed my guess. I skipped to Lara's bedroom, finding my child, her neck bloodied, lying on the sheets of the bed. Eldevik had been rough with her. Karzac was behind me, as was my father, Edan, and both moved to work on Lara, healing and cleaning her up. Kifirin appeared right behind me to survey the aftermath of the claiming.

"Say anything and I'll punch you," I growled as I stalked out the door. Another roar came. I walked into Kara's room. She'd been left in better shape. Only a bit of blood left on the back of her neck where Sheldevik's canines had held her. Raedah and Tara were there behind me, moving to tend their sister. "Keep me updated on their recovery," I told them, giving them a brief hug.

"Mom, do you have to go?" Tara asked.

"I'm going," I replied and skipped away.

"You don't have to say it's my fault. I know it's my fault." Garde was back in the kitchen, helping himself to more bourbon. Kifirin had pulled up a barstool and was having a drink, too, something he seldom did.

"One of my better decisions," another creature appeared, shining brightly before he dimmed his light as the others present couldn't bear the brightness of it, "One of my better decisions," he repeated, "is not allowing love to be forced. It is either given freely or it isn't love. Otherwise, all three of you would have forced Reah back, wouldn't you? Love must be coaxed. And once it comes, it must be nurtured and protected. I do not interfere with personal decisions. Or generally the consequences of such."

"To whom are we speaking?" Jayd asked carefully, not wishing to offend.

"This is the one who made me," Kifirin drank the rest of his bourbon and poured another.

～

"Here is the newest version comp-vid we give to our field agents," Lendill handed it over. I was shocked to see that Ry had come with Lendill, and even more so when I learned that he'd volunteered to work the assignment with me. A part of me was glad; I hadn't worked an investigation in twenty-six years. I was also glad that my new hotel room had two beds; Ry had brought two bags filled with clothing and necessities. I would have to go out and purchase clothing the following day unless I wanted to ask questions dressed like a farmer.

Ry got a comp-vid as well, and we both received the latest technology Ranos pistols and rifles. The rifles came in three parts that fit together easily and quickly, breaking down to fit inside a small bag if necessary. Both of us carried ID that allowed us to have the weapons Lendill handed to us. "My father wishes you to visit when this assignment is over," Lendill said.

"I'll do my best." And I would. I liked Kaldill Schaff, even if he was very plainspoken at times. I preferred the honesty, actually.

"And we'll take some time when this is over. I promise." Lendill leaned in to give me a kiss.

"Lendill, don't make any promises you can't keep."

"Reah." He took my face in his hands. "I swear it, breah-mul."

"Fine." In twenty-six years, Lendill hadn't taken a vacation. I guess it was a good thing he was immortal. On his father's side.

"I have to go." Lendill kissed me again and folded away.

"Well, Ry," I said, looking at my warlock investigative partner, "which bed do you want?"

## CHAPTER 4

*R*y did a little catching up while I went out to buy clothing. We were in Quezlos, the capital city of Surnath. Darletta and her father lived on a wide expanse of land just outside the city. Dantel Schuul had given up his political career a few years earlier in favor of making more money than anyone had a right to, manufacturing comp-vid components. He had the newest technology and everybody bought it.

I figured Darletta had gotten tired of Tory and was searching for new blood. Surnathans lived around one hundred fifty years, and Darletta was around forty-six or so—in her prime and likely looking for a little spice. Although Alliance law held here, Surnath frowned on multiple mates. Therefore, there was plenty of divorce. I'd looked into the state's records regarding Darletta and Tory's writ of detachment, and they'd mutually agreed to separate, leaving one another's property with the original owner. In my opinion, Tory should have held out for a settlement. He'd been married to her for twenty-five years, after all.

But that wasn't why Ry and I were there. Bel's last known communication had come from Quezlos. We were planning to go through Bel's hotel room and look through any belongings he left behind. Lendill had managed to quarantine the room, although it had

50

been more than a month and the hotel manager was a bit grumpy over the whole thing.

"I need working clothes, not that." I shook my head as the salesclerk tried to sell me a dress. Pants, shirts and plenty of underwear was what I needed. I wanted new leathers, too, but Falchan was far away and I didn't have time to wait on them to be made.

"Yes, several pairs of the denim, plus some good slacks that won't fall apart if I wash them," I said, waving the girl away. She was a girl to me, in her late twenties. I was more than twice her age. My High Demon immortality would ensure I always looked young, but inside I felt older than I should.

After getting enough to wear, I went looking for shoes. Things had changed a little since the last time I'd gone shoe shopping. I bought plenty of socks and hosiery to go with serviceable flats and low-heeled boots. Some athletic shoes went into the mix as well. Now I needed bags to carry everything, and after I found three that would do, I skipped everything back to the hotel room, finding Ry still searching through the comp-vid and reading information Bel had transmitted on the killings before he'd gone missing.

"We still have time to go look at his hotel room this afternoon," Ry said, standing up and stretching. I figured a woman had delivered room service; the women always stared at Ry. Some even followed him around at times. Ry was quick to throw on a disguise if that happened. The remains of a nice lunch were scattered over a tray on the edge of the hotel desk where Ry worked. I remembered that I hadn't eaten while I'd been out shopping.

"Get what you needed?" Ry asked, eyeing my one and only farming outfit that I'd brought with me and had worn to go shopping.

"Yes. Now I just have to change. Is there anything left of your food?"

"Reah, it has gone cold. I'll order something else for you."

"No, I can grab something while we're out," I said, sorting through the clothing for something suitable to wear. Grabbing a blouse and slacks, plus new underwear, I walked into the bathroom and shut the door.

"Much better," Ry nodded when I came out, dressed in new clothing. Hastily I slipped into new shoes after donning socks—my stomach was telling me it wouldn't wait much longer to be fed.

"Someday, I'd like to eat another meal that you cooked," Ry said, grabbing his comp-vid and stuffing it in his pocket. I slipped my Ranos pistol into my new handbag and slung it over a shoulder. Normally I didn't carry a handbag, but I figured people would stare if I wore the pistol in a holster strapped to my thigh. I could still shoot; snakes lurked throughout the gishi fruit groves. If I found them, they didn't live over it; they were poisonous and threatened my workers. Well, Garde's workers, now. Briefly I hoped my daughters were all right and not in too much pain.

"Ry, I'd be happy to cook something for you. Find us a kitchen while we're out and you'll get whatever you want."

"I'll hold you to that." His smile was a blast of sunlight after a very dark night.

"Come on, handsome man, let's go see Bel's hotel room." Ry let me steer him out the door.

Bel's bags were still sitting on the rack, looking as if he'd sorted through them to find something to wear. He hadn't intended to leave anytime soon, I saw that right away. The ASD had sent a small team in to do perfunctory work, checking for blood, fingerprints and such. They'd found plenty of fingerprints, most Bel's, a few belonging to the cleaning crew. No blood. His comp-vid, weapons and a few other items were missing. They'd tried to triangulate on the comp-vid, but got nothing. That could mean it had been destroyed or reprogrammed, somehow. And since it was ASD issue, reprogramming would have been very tricky. They were designed to emit a locating beacon if someone tampered with it. Nothing had been sent.

Carefully, Ry and I went through all of Bel's belongings. I sorted through his shirts, pants and other clothing, feeling certain that if I held the shirts to my nose I still might catch a faint whiff of my old friend. I hoped he was alive somewhere, although my fears in that direction were rising. He would have sent mindspeech if he were able.

Now, Ry and I were trailing down a path gone cold, with little hope of finding anything at the end of it.

"There's nothing here." Ry had used his warlock talent to search while I'd done the physical part of it. Bel had slept here and very little else. We had his records—what he'd turned in, anyway. We'd found a reprimand or two in his files that said he wasn't the most prompt person to file reports. I knew that; Bel hated what he termed paperwork. I'd done it for him long ago when I'd first met him on Mandil. Now, Mandil had buckled and joined the Campiaan Alliance.

"It's a little late in the day to show up at those two businesses," I said. "But we can make appointments for tomorrow." One was a legal firm, the other a small electronics manufacturing concern. Hauling out my comp-vid, I called the legal firm first.

"We've already spoken with someone from the ASD," the receptionist was bordering on rudeness.

"And we're still investigating. Do you want answers or not?"

"Yes. But we wanted them a month ago."

"I understand that, and we'll do our best for you now," I said.

"Be here at ten bells tomorrow morning," she tapped the appointment into her scheduling-comp.

"Thank you," I nodded and terminated the communication. "Now, for the electronics plant." I figured this one survived because they made small household appliances—nothing that Dantel Schuul wanted to dirty his fingers with. He'd bought most of the competition long ago. I was more than grateful that I didn't have to deal with him or any of his employees. It would just be too awkward.

"Pripps Electronics," the face appeared on my comp-vid, mouthing the words at me. I wondered how often the young man said the same words every day.

"Hello, I am Reah Nilvas with the ASD," I held up my badge so the red-haired and freckled youth could examine it. "I need to make an appointment to ask questions about the murders at your business."

"Sure. We were wondering if the ASD had forgotten us. That attack wiped out most of our day crew," he said. "My name is Nirif, and my father was killed on that crew."

"Nirif, I am very sorry for your loss. May I make an appointment to come in and talk with someone about it? We're still trying to determine a cause for this."

"Sure. I wouldn't have pegged Jaske as a murderer, but he was." Nirif sounded angry. I would be, too. "You can come in tomorrow afternoon if you'd like, around third bell, if that's acceptable."

"That's good," I agreed. "We'll see you then." I tapped the comp-vid to end the call.

"How do we hedge around asking them about the information Bel got, without saying he's missing?" Ry asked. We sat inside a restaurant near our hotel, having sandwiches made with shaved ox-roast.

"I think I'll ask if they recorded the questioning," I said. "Just as a review, so we won't go over too much of the same ground."

"Good idea. Let's hope they thought to do it."

"I want to go over the records of the pirating activity for the past six months or so," I said. "Tonight."

"Good luck with that. I thought I'd fold to Le-Ath Veronis and check on a few things." I knew right away that Ry was going to see Tory; he just didn't want to upset me with that news. That didn't bother me; Tory was his brother, after all, and I certainly wouldn't interfere with that. I just nodded at Ry's words and we walked to the hotel in silence. Ry left shortly after we arrived.

I thought about contacting Lendill to see if he had half a click to spend with me, but changed my mind. He was busy with pirates. I was about to do a little research on them. I settled back against the headboard and pulled up the information stored in the ASD's archives.

"Did you know that between the two mass murders, two of Schuul Enterprises' ships were captured by pirates?" I asked Ry the following day over breakfast. He'd been out late and gotten around six clicks of sleep before we rose. Somehow, it didn't even bother me that Ry paraded around the room half-naked, brushing his teeth or drying his hair with warlock ability, running his fingers through the thick blackness until it was styled just right.

"I hadn't heard that," he said, biting into a breakfast roll. "I guess the two mass murder incidents drowned it out on the local news-vids. Plus, I figure everybody thinks Schuul Enterprises is wealthy enough to take dozens of hits before they even feel it."

"Yeah. That's probably true. I wonder what those chips are selling for on the black market," I said. "I'll have to look into that."

"If they're selling them. They could be keeping them for their own use."

"There's that," I agreed. "I'll check on that later, after we do our interviews."

The receptionist at the legal firm was falling over herself to be nice to us the moment she saw Ry. "My name's Genita," she gushed, holding her hand out for Ry to take. He gave her a charming smile and squeezed her fingers. He wasn't the best diplomat in either Alliance for no particular reason.

Genita led us to the cubicle belonging to the secretary who'd killed six of her coworkers. All the dead worked in the spaces surrounding hers. After the killings, she'd turned the laser pistol on herself, blasting her head off. According to the records I'd read, an ASD cleanup crew had picked up as much of the tissue and bloody matter as they could, hauling it to one of their labs for examination. They hadn't found anything.

"Maris even killed her own sister," Genita sighed as we examined Maris' cubicle. Bloodstains were still on the carpet and chair upholstery. The ASD hadn't given the firm permission to clean it up, yet. I knew about Maris Krastel's sister, Lethia. I couldn't fathom how Maris, the older sister, had been able to shoot her younger sister in the head and throat, killing her instantly. According to other relatives, the two had been very close.

"Do you have vids of the interviews the other agent did with the employees?" Ry asked.

"Oh, yes. We record everything. We're a legal firm, you know," Genita was smiling and running a finger around the low-cut neckline of her dress.

"Would it be a bother to get a copy of that?" Ry leaned closer to Genita and smiled back.

"No bother. Follow me," Ry walked beside Genita, I trailed behind, happy to do so. Ry was getting everything we wanted with a smile and a leer. We did perfunctory interviews with witnesses inside the office, asking if they'd remembered any other information since Bel had spoken with them. Two had minor information and we dutifully recorded it on comp-vid before thanking them and leaving.

"Do we have time to watch this before going to Pripps Electronics?" Ry held up the tiny case that held the data chip recording.

"Maybe, if we eat lunch while we're watching it," I said. Room service delivered soup and sandwiches while Ry and I settled in to watch the interviews that Bel conducted with Abinger's Legal Firm. The story didn't deviate much—Maris Krastel didn't have a grudge against anyone—at least to her coworkers' knowledge, and she and her sister had teased one another earlier in the day, laughing over some silly thing. After lunch, Maris had gone crazy, shooting her sister and five others with an unregistered weapon before taking her own life.

"Did they pick up Maris' comp-vid when the investigation was done?" Ry asked as we listened to one of Maris' coworkers say that Lethia, Maris' sister, had talked constantly about a vacation to Stellar Winds. In business for fifteen years, Stellar Winds was a social planetoid where singles could meet other singles and young couples could go to party. Mostly that's what it was—one continuous party.

The planetoid held one large city, with every business constantly serving drinks. Nothing ever closed, there, and if you weren't drinking, you could lounge around a pool at your hotel, get massages, book a mate-finding class, sign up to meet others with mutual interests or play any number of popular games, physical or mental. Everybody knew, though, that Stellar Winds was the place to go if you were looking for sex.

Brothels abounded across Stellar Winds, catering to any whim. Elegant dining was also offered there and many of the best master cooks now worked for restaurants on Stellar Winds. They were paid outrageous amounts for their work, too. Fes had lost two assistants and Radolf one that way.

"Wonder why her sister didn't go to Stellar Winds with her," Ry muttered as we listened to the secretary prattle on about Maris and Lethia.

"Maris' records say that she had a lover," I offered, still listening to the interview. "He was interviewed, too, and he said that he couldn't believe that Maris would do anything like this. He said that Lethia was Maris' best friend and confidant, besides being her sister."

"So, nothing in the records about the laser pistol used?"

"Not much. No identifying numbers or anything. It looked to be contraband from the old Campiaan Alliance." That's how everybody referred to it, now. There was the Campiaan Alliance, the one Teeg formed twenty-five years earlier, and the old Campiaan Alliance, referring to the scattering of nearly lawless worlds where strength and power ruled by force.

Plenty of older weapons found their way into both the Campiaan and Reth Alliances from many of those worlds. The ASD and CSD both worked toward eliminating them, but there was still plenty to be had if you had the right connections and the proper amount of non-identifying credits. The trouble was, Maris had neither of those things. Not that anyone knew of, anyway.

"And Maris' lover worked for?" Ry was prompting me.

"He's in lower-level management at one of Schuul Enterprises' many small electronics plants. I think they make sensors for home security alarms. He's so clean he squeaks when he walks, Mr. Faldin Bierla is."

The truth was, nearly half of Quezlos' population worked for some subsidiary of Schuul Enterprises or other. Quezlos, as the capital city of Surnath, boasted a teeming population of fifteen million. High rises rose far into the sky, filled with living quarters or multitudes of businesses. The largest and tallest, of course, belonged exclusively to Schuul Enterprises and all their business operations were located there.

On the recorded vid, Bel's questioning was thorough, and he didn't look much different from the last time I'd seen him. Mandil's population lived around two hundred twenty years, but their wizards lived around five times that long. Something about the power they held did that for them. Bel, according to the records, was barely three hundred. He had many turns left, if he still lived. I found myself sighing and worrying for my old friend again as I watched him on the vid.

I rushed to brush my teeth before we went out the door to visit Pripps Electronics. Nirif greeted us, and this time it was my turn to exude charm as much as I could, although I didn't have Ry's talent for it. Nirif didn't seem to mind, he wanted to fawn anyway. He was such a sweet young man, I didn't mind. And now he was fatherless and that got him an extra bit of sympathy. He also had a vid copy of the interviews Bel had done. I wanted to hug him for that.

Nirif produced vid-images of Jaske, too, something the legal firm hadn't done for us. Jaske worked as a supervisor on the assembly line. Mostly he supervised the employees who monitored assembly robots, and those employees were the ones he'd killed. Nirif was correct; Jaske had nearly wiped out the entire day shift that Pripps employed. Ry and I questioned the employees again, asking for any additional information. We got a bit more, just as we'd done at Abinger's Legal Firm.

"Here, the owner wanted to give these to you, they're prototypes of something we're developing," Nirif smiled and handed two packages to Ry and me.

"What's this?" I smiled at Nirif. I hadn't expected a gift.

"We're trying our hand at comp-vids," he said. "We're not ready to compete with Schuul, don't worry about that," he smiled. He'd seen Ry's and my comp-vids already. He knew who'd made them. "These are geared toward the ones who like to play games. The software helps with puzzles and such." He tapped the box I held in my hand. Schuul comp-vids were capable of loading any game imaginable, but none of them helped with the puzzles and such. You had to figure that out for yourself or buy additional programming that helped a little.

"Thanks," I said, waving at Nirif as we walked out the door. Ry and I slipped the information chip into our reader as soon as we made it back to our hotel, and settled in to watch as Bel interviewed Pripps employees. Turns out Jaske's mother worked for Schuul Enterprises. Still not a surprise. I was surprised that more of the employees didn't have a spouse or sibling working for Dantel Schuul in some capacity.

"Want to interview Maris' lover and Jaske's mother tomorrow?" Ry sighed as we shut off the comp-vid-images later. It was long past dinner and we'd have to find something to eat somewhere. Neither of us wanted sandwiches again.

"Sure. Bel talked to both of them, I know," I nodded. "Feel like that meal I promised to cook for you? I haven't gotten good fish in a long time."

"Where are you cooking?" Ry asked.

"How about going to Dee's? We can eat in the kitchen. If Radolf complains, I think I can take him." Ry grinned at me and folded us to Dee's.

"Reah, what's this I hear that you left Kifirin for good?" Radolf was hovering. He was still my mate, he just didn't feel up to having sex with a female and probably wouldn't for the next ninety-five years. Ilvan had come for a day off and was helping Radolf around the kitchen.

"You heard correctly," I said, pulling yaris fish from Radolf's industrial fridge and setting about preparing it for Ry and me.

"Are you sure that's wise, cutting yourself off like that?" Radolf fretted. I didn't point out that he'd done the same thing when he'd renounced his Karathian citizenship, just as Ry and I had.

"Rad, this is my decision and it was long overdue," I said, pouring a bit of oil into a skillet and dredging the fish in the flour, herb and spice mixture before laying it gently in the heated pan to cook. The sauce was what truly made the fish, and I'd already slapped it together. Thankfully, one of Rad's kitchen employees was putting a vegetable dish together for Ry and me.

"Who will you live with?" Radolf demanded to know. Now I knew why he seemed so concerned. He and Ilvan were in my house there on Tulgalan. He didn't want to be turned out of it or forced to share. It made me sigh. They'd taken it over as theirs, although it had been a gift from Teeg twenty-five years earlier.

"Rad, if you want the house, I'll sell it to you. Although it's probably still in Teeg's name. You'll have to work it out with him." That caused a lifting of eyebrows, both his and Ilvan's. I never stayed there anymore and none of my things were there any longer. I figured Rad and Ilvan had taken over the master suite long ago.

"Reah, it may be out of our price range," Ilvan pointed out. He was my uncle and Edan's younger brother. He'd been afraid to admit his sexual orientation to his father, Addah Desh, as long as Addah was alive. To say Addah was prejudiced might have been putting things in much too mild a perspective.

"Talk to Teeg. I'm not going to jerk it away from you," I assured him. "Stop worrying about it. I can stay at Aurelius' or Lok's. They're never home anyway."

"I'd like for both of you to stop bothering Reah about this; she will have a place to stay," Ry sounded angry for some reason, and he never angered. He was always diplomacy and discretion, in the highest measures. I was a little miffed, too, but I'd let them live in the house rent-free, so why should things change now?

I finished the fish, we got the vegetables onto our plates and Ry and I sat in the kitchen and had a nice dinner while Ilvan and Radolf kept working. I'd found a good bottle of wine to go with our fish, and Ry and I took the rest of it back to our hotel room in Quezlos.

"Reah, you have to stop allowing them to walk over you," Ry gave me a hug and poured more wine into two glasses the hotel provided. Handing one to me, he bumped his glass with mine.

"I guess I should reevaluate my relationships," I gulped half my wine. "In ninety-five years, we'll see if Radolf wants me again."

"Reah, he should want you now. That's how those relationships work."

"Could have fooled me." I gulped the rest of my wine. "All he sees is Ilvan, now."

"Ilvan is your uncle. He needs to see past his lust for a moment or two. If somebody were homesteading in his house and he needed it, you can bet he'd be having a fit."

"I allowed it for the past five years. They're entrenched, now."

"You have to stop letting people take advantage like that." Ry held my face in his hands for just a moment.

"Yeah. But that's not likely to happen anytime soon, is it?" I walked away from him. He'd taken the bed closest to the door, so I went to flop on mine, wishing I'd taken a second bottle of wine from Dee's. Yes, it was named after Dee, Teeg's surrogate father and right-hand vampire. He'd bought the restaurant for me, initially, with Teeg's money, but all the profits went back into the business, according to the books I saw. I seldom saw any of the money, and what I did see usually went to help the disabled on Kifirin. I worried whether they'd have proper care, now. Slapping a hand over my eyes, I moaned softly over how my life had gotten so complicated.

"Stop worrying about it," Ry said softly. "Get into your pajamas, Reah, and go to sleep. Dinner was incredible, by the way. It would have been the best ever, if we hadn't had Ilvan and Radolf to contend with."

"Ry, don't let them upset you. We'll just pretend they weren't there." I heaved myself off the bed and went to find my pajamas.

"I want to see Reah."

"Tory, I don't think that's a good idea, right now. Besides, she's working an assignment for Lendill."

"I have to see her. Soon. How will she know I want her back?"

"This is going to take time." Lissa brushed hair back from Tory's forehead. They were sitting in a nearly-dark kitchen, eating ice cream from Niff's.

"How much time, Mom? I don't think I can wait very long. It feels like years since we—you know."

"Honey, I'm sure it feels the same to Reah, too, and that's not a good thing. You know Wylend didn't give you the whole conversation, don't you? He wasn't being completely truthful when he came to you. He regrets that now, because Reah hasn't spoken to him for a very long time, either. Not really. And she renounced her Karathian citizenship."

"Yeah. Ry told me." Tory dropped his spoon into the empty ice-cream dish. "How could he do this—Em-pah Wylend, I mean? He could have broken Reah and me up forever. Looks like he broke Reah up with him forever."

"He did, honey. She won't ever go back to him. I think that's pretty much a given. Corolan has been heartbroken over it. He won't come around her because he doesn't want to be rejected."

"What about Em-pah Wylend? Is he heartbroken?"

Lissa sighed at her son's question. "Hon, I can't answer that. It doesn't look like he's debilitated or anything."

"I made a mistake, Mom. Darletta was the worst kind of mistake. She was pretty and she turned my head. Reah is beautiful. Darletta thinks she is, but there's so much ugly inside her."

"Torevik, there's no comparison between the two."

"Yeah. I know that now. When will I see my two babies?"

"That may take a little while. They don't know you, so we need to take it slow on that, all right? Give us a little time to prepare all of you. This is a big adjustment. Are you ready to be a father? Do you want to be? You have to prepare yourself for that."

"That's what upset Reah to begin with. I wasn't ready. I realize that now. But I'm getting there. I think I wouldn't mind holding a little person. Especially if that little person is part of me." Tory raked a hand through his dark hair, his gray eyes troubled.

"Then we'll work on that, baby." Lissa rose from her seat and hugged her second-born.

"Are you going to tell me where Reah is?"

"Not right now, Tory. She's busy and we don't need to upset her any more than she is already. Give it a little more time. Then we'll try to work this out. With her and with your daughters."

"Who's taking care of them? My babies?"

"Your Aunt Glinda and Uncle Jayd are watching over them, as is your father. They're well cared for. You don't have to worry."

"All right. But I want to see them soon."

"You will. I promise."

Zendeval Rjjn breathed out a sigh as he looked around him. Music thumped so loudly through the nightclub portion of Galedaro's that he couldn't hear himself think. Strobe lights in a rainbow of colors flashed across the dance floor and the usual capacity crowd was drinking, dancing and likely engaging in either sex or drug activity of some kind. He couldn't say that he liked any of it. He certainly had no appreciation for any of it and generally despised those who walked into the place, looking for titillation or escape.

Yes, he'd volunteered for the job, because it was so much better than the alternative. He didn't like the alternative. At all. He felt it cheapened what remained of his race. All seventy-two of them. His father told him long ago that things were better in the distant past, but that was so far in the past as to be nearly myth, Zen figured. He'd never seen the good times, when the race had inhabited their own planet. His cousin Nedrizif held himself as King, now, although he bore no royal blood.

Zen's father, Zondilir, had been the last of a long line of Kings. Zen suspected Nedrizif of killing his father, but he could prove nothing. Ned's story was that he'd found Zen's father, bleeding from many wounds delivered by a monster that disappeared conveniently when Ned showed up. Ned also claimed that Zond passed the kingship to him, since he was with his uncle when he died. Either way, Nedrizif wore the ring that made him King. Zen had been far away at the time of his father's death. A convenience for Ned, a decided inconvenience for Zen.

Zen sighed again and walked toward the door that led into the employee's catacombs. Passed dressing rooms for visiting musicians and performers, passed temporary sleeping quarters for some of the others that were on call. Walked by the door leading into the constantly busy kitchen. Three master cooks worked the kitchens at Galedaro's, and Zen was looking for one more to handle another shift so the others could have days off. If he didn't find someone suitable, he stood to lose at least two of his current cooks. He couldn't afford that; good master cooks were extremely difficult to find.

Tapping numbers into the keypad to bring his private elevator down, Zen stepped onto it and let the doors swish shut behind him. The conveyance operated on voice command—his voice and very few others. "Penthouse," he directed and was whooshed upward at a tremendous rate of speed. His comp-vid was going off before he set foot inside his quarters.

"Yes?"

"You'll have important visitors in seven days," Nedrizif informed him. "Six of them. Please ensure that they have the top suite and the best of everything. Have you hired the cook, yet?"

"I interviewed three today, and none of them was suitable. We have a standard to maintain, my King."

"Of course. Are there more interviews?"

"Yes. And I will place the advertisements again. I want the best we can get."

"As do I. Only the best will suit our guests, I assure you. I leave this task in your capable hands, cousin."

"I will do my best, my King."

"I depend upon it." Nedrizif terminated the communication. Zen punched the button a little slower and sighed again, tossing the comp-vid onto the hall table. His suite was sumptuous and he wanted for nothing, unless it was a bit of peace away from his cousin and the others. All of them postured and vied for position. Zen cared for none of it, but they were all that remained of his kind.

His father had told him once that they'd numbered in the millions before the fall of the race. A handful was all that was left, now. And here he was, the son of a King, taking orders and bowing down. *At least,* he thought for the second time in the same night, *it's better than the alternative.*

# CHAPTER 5

"Mrs. Trispe?" Ry's voice sounded so sympathetic. I wish I had his gift, at times. He knew just the proper tone to take, every time. We'd come to speak with Jaske Trispe's mother the following morning, and had an interview with Maris Krastel's lover, Faldin Bierla, in the afternoon.

"You're from the ASD?" Shedrith Trispe seemed surprised that Rylend was an agent. I might agree with her, if I were in her place. Ry could grace any number of vid-mag covers, modeling the latest fashions or hairstyles.

"Yes. We've come to follow up on the case. We're still trying to determine what happened that would cause your poor son to deviate from his normal behavior."

"You do understand," Shedrith Trispe whispered, her eyes watering.

"Of course. Everyone says that this was so unlike him." Ry could have the worst of the worst eating from his hand in three blinks, I imagine.

"Please, come in." She held the door open for us. I followed Ry, not saying anything. We were led to seats in a small but tidy sitting room and drinks were offered. "He was such a good boy, even though he refused to work for Schuul Enterprises," Shedrith Trispe sighed as she sat across from us. "I didn't argue with his bid for independence, you know."

"Such a good parent," Ry said sympathetically. "Do you remember the other agent who came to speak with you?"

"Yes. He was nice as well, but not nearly as sympathetic. And I must admit, I'd just lost my boy, so I'm afraid I was weeping during the interview."

"Do you remember anything you talked about?" Ry asked.

"He just asked about Jaske. What he liked to do, where he liked to go. If he had any friends, that sort of thing."

"What do you think happened, Mrs. Trispe? Did something upset your son?"

"Not that I noticed," she said. "He was supposed to go out with a girl that he'd dated twice before, and he was looking forward to it. That's why all this is such a mystery. His life was opening up and he had such a good future, I think."

"Do we have the name of the girl?" Ry asked. "Just for my information," he added.

"I didn't have it for the other man; I told him I'd try to find it. Jaske was so secretive about the whole thing." She smiled, rose from her seat and went to a drawer, pulling out a comp-vid. "This was his, you know," she informed us and powered it up, scrolling through the menu. "Here it is—her name is Sedra." She handed the comp-vid to Ry with the information displayed.

"May I keep this for a day or so, just in case?" Ry asked. He could demand it, and I wondered why Bel hadn't asked for it. Perhaps it had slipped past him, somehow, during the questioning.

"Of course. I didn't find it until recently, I heard it ringing and found it tucked beneath Jaske's mattress. I'd have turned it over to the other man if I'd known about it before. I thought it was with Jaske when he—when he," she couldn't finish, she was weeping. I pulled tissues from the small handbag I carried and offered them to her. She took them and wiped her eyes and face. Jaske had killed himself, much like Maris Krastel had, by shooting himself in the neck and head with the laser pistol he had. More and more I found the similarities between the two cases curiously disturbing.

"Mrs. Trispe," I said, once she'd gotten herself back in hand, "I know this has no bearing on the case, but I heard that two of Schuul Enterprises' ships were hijacked by pirates shortly after your son died. I imagine that was a terrible blow to the company you work for."

"Yes. An entire month's work, stolen," she nodded. "We were all upset over it, and many of us had to work double shifts afterward to replace the orders. Thankfully, the second shipment wasn't intercepted."

"They asked you to work overtime, after such a grievous tragedy in your life?" Ry asked.

"I know. Maybe it was better that I didn't have much time to dwell on my sorrow," she said, wiping her cheeks again. "And we earned a small bonus for getting replacement chips manufactured so quickly."

"You're a strong woman, Mrs. Trispe," Ry said. "If you would, think back to the questioning by the other agent. Did he ask any unusual questions? That you recall?"

"He did ask one strange question," Shedrith Trispe replied, her brown eyes red from weeping, and a bit of gray showing in dark hair that I imagined hadn't been there before the death of her son.

"And what was that?" Ry asked.

"He asked if Jaske had ever gone to Stellar Winds."

"That is so strange," Ry agreed, as we discussed Bel's question to Mrs. Trispe. Why would he want to know if Jaske had ever gone to Stellar Winds? Mrs. Trispe said that Jaske hadn't.

"The local ASD office has Maris' and Lethia's comp-vids. Maybe we should ask to look at them, too," I said. I was going through Jaske's, trying to determine if he'd gotten any calls or messages that might have set him off. So far, I hadn't found anything, but personal communication was password protected. I'd need the computer at the local ASD office to get past that.

"And we can ask if they confiscated a second comp-vid off his body," Ry said. I nodded—I'd been thinking the same thing. Nobody went anywhere without a comp-vid. It was foolish to do so.

After a quick lunch, we took the transit train to the western edge of Quezlos where Faldin Bierla had an apartment. It struck me as strange that Maris hadn't moved in with him and that they lived so far apart. I shrugged it off for the moment—Ry could have folded us or I could have skipped us over, but for some reason he was content to ride public transportation. Sometimes it's interesting and informative to do so.

I'd once killed a half-crazed Ra'Ak who'd gotten onto a bus, intent on killing all on board. He hadn't counted on a High Demon being there, who'd beaten him to the punch. He'd dusted after I'd taken his head in my smaller Thifilatha, blowing out the windows in the hoverbus and injuring many of the passengers. At least nobody died; Lendill and Norian had confiscated the vid-recording and explained it away as an accident.

This time, there were no homicidal Ra'Ak to deal with on our bus trip, just mothers with small children on their way home after finishing a day in early-school, or those with physician's appointments or some such. A young unmarried couple was on their way to the space station terminal. They were traveling to Stellar Winds and discussing their trip excitedly. Somehow, they'd gotten a discounted trip to the popular party planetoid.

Ry and I glanced briefly at one another as the couple talked. Some people (and I wasn't one of them) looked forward to drinking until they were sick, having sex until they passed out, or both. Stellar Winds was an all-inclusive resort planet, but if one wanted to visit the better nightclubs and restaurants, one had to purchase an upgrade, which included a chip that granted access to the exclusive spots. It was a point of pride and an indication of wealth if the visitor could afford the upgrades.

Our stop came up long before the one for the space station, so we didn't get to see the couple off on their vacation. Instead, we walked toward Faldin Bierla's high-rise apartment to question him about his deceased lover.

"I told the other agent everything I know," Faldin was rude from the start. I could tell when someone was lying, and Faldin Bierla was concealing something. I just didn't know what it was. He lived well for someone of his station, but he was nearing sixty. Plenty of time to put together enough wealth to afford such a nice apartment.

"I'm very sorry for your loss," I said. "And I hope you'll forgive us if we ask a few of the same questions," I added, disliking him quickly.

"I will protest this treatment," he snapped. "I'll go straight to the Director myself."

"Go ahead. Would you like to speak to him now?" Ry called Faldin's bluff by hauling out his comp-vid and tapping in Norian's code.

"What do you want to know?" Faldin grumbled angrily.

Neither Ry nor I asked any questions about Stellar Winds; we asked instead about the relationship he had with Maris, when he'd seen her last, that sort of thing. To Faldin, his and Maris' relationship didn't seem to be anything other than casual, although Maris' coworkers had made it sound quite serious. Maris may have presented it as more than it was; therefore, the employees at Abinger's Legal Firm thought it to be a significant relationship.

Faldin pointed out that he'd only seen Maris twice during the month leading up to the murders, and said what the others did about how close she'd been with her sister. It made me wish I could have questioned Lethia, but she was dead. Maris and Lethia's parents were also deceased—killed in an accident years earlier. Faldin didn't volunteer anything and didn't answer anything, other than what he was forced to. We left him behind roughly a click later, feeling unsatisfied, somehow.

"I want to get into the information supplied by the legal firm—you know, the cases that Maris researched. And Lethia, too," I said.

"I'll help," Ry said. "I sent a request to the local ASD office; they've got the comp-vids they took from Maris, Lethia and the one they found on Jaske."

"So, he did have a second one," I said.

"Looks like it. Come on, Sherlock, let's do a little sleuthing." Ry gave me a brilliant smile and led me toward the public transportation kiosk.

"Sherlock?" I lifted an eyebrow.

"A fictional character. Reah, you really need to brush up on your English reading skills."

"Uh-huh." That colloquialism had Ry grinning at me. "You could brush up on your cooking skills at the same time."

"Point taken," he nodded and ushered me onto the next transport.

"You're welcome to look through that box of tangled mess that Bel left behind." The supervisor at the local ASD office led us to one of the locked steel cubicles inside the facility. "There's a desk comp in there as well, to get into the other files you want. Just enter your codes and you'll get it."

"Thanks, Supervisor Steeb," I said. This one was looking at me the whole time. Ry had already sent mindspeech, telling me she preferred women. I'd figured that out quickly on my own. Bel had certainly left a box of tangled objects inside the cubicle. Maris' comp-vid, Lethia's comp-vid and a few other things were lying on a steel table inside, along with clothing and other evidence. The box Doras Steeb mentioned was in a corner of the room. Usually, evidence was sequestered in a basement, inside a much smaller space. A killing such as this, as odd and as violent and deadly as it turned out to be, rated its own cubicle above ground.

"Look at this—there's at least six comp-vids in this box." Ry held up one of the small, rectangular electronic devices. I stared at it; it looked as if it had been gutted, with the back missing, the battery pulled out of it and what looked to be part of a data chip hanging out and damaged.

"You think Bel was hard on his comp-vids?" I asked. "We can pull up the registration on all of them to see for sure."

"I'll do that, you get into the comp," Ry jerked his head at the chair.

I scooted into the padded seat and booted up the desk comp, entering my clearance codes as soon as the screen appeared.

"Here—it looks like Maris was working on files submitted in that Prekisule Company case," I said, reading through information on the screen.

"The one that said they were not only making the screens for the comp-vids, but the cases as well, even though the case company is listed under a different name?"

"Yeah. That other company is Meldrim Enterprises; it's mentioned here, too. The case was dropped in the last three weeks from lack of evidence," I said.

Everything was in the file that I'd pulled up from Abinger's Legal Firm. Someone from Meldrim had come to the ASD, claiming that the two companies were actually owned by the same conglomerate, which couldn't be. It violated the anti-trust laws of the Reth Alliance. The chips were manufactured by Schuul Enterprises, the screens by Prekisule, the cases by Meldrim, and other parts and pieces by this company or that, not all of which were on the same worlds. Prekisule and Meldrim were certainly not on Surnath, I knew that much.

"So, Maris was doing the legal legwork on that, then," Ry grunted, digging through Bel's box of stuff.

"Looks like it. And then she went crazy and shot up the office." I turned to her comp-vid next; it was carefully labeled as such. A bit of dried blood was on it, too. I handled it gingerly, although it had already had any fingerprints scanned by the locals. Syncing it with the larger system in front of me, I entered my security codes to get the larger comp to sort out Maris' passwords. They pulled up quickly—someone had already done this, as I'd expected. Likely, it had been Bel. I scrolled through personal messages Maris had sent and received just before the murder; there wasn't anything unusual about any of them, so I worked my way backward, until I came to one she'd sent to her sister about two eight-days prior to the murders.

*I saw him with her again. At Starshine.* Maris had sent to Lethia.

*He's scum,* Lethia had sent back. *You need to dump him.*

*Thinking about it,* Maris had replied. *I can do better.*

"Faldin was fooling around," I held up Maris' comp-vid and turned in my chair to look at Ry, who was trying to piece a comp-vid back together. This one looked as if Bel had stomped on it.

"Big surprise," Ry muttered, trying to force pieces of the case together again.

I went through other messages, back two months, at least, and didn't find anything else worth mentioning. Faldin was correct in one sense; he and Maris weren't that close. Only a handful of messages were recovered between the two of them and there was nothing noteworthy in any of those. I turned to Jaske's comp-vid next. I got a hit from the girl he was seeing right away—she'd sent him something only a few clicks before he went crazy. The message had an eyebrow lifting.

*See you tonight at Starshine*, she'd sent. Poor Jaske had sent *I love you* as a reply. Those were the last words he'd sent to this girl, who apparently meant so much to him. Images were compiled in the comp of all the dead, both shooters and victims. Jaske wasn't that much to look at. I went searching for the image of his girlfriend, Sedra Prade, finding it at the end of the others.

Sedra was very pretty, with shoulder-length, dyed red hair with blue tips, cut unevenly at the ends—one of the current styles popular with the younger ones. She was dressed in a shiny red outfit that had the Starshine logo printed on the left breast. She worked for the most popular nightclub in Quezlos, and likely on all of Surnath. Some called it little Stellar Winds and all the popular and wealthy among the younger set went there to meet and mingle. Opening later in the evening, it stayed open until nearly dawn, with loud music thumping through the place while alcohol (and drugs, more than likely) flowed freely.

A legal brothel was onsite, too—licensed by the Surnathan government, of course. Some drugs were legalized in the Alliance, but employers weren't allowed to let their employees work if they were under the influence. Most had scanners nowadays, located at employee entrances. If an employee set it off, they were sent home. Too many times being sent home and they lost their job. There was always some abuse, but the businesses faced very stiff fines and regular visits from the local constabulary if found in violation.

Personal hovercraft was also equipped with the same type of scanners. You couldn't drive on manual if you'd imbibed—either alcohol or drugs. Jail time was assigned if the sensors were tampered with in your conveyances. Most people didn't own anything like that, depending upon public transportation instead.

"Tell me why this girl would be seeing Jaske," I said, moving aside so Ry could get a look at Sedra Prade, and then flipping over to Jaske's image.

"He looks like a nerd," Ry nodded. "Not that stranger things haven't happened," he was still working on the comp-vid, I think, trying to shove parts back together. Finally, he gave up and used his extensive warlock gift. The thing floated in midair and went right back together, as it should be. "There," Ry grinned and floated it to me.

"Why didn't you do that to begin with?" I wrinkled my nose at him.

"You know, we men have to try brawn first."

"Uh-huh." I turned back to Sedra's image. "You know, since Maris saw Faldin at Starshine with someone else, and Jaske's girlfriend works there, I think we should go out tonight," I turned to look at Ry.

"Sure. Do you have a hip outfit and dancing shoes?"

"Hip?" I was completely lost at his jargon.

"You know, sliding."

"The term that means trendy and appealing to those younger than twenty-five?"

"Yes. Sliding. Do you have a sliding outfit?"

"Sure. As soon as I go out and buy it," I grumped.

"I'll come. It has to meet with my approval."

"You're the fashion constabulary, are you?"

"You got it." Ry's grin would have stopped many a female heart. I just grinned back at him.

I lifted the comp-vid he'd reassembled with power and synced it with the comp, pulling up any records that might be on it. Bel had used this one; I could see that right away. Several appointments were listed, showing the dates he'd interviewed the workers at Maris' legal firm, and then when he'd gone to question those at Pripps Electronics. I pulled up all his interviews, the ones we'd seen already, anyway, through copies provided by both businesses. Bel hadn't used this one long, as it turns out.

"Is there any saving of the others?" I asked, turning to Ry again.

"Parts are missing," he said, tossing the last one into the box. "Mostly the chips. Can't pull anything up if you don't have those."

"Did he remove them, or did someone else?" I asked.

"I already did a scry. Bel did it. On all five of the others. The one you have is the only one that had all the parts there."

"What was he thinking?" I muttered, mostly to myself.

"What were Maris and Jaske thinking?" Ry's dark eyes met mine.

"I don't know." I shook my head.

"Reah, that one is incredible." Ry walked around me as I stared in the mirror at the short, tight-fitting black dress I wore. I'd have been happier if it didn't glitter with thousands of tiny, jet-black beads. The shoes were almost as bad, with heels twice as high as I felt comfortable wearing. Tiny, gold straps hooked around my ankles, and gold beading glistened around the edges of the soles. The rest was black, to match my dress.

"And see, since you've had those babies, this is filled out perfectly." He stood behind me and cupped both breasts in his hands.

"Rylend Morphis, you lech," I turned and smacked his hands lightly. He laughed.

"This jewelry will go well with this," the female clerk was back, offering a long, beaded necklace in black and gold, with matching earrings.

"Pack it all up, we'll take it," Ry said, without waiting for me to say anything. He bought a shirt but already had pants and boots to wear, and that's how we found ourselves walking up to the line waiting outside Starshine later. Someone was going down the line, picking out the prettiest people to let in first. Unless you were wealthy or well-known, or both. Those were escorted in without standing in any line. Ry smiled down at me.

*Remember, we're together, so act like you like me, all right?* he sent.

*Who's acting? I love you, you pompous, handsome ass*, I returned.

*Just remember, you said it first*, he informed me silently. I did love him. Had always. He was like a brother. The one I grumbled to about Teeg or Tory or any other number of people or things. Whenever Teeg had a function, Ry was my escort for at least part of the evening. He asked about the girls. They adored their uncle Ry. He bought them gifts, even when I said no, sometimes. We ended up never arguing about it.

"What do we have here?" The Starshine employee, wearing a shirt that proclaimed him *Gate Keeper* and backed up by two rather large security guards, was standing in front of Ry and me. "These two are in," he jerked his head at one of the guards, who escorted us right to the front and even opened the door for us. Yes, Ry's face opened a lot of doors.

*What does Sedra do here?* The music was so loud Ry was back to mindspeech.

*Bartender*, I told him. Ry tucked my hand in the crook of his arm and led me through the crowd toward the bar. Sedra, in her sliding outfit, was pouring a line of shots for an appreciative male crowd. Her top revealed most of her breasts and hugged her like a second skin. Hair tips were dyed purple, to match the Starshine top worn over very short, black shorts.

*What do you want, pretty girl?* Ry asked.

*What are you having?*

*Yadeli*, he replied. Yadeli was a particularly fine bourbon. Not the most expensive, but better than that, in my estimation.

*I'll take a cloudy sunset, then*, I returned. A cloudy sunset had bourbon and two other types of mixers in it, the layers making it look like gold and purple clouds. It was good, too. I made them now and then, for the supervisors on my work crews. Well, Garde's work crews, now.

Ry stepped up to the bar and had Sedra's attention right away. He ordered and then laid a casual arm around my shoulders when Sedra attempted to get friendly while she made our drinks. Sedra didn't give up, though, chattering away with Ry, even though it was difficult to hear inside the massive bar. Ry grabbed our drinks and walked away, leaving Sedra talking to empty space.

"Hello," another Starshine employee appeared at our table the moment we sat down. "We're offering discounts to Stellar Winds to some of our best customers," the young man said, handing me a recycled plastic brochure. Paper wasn't used much in the Alliance any longer. "Just enter the code number here," he pointed to a number listed at the bottom of the ad, "when you book your reservations. This is good for half off your trip." I blinked up at him—he was nice-looking, no question about that, with black hair, cut in the latest style and vibrant blue tips spiking up here and there. He wore lenses in his eyes, making them a striking yellow. Going for a feral look, no doubt.

Ry thanked him while I stuffed the brochure into my small handbag. I watched the young man walk away, noticing that he wasn't giving brochures out to everyone. I sat up straighter and paid attention, watching while he handed out another one to a handsome couple seated at a table six away from ours. He'd ignored the average-looking customers in between.

*Ry, what are they doing?* I asked mentally. He'd seen what I'd seen, his eyes following the young man as he made his way through the bar. Just as the pretty couples were allowed inside the bar first, now they were offered half-price trips to Stellar Winds. There was a connection between the two, and I wondered what it was.

"Reah," Ry jerked his head to the side. He'd seen them first. I followed his gaze, drawing in a breath. Faldin Bierla was there, escorting a date. I recognized her, all right. Darletta Schuul was with Faldin, dressed in something that I couldn't have afforded with five years' pay in the gishi fruit groves.

Now I knew where Maris had seen Faldin with "her." Faldin was listed in our files as a low-level supervisor for Schuul Enterprises. Somehow, he'd managed to snare the biggest fish in Surnath's pond. *He must have other talents,* I thought to myself. Tory was so much nicer to look at. It made me wonder if Tory and Darletta had come here while they were still together. The thought made me shudder.

*Reah, hold it together, sweetheart,* Ry's voice was gentle in my mind. I doubted that Darletta would recognize Ry or me—she'd only seen us once before and that was nearly twenty-six years earlier. Faldin and Darletta were too old to be in this crowd, too—I saw the young ones all around them staring.

Darletta was nearing fifty and Faldin was in his sixties. In their prime but still too old for here. Ry and I would always appear to be in our twenties. That's what immortality did for our kind. Someone else came to speak with Faldin, someone else who was also older in appearance. He wore a badge indicating that he was a Starshine employee. Likely the manager, I thought, as I watched Faldin lean down to say something to Darletta. She went to sit at the bar while Faldin followed the employee. Ry, watching just as I was, patted my hand and rose to see where they went.

*They just walked into an employee entrance,* Ry sent, sitting down again.

*We need to find out who owns this place,* I replied.

*Yeah. I think we do,* Ry agreed, emptying his drink in one swallow. *Let's go.*

We'd barely gotten out of the place before receiving mindspeech from Lendill. The local ASD office had been broken into and ransacked. Lendill and Norian were already there; both could fold, so it wasn't surprising.

Ry folded us to the location, where two overly-zealous ASD agents thought to keep us from going inside. When Ry and I hauled out our IDs, we were allowed through. Lendill met us in the lobby.

"It's difficult to pinpoint ASD offices," Lendill rubbed the back of his neck as we surveyed the wreckage inside the building. The lobby had been destroyed by an explosion—that's how the perpetrators had gotten in. Then, they'd methodically tossed several cubicles, including the one Ry and I had been inside earlier. Ry and I blinked at one another as we stopped outside the entrance. The locked, metal door had been blasted off its hinges and everything inside was broken and scattered.

"Lendill, this is the room that held all the evidence from the shootings we're investigating," I said.

"Was anything taken?" Lendill crunched across bits of debris to poke his head inside the door.

"We'd have to get in there to see," I sighed. The place was wrecked and the desk comp had been shattered and tossed in a corner.

"The box of junk is gone," Ry said. I stared up at him; his eyes were unfocused, indicating that he was scrying the area. I envied his talent, at times. It would have taken time for me to go through everything in the room to determine that.

"What was in it?" Lendill waited until Ry was back with us.

"Comp-vids that Bel destroyed for some reason," Ry answered. "He'd torn chips out of several. I had to use power to put one back together that looked as if it had been stomped on."

"If he wanted to destroy it, why didn't he use power?" Lendill asked.

"No idea. I wondered the same thing," Ry shrugged.

"Reah, you look incredible," Lendill sighed softly at my side. I'd forgotten how I was dressed.

"We took a little investigative trip to Starshine, and found Maris Krastel's lover boy, Faldin Bierla, there with Darletta Schuul," Ry gave Lendill a look. I figured Ry was also sending private mindspeech. That was all right with me; the less I heard about Darletta, the better.

"A bit old for that place, don't you think?" Lendill said aloud.

"We'll research all of it," Ry said. "Do you need our help here with this?"

"Not since I know what's missing, now," Lendill shook his head. "Write a report and get it to me by the end of the night."

"We will." Ry steered me away from the wreckage.

"Here, it lists the ownership of Starshine," Ry handed his comp-vid to me after I walked out of the bathroom dressed in pajamas. I took it and scrolled through the names. Six investors were listed, and Darletta Schuul's name was one of them.

"Big surprise, but why was it Faldin and not Darletta who was asked into the back?" I said, handing Ry's comp-vid back.

"Maybe they had a technical problem and needed his assistance."

"He does work for the alarm side of their business, doesn't he?"

"Yeah. He does." Ry didn't sound convinced to me. I wasn't convinced, either. The employee hadn't spoken to Darletta at all. He'd gone straight to Faldin, and if Darletta was an owner, he should have bowed and scraped to her, first.

"Ry," I said, grabbing the purse I'd used earlier and pulling the brochure for Stellar Winds out of it, "why is Starshine promoting Stellar Winds? Does Darletta have a piece of it as well?"

"Good question," Ry said, tapping on his comp-vid. Obviously he had clearance codes, just as I did. "Here." He offered the comp-vid to me a second time. Seven names were listed, and right in the middle was Darletta Schuul's.

"So, Daddy makes comp-vid chips and Darletta does sex and sin," I grumbled.

"Both lucrative," Ry said.

"No doubt about it," I agreed.

"I think Lendill wants to see you in that dress again sometime," Ry said as I pulled the covers back on my bed.

"He might find time for that in a year or two," I said, climbing into my bed and turning out the light on my side. Filing the report and fretting over the break-in had worn me out. Why had thieves taken the box of junk Bel left behind? Why?

~

"Mom, I left Reah asleep in our room." Ry settled on the sofa inside Lissa's private study. She was working late and told Ry where to find her when he'd sent mindspeech.

"What's up?" Lissa looked at her firstborn (by a matter of days) who sat across from her desk.

"I think I know part of the reason why Tory's memory has gaping holes in it."

Lissa's eyes widened. She was dressed comfortably in fleece as she worked over the information for the next Reth Alliance Conclave. "What did you find? Do you know how it happened?"

"I don't know the how, but I may know the why," Rylend's sigh was heavy. "Darletta has her fingers in Starshine on Surnath, and is one of the owners of Stellar Winds. When she and Tory married, she didn't have anything – Daddy owned all of it. That has obviously changed through the years. She didn't want to give Tory any part of that when she sent him packing. And it was her choice, I'd bet on it," Ry's handsome face held worry.

"She's already going around with someone else. Reah and I saw both of them tonight at Starshine. The thing is, the man Darletta was with is the former lover of the woman who shot several of her coworkers at Abinger's Legal Firm in Quezlos."

"That's weird," Lissa said. "Are you and Reah working on all that?"

"Yeah. That's what we're working on, Mom. Bel was doing the investigation, and he disappeared. Lendill asked us to find Bel, so we're backtracking his last few steps. This is turning into one of your cans of worms, Mom."

"Sounds like it. You think Darletta and dear old Dad had something to do with Tory's loss of memory?"

"Yeah. How else can we explain it? How's Tory doing?"

"Connegar says that they've got him to the point where he believes Raedah and Tara are six," Lissa said, standing and pushing her chair in. "If I find out the Schuuls did something to him, I may have a few words to say."

"You can't interfere, can you?"

"No. Belen and the others say no. They say that this has to play out as it does. It will alter the timeline if I try."

"So, no sense *Looking*, huh?"

"I haven't even tried."

"Then Reah and I will do our best to piece this together. Don't worry, Mom, we'll get to the bottom of it."

"Please do. Get good, hard evidence for me, honey, and I'll see that they're prosecuted."

"We will. I need to get back."

"Let me know if you need anything," Lissa stood on tiptoe to kiss Ry's cheek.

"Will do." Ry folded away.

~

"Have fun?" I asked sleepily when Ry appeared in the darkness inside our hotel room.

"Went to see Mom for a few minutes," he replied, pulling his shirt off and wandering into the bathroom. "Besides, you're supposed to be sleeping."

"I need a glass of water," I said, tossing back covers and sliding out of bed. Ry was brushing his teeth at the sink as I held a glass under the running water when the blast hit, and if I hadn't gone to smaller Thifilatha and skipped Ry away after we got knocked against the shower wall, he might have been badly burned at the very least.

# CHAPTER 6

No heat or fire can harm a High Demon's Thifilathi. Or Thifilatha, if the female can turn. Most didn't. My daughters hadn't. At least not yet. I'd wrapped myself around Rylend Morphis and hauled him out of our burning hotel room, skipping to the first place that came to mind—my house on Kifirin. The cottage was empty, thank goodness, else we might have had to explain why I was naked and Ry's clothing was smoldering.

"Fuck!" Ry shouted, pacing and flinging his arms this way and that. I'd never seen him so angry. I wasn't arguing with it, though, opting instead for going to the closet in my old bedroom and pulling something out that I could wear. My new clothing had been inside the hotel room, and all of it was now obliterated.

*Reah?* Lendill's frightened mindspeech came as I was slipping into an old pair of shoes. *We're on Kifirin, both of us,* I reassured him. He appeared, seconds later.

"Reah got us out, I wasn't expecting anything of the sort and was unprepared." Ry was as angry with himself as he was with whoever had bombed our room.

"This is no coincidence," Lendill muttered, watching Ry pace. "The moment my agents begin to look into this again, someone tries to kill them." I'd been thinking the same thing, and that had me frightened for Bel. Again. I was hugging myself without realizing it.

"Reah, don't worry, we'll deal with this," Ry put his arms around me. "Lendill, can you release a statement saying we got killed? And can you salvage anything inside the room and bring it to us at my chalet on Campiaa?"

"Sure. Norian is on Quezlos and about to pitch the biggest fit, so I'll go calm him down," Lendill nodded at Ry and me before folding away.

"Ry, what does this mean?" I looked up at him. My back was to his chest and he was squeezing me gently, his chin resting on the top of my head until I moved.

"No idea. Come on, there's plenty of room at my place." Ry folded me to Campiaa.

"Is this the best you could find?" Zendeval glared at his assistant, who was as efficient as any assistant could be. Zen had just finished interviewing four master cooks and didn't like any of them. They'd cooked for him, he'd tasted the food and none of it was up to Galedaro's standards. It would do at a lesser restaurant, and Zen fumed over that. He oversaw the five best establishments on Stellar Winds. Galedaro's was the best of that five. That's where he had his offices and suite. Jerves, his assistant, lived on one of the lower levels and kept things running smoothly for the most part, bringing only the most important decisions to Zen for approval.

"Sir, I can only bring you the best of those who apply," Jerves was worried, Zen could tell.

"Did you contact those on Tulgalan, as I asked?"

"I did. They politely turned me down," Jerves was shaking slightly, Zen noticed.

"Jerves, calm yourself. All right? You're not about to lose your job. Go back to the ones I mentioned and offer more money."

"I will, but I don't know if that will mean anything. They're a close-knit family, and quite loyal."

"Then we'll work on that," Zen sighed. "Go. See what you can do. We need to hire someone in the next two days."

"Of course, sir. I'll let you know as soon as I have anything."

"See that you do." Zen watched as Jerves hurried out the door to his private office. He had the list of seven visitors in front of him—Nedrizif had finally sent it. The seven official owners' names were displayed on Zen's comp-vid. There were two other owners who wouldn't (and couldn't) be listed. Nedrizif was one of those. Zen ran fingers through his dark-brown hair and tugged.

Ry has a beautiful chalet, high in the mountains surrounding Campiaa City. I was leaning on his kitchen island, a cup of tea in my hands and staring out a huge window overlooking the mountain and the city below.

"Sleep well?" Ry came in wearing pajama bottoms only and poured tea for himself. If more women could see the body, coupled with the face, they'd have multiple orgasms on the spot. Ry usually worked out with someone; either Drake, Drew or their father or uncle, two or three times a week. Rylend Morphis was a master swordsman, even if he never talked about it.

"Tossed and turned," I said. My eyes felt gritty as a result.

"Yeah. Me, too." Ry went to turn on the small vid-screen that sat on a corner of his kitchen counter.

"Philis' sister, Jilis, disappeared nearly a moon-turn ago," a journalist said. "The twins did everything together, according to their parents." I turned, mildly curious as to why twins would be kidnapped in separate incidents, if they were together most of the time. An image of the twins in question, both very pretty blondes, I noticed, was displayed on the screen. The other thing that interested me was that both were wearing identical Stellar Winds logo shirts—the kind the tourists purchased. Those shirts were a status symbol and quite popular.

"Ry, do you see that?" I asked.

"See what?" I was moving closer to the vid-screen, coming to stand beside him.

"They're wearing shirts from Stellar Winds."

"Reah, lots of people have those shirts."

"I know. Do you have a comp or a comp-vid here?" I asked.

"Here." He opened a drawer at the kitchen island, handing an old one over. "That one's ancient, but it still works."

"I can see that," I said, poking him in the ribs. He grabbed me and swatted my behind.

"Careful, I have these things tied as tight as I can," I said. I was wearing some of his pajamas and they hung off me. I'd rolled up the legs a time or two, just to walk in them without tripping.

"What are you looking for?" he asked, letting me go.

"Other disappearances," I said, scrolling through names from the past year. Actually, it was sun turn instead of year on Campiaa. I dismissed that thought and kept looking, sorting through information and images that popped up, courtesy of the ASD files I was accessing. Although they didn't investigate kidnappings and such, leaving that to locals to sort out, they did keep files on all of it, in case some of their criminals were involved.

"How are you picking and choosing?" Ry was mystified as he leaned over my shoulder to watch.

"I'm picking out the pretty ones," I said. After I'd collected about twenty-five female victims out of the dozens of records I'd scanned, I then went searching into their backgrounds. "Ry, look at this," I pulled up sixteen of the twenty-five records. "All of these girls visited Stellar Winds less than a year before they were abducted. And all these cases are unsolved."

Ry was now staring at me, his mouth open in shock.

～

"Do you think this is what Bel stumbled upon, working the other investigation?" Lendill asked later as we sat in the office he kept inside Ildevar Wyyld's palace.

"I think it's possible," I said. "Starshine certainly played a part in the investigation, and Bel may have gotten information somehow, since they only hand those brochures to the good-looking couples. They offered Ry and me half off our visit." I handed the brochure to Lendill.

He'd managed to rescue my purse and a few other items from our bombed hotel room, including the two boxed comp-vids that Pripps Electronics had given us. No pictures were shown of Ry and me, but the information that Lendill released said both occupants of the hotel room were dead, with two others in an adjoining room injured.

"Then I want you to go to Stellar Winds," he said. "Only not as guests. I want to get to the root of this." He pushed a comp-vid across his desk toward me. "There's a master cook's position open at the best place on Stellar Winds, and another job available in Guest Relations," Lendill looked at both of us. He'd been busy since I'd first contacted him with my hunches. "Reah, the first gishi fruit shipment from Kifirin was hijacked by pirates," Lendill added as I read the ad for the cook's position.

Raising my eyes, I stared at Lendill. "Hon, tell Garde to list the shipment as nannas next time. Both fruits need the same type of cool environment to ship, and I'll lay money on the odds that a nanna shipment won't get attacked."

"Code, Reah?" Lendill asked, frowning at me.

"If you want, yes," I said. "And tell them to seal the cartons, so nobody on board the ship can see what's inside."

"I'll do it, as a test run," Lendill agreed.

"I'm submitting my application now," I said, tapping the required information into Lendill's comp-vid. I had my master cook's license, now. Had it since I'd been pregnant with Raedah and Tara. I altered my official records on the application, using the codes I had. I now had worked for Dee's as an Eight-Day cook for three years, instead of only a few weeks.

Of course, I used an alias that Lendill gave me. I was Reah Windle, now. What surprised me, though, was that Ry was Ryliff Windle, my husband. According to the records now, anyway. He had work experience on Le-Ath Veronis—in the palace. Let anybody argue with the Queen that he wasn't who he said he was. Lendill had grinned wickedly when he said he didn't want us separated on Stellar Winds. I didn't, either. I'd worry about Ry's safety, otherwise. Therefore, Lendill was sending us in as a married couple. Lodging was part of the compensation package, after all.

"You're going in undercover, I can't help with the jobs, you'll have to get those on your own," Lendill sighed. "I honestly hope you find nothing wrong, but this has me worried."

I stared at the comp-vid; I already had a reply to my application.

"They're asking if I can be there tomorrow afternoon to interview," I said, turning the comp-vid around so Lendill could see.

"Then tell them you'll be there," Lendill said. I sent the reply.

"I have one, too," Ry grinned at me. Of course he did. I'm sure they got one look at his vid-image and made the decision based on that.

"I have three interviews set up for tomorrow," Jerves was jittery with nerves as he stood in front of Zen. "Two of them look very good. One worked as master cook to the Governor of the Realm on Refizan, the other was an Eight-Day cook on Tulgalan.

"Put those two up first," Zen ordered.

"I already did, the Refizani first," Jerves nodded. "He has more experience, according to his records."

"Good. I'll see both of them for sure. We need another pastry and dessert cook, if I like both of them."

"Yes, sir." Jerves nodded respectfully and scuttled away.

"You look fine, stop fidgeting," Ry said softly as I dressed for my interview. We'd rented a room at one of the many hotels located on

Stellar Winds. Lendill had ship's records altered, showing that we'd arrived in a conventional manner. Only we hadn't. Ry had folded us to the Starship Station and we'd mingled with the crowd getting off a ship. We'd brought one large bag each, and I had a new wardrobe, thanks to some quick shopping with Ry. He'd practically flung clothes in my direction, barely giving me time to try anything on before buying it. I gave up after a while and let him have his way.

"You always look perfect," I said, giving Ry the once-over. He did. His interview was on the third floor of Galedaro's, mine was in the kitchens. Just as well; my cooking spoke for me, most of the time. "I'm ready," I turned for Ry's inspection. I dressed in a nice suit that would do for any interview. The outfit was made of a deep-green fabric, with a pale-green blouse and short-heeled pumps. Nobody should ever wear high heels in a kitchen. Not if they had any sense, that is.

"Very nice. Wear an apron," Ry grinned.

Jerves Lidris, Zendeval Rjjn's personal assistant, met me outside the kitchen. "He'll be ready for you in just a moment," Jerves said, looking me over appreciatively. I wore a ring on my right index finger, indicating my supposed marriage to Ry.

"Would you like something to drink?" Jerves offered politely.

"No, but thank you for offering," I said. He led me to a seat in the hallway outside. I could hear the normal sounds of any kitchen while I sat there. A master cook was shouting at an assistant and at a waiter. I'd heard it all before. Jerves paced a little while we waited, and it was nearly half a click before Zendeval Rjjn walked out, another man beside him. "I'll have the paperwork sent to your hotel this afternoon. Welcome to Galedaro's," Zendeval said. I knew then he'd already hired the man. I was ready to stand and walk out when Jerves grabbed my arm.

"Sir, this is the cook from Tulgalan," he said. The poor man was fidgety for some reason, and I wanted to jerk my arm from his grip. I didn't. Only then did Zendeval Rjjn turn in my direction. He drew in a breath.

"I won't take up your time," I did pull away from Jerves, then. "I see you've already hired someone." I stared Zendeval in the eye. They were dark, those eyes. Black, perhaps. The light wasn't good enough in the hall outside the kitchens to make an accurate assessment. It was the poorest of manners to set up interviews and then hire before all of them were completed. And announcing the hire in front of another candidate was the height of rudeness. Zendeval Rjjn, I decided, was quite rude indeed.

"No, didn't Jerves tell you? I'm looking for a pastry and dessert cook as well." Zendeval was trying to cover his mistake, I could tell. He was giving a partial truth, but only partial.

"I'm sure I can find another place to hire me," I pulled my purse strap over my shoulder, preparing to leave. "And you can wonder then why your customers will come to my restaurant instead."

"No, please, I intend to compensate just as well if I find the right cook," he said. He was saying please, and I didn't think that word came out of Zendeval's mouth very often. "Come, you will make dessert for me. Master cook Crade made my midday meal."

"Then come back in two clicks," I said. "I need some time to prepare a sampling of my work."

"I'll be back in two clicks," Zendeval smiled slightly. "Jerves, take her to the pastry kitchen and see that she has everything she needs."

"Of course, sir." Jerves nodded to Zendeval Rjjn, who walked away. "This way, Mrs. Windle," he held out a hand.

I surveyed the kitchen as I tied an apron on, just as Ry asked. Crates of oxberries, gishi fruit, redberries and a few other items, all fresh and in season, were available for my use. The usual items needed to make pastry and desserts were also waiting. I set temperatures on ovens first and went to work.

"I got out of her way," Perdil, the overworked pastry cook complained to Zendeval a click and a half later. "She asked if I had ice-cream makers. I showed her where those were and went to work on the other side of the room."

"Did it look as if she knew what she's doing?"

"Better than I do," Perdil snorted. Perdil was a dwarf from Liffel II, a world that refused membership in either Alliance. Perdil was a good pastry cook. Perhaps not the best but good, regardless.

"Then we'll both taste what she makes, and you can help decide," Zendeval said.

"I thought Jerves was going to drool on her," Perdil grumbled.

"We'll make sure Jerves keeps his drool away. If we hire her. Come, it's nearly time."

"This is a raspberry and chocolate cake, with a cream center, redberry sauce and fresh cream drizzled over it," I handed a piece to Zendeval Rjjn and another to Perdil, the pastry cook. I had Perdil on the first taste.

"This cake is exceptional," he mumbled around a mouthful.

"Save room for other things," I told him. Zendeval was nodding immediately over the cake, so we moved down the stainless-steel prep table and I offered them the oxberry pastry, with cream and a light frosting.

"Oh, my, this is even better," Perdil was extremely happy, stuffing nearly half the pastry in his mouth. I didn't stop him; most dwarves could eat any other race under the table.

"Excellent," Zendeval said, nodding.

"And this," I pointed to the third item I'd prepared, "this is the most expensive dessert you'll ever serve." I scooped out a big portion of the fresh ice cream I'd made and put it on the first plate, then placed a second scoop on the other. "This is black chocolate cake, thinly sliced, with fresh oxberries and raspberries, a sprig of mint and a scoop of gishi fruit ice cream." I handed both plates over with a flourish.

Nobody else made gishi fruit ice cream. I'd worked on it over the past twenty years, and it was served after every harvest on Kifirin. Except for this year. I'd learned how to make ice cream at Niff's; Lissa allowed me to have the recipes, and I'd developed the gishi fruit ice cream after I'd grown the trees. The thin slice of dark chocolate cake was extremely rich, so the berries and ice cream lightened it to just the right taste. Each of the plates my tasters held could bring at least three hundred Alliance credits, easily.

"Oh, my uncle's beard," Perdil breathed a sigh and then kept eating.

"Does anyone else serve this?" Zendeval asked, taking a second bite of the ice cream.

"None that I know," I said. "I developed the recipe."

"I want this served tomorrow evening; we have special guests coming for dinner," Zendeval said, finishing off his ice cream. "How much of this did you make this time?"

"Only enough for six servings, since the gishi fruit is so expensive," I said.

"I want the rest of it," he said. I handed the small container over. "I'll have your contract ready in a click. Jerves, show her to one of the suites on the fifth floor."

"Here," I handed one of the oxberry desserts to Jerves; he'd not gotten to taste, although he'd been standing there most of the time, watching Zendeval and Perdil eat.

"This cake is marvelous," Perdil was still eating as Zendeval walked out of the kitchen with his container of ice cream.

"What's this?" Nedrizif stared up at Zen when he set the small container of ice cream on Ned's desk.

"The best ice cream you'll ever eat. And the most expensive," Zen smiled at his cousin. "Here, I brought a spoon for you." He handed the utensil over.

"What kind of ice cream?" Ned loved ice cream, and dipped his spoon in for a generous bite.

"Gishi fruit ice cream," Zen said as Nedrizif rolled his eyes in pleasure at the taste.

∼

"Here is your schedule; you'll work from fourteen bells to twenty-four bells each day, unless Mr. Rjjn specifies," Jerves handed over a small comp-vid that held my schedule. "Every other Eight-Day off—you'll switch with Master cook Perdil. You'll get First-Day on the other weeks." I nodded; that was standard if you had two pastry cooks. And my shift would cover the hours when dessert was likely to be served. He'd shown me a nicely appointed suite on the fifth floor, completely furnished, with room service available since I worked in the kitchen as a master cook. Most other employees didn't get that. The pay was good—what a master cook might expect at Desh's, and for a pastry cook, that was very good.

"We'll supply aprons with our logo, and launder them. Yours should be ready and in your locker tomorrow when you report for work. Mr. Rjjn expects enough of the gishi fruit ice-cream dessert to feed fifteen people tomorrow evening. We'll be offering it as an exclusive to special guests first, and then place it on the premium menu for an additional cost. And Mr. Rjjn wants you to sprinkle edible gold flakes on the chocolate cake and charge even more for it. It truly will be the most expensive dessert available." Jerves was smiling widely.

"Then you need to make sure you get some of it next time," I said.

"Mrs. Windle, do you cook other things as well as you make desserts?" he asked.

"Perhaps you can be the judge of that, if you'll come to dinner some night when I'm off," I said. I was hoping Ry and I could get information from Zendeval Rjjn's personal assistant, without making it obvious.

"Just tell the kitchen what ingredients you want, and they'll supply it. At least they won't have to cook it and carry it up," he said, nodding enthusiastically.

"I will. How much is Mr. Rjjn planning to charge for the dessert?" I asked.

"Five hundred credits," Jervis said. "And he says it's worth every bit of that." I could tell that Jerves was upset that he hadn't gotten to try that particular dessert. "Now, this will allow you to eat at or visit any of the clubs or restaurants," Jerves handed a chip necklace to me. "And Mr. Rjjn mentioned that he would like for you to visit the other four clubs and restaurants that he supervises, to let him know how their dessert menus rate. In your opinion," Jerves added.

"Does he have a particular time period for these visits?" I asked.

"He says within the next two eight-days. I can relay the information; just contact me by comp-vid. Here's my code," he passed that to me on a data chip. We were standing in the small kitchen inside the suite I'd been given. Ry chose that moment to walk through the door with our luggage, his own version of Jerves leading the way.

"I see your wife is already here," the assistant said, smiling at Ry. The man was smitten, that's all there was to say.

"Wife, what will we do for dinner this evening?" Ry was grinning at me, the scamp.

"I thought we might go next door and check out their menu tonight," I said.

"Good. I've been asked to evaluate the service I get in this complex of five clubs and restaurants," he nodded.

"Great. We'll check everything out while we eat," I replied.

"Mrs. Windle, welcome to Galedaro's, and if you have any issues, please let me know." Jerves gave a brief wave and left. Ry's escort was slower to go out the door, but he did eventually leave.

"Any trouble getting the job?" Ry asked, coming over to give me a warm hug.

"The Master Cook's position was filled during the interview before mine," I said. Mentally I added, *and the jerk, Rjjn, was callous enough to tell the man that he had it right in front of me.* "But I got the pastry and dessert cook position," I added aloud.

"Sweetheart, if they'd tasted your cooking, you'd have the other job now," Ry told me. We knew not to say anything aloud that we didn't want overheard. If there was something going on, it was a safe bet that everything was bugged in some way.

"I invited Jerves to dinner some night when I'm off," I said. "I was thinking about making the stuffed duck, or maybe the ox-roast."

"Make the ox-roast. I haven't had that in a while." Ry was hungry, I could tell.

"Hon, let's go next door and get something to eat before you cave in," I patted his stomach.

"You noticed, huh?"

"I did."

"Did you want to change?"

"Do you think I should?"

"No, you look great. Let's go." Ry walked me out the door.

"Reah suggested this, but I'm varying it just a little," Lendill said. Garde sat across the table from where Lendill sat, at Lissa's formal dining table. Everyone had come to dinner, almost, including Tory.

"What is it, and how are you varying it?" Garde asked. He was still angry about the hijacked gishi fruit shipment, and blew smoke whenever he thought about it.

"We'll label the next gishi fruit shipment as nannas, as she suggested, and when we ship the nannas out, we'll say it's gishi fruit. That's how we'll list it with the ships, too. All the crates will be sealed, and we'll see which ones get hijacked."

"It's worth a try," Garde blew out a slightly smoky sigh. "Where is the little thing, anyway?"

"Can't say, it's top secret," Lendill replied. "We're tracking down a hunch at the moment, but it might be a very viable hunch. If it turns out as I suspect it might, some mighty big heads might roll over it." Lendill refused to discuss it further.

"When did Kifirin start growing gishi fruit?" Tory asked. He now believed his oldest twins were eight. He'd come quite a way in only a few days. Lissa smiled at her second-born. She was waiting for

Connegar to heal Tory's memory well enough to explain that he'd had a second set of twins. She hoped the information wouldn't be too difficult for him to accept.

"It was an experiment just a few years ago, son. Reah thought the Southern Continent would support the fruit. Turns out she was right," Lissa said gently. "Gishi fruit has become Kifirin's top export."

"Really? That must bring in a lot of money, since gishi fruit is so expensive."

"It does," Garde agreed. "We may be able to pay off Kifirin's debts, just by selling gishi fruit."

"Dad, that's great. I know what a burden all those loans were," Tory recalled the crushing debts that Kifirin faced after the comesuli were brought home to Le-Ath Veronis.

"They'll all be paid before you know it," Garde said. "Just give us a few more years and we'll be completely in the clear."

"We have Reah to thank for that idea?" Tory blinked at his father.

"Yes. We have Reah to thank," Garde dipped his head. "But on another note, we can plant some of your holdings on the Southern Continent now, and you can raise gishi fruit. It's a lucrative enterprise, son."

"You didn't do it before, so the bitch wouldn't get her hands on any of it," Tory blew out a little smoke of his own. "How are my babies? I can't believe they're eight, now."

"They're growing up fast," Garde acknowledged. "You'll see them soon, I think."

"Lendill, are you spending the night?" Lissa asked to change the subject.

"I'm going to visit my father after dinner. I think he'll announce which of my brothers is next in line for King sometime soon."

"I hope it's somebody you can live with," Lissa said and turned back to her dessert.

"Me, too," Lendill agreed.

～

"Too dry," I pushed the cake away with a sour face. "And the raspberry sauce is too tart. How's yours?" I looked expectantly at Ry, who'd ordered a puff pastry with redberries and cream.

"Nothing near yours," he pushed it toward me. I took a bite and agreed with him. The pastry was too thick around the filling and the cream not quite sweet enough. I could only imagine the other desserts also needed work. We'd asked the waiter to bring us their two best desserts and this is what we'd gotten.

"We're ready to pay," I said when the waiter appeared at our table. He scanned Ry's employee chip, we left our unfinished desserts on the table and left. "At least the waiter was good," I said as we slipped out the door of Chrestin's, the second-best resort on Stellar Winds. The food had been decent, if not of the highest caliber. I'd ordered a chicken dish, Ry had asked for steak.

Stellar Winds was in the fall season upon the tiny planetoid, but one wouldn't know it unless one walked outside the glassed-in tunnels and tubes that ran from one place to the next, all climate-controlled. Trees, plants, waterfalls and small ponds were scattered here and there, decorating spaces inside and out of the resorts. Some even had exotic animals held behind clear plexi.

"Feel like going to the bar inside Galedaro's?" Ry asked as we took the turn that would lead us to the main building. The hotel portion was attached on the left side. All five of Zendeval Rjjn's properties were in a circle, with other glass tunnels leading away from each of them to get to the other resorts, brothels and game facilities. Gambling was prohibited on Stellar Winds; it wasn't licensed for it. I figured there was some going on somewhere, though, legal or not.

"We can go for a little while, but I'm tired and I've got a long day ahead of me tomorrow," I told Ry, slipping my arm inside his. He lifted my fingers to his lips and kissed them. "After this, I'm going to put you out by a pool somewhere and make you sleep for a week," he said.

"You'll make me?" I lifted an eyebrow at him.

"Absolutely," he grinned. Two women, passing by, ran into one another while staring at Ry. "Ladies," Ry nodded to them. They were whispering furiously when they went on their way.

"Is it good to give women orgasms just by smiling?" I laughed up at him.

"I'm working on perfecting my art," he said. "Want another cloudy sunset?"

"I'll take one. Two will put me to sleep," I said.

"We'll order two, then," he told me. Normally it would take more than that, but I was truly weary. Ry and I had a tough road ahead of us, if we were to learn anything about the disappearances, Bel's included. Lendill was now keeping track of all the people who booked passage on ships bound for Stellar Winds. He was prepared to watch for further disappearances to check against that database.

"Two cloudy sunsets, with Yadeli," Ry ordered as we took seats at the bar. We'd passed several drunken (or drugged) people in their twenties. Some had undressed, one completely, and were dancing beneath the strobe lights on the dance floor.

Security was discreet but present. If anyone became a disturbance, they'd be hauled off to a drunk room to sleep it off. If they became violent, they stayed inside a padded cell until the drunk wore off. Two infractions meant a dismissal from the planetoid with no refund. Everyone signed a release before setting foot on Stellar Winds.

"I have to inspect the voyeur parlors tomorrow," Ry grimaced as he sipped his drink. I didn't think it was the drink—mine was very good. Some visitors agreed to participate in sex acts while others watched behind one-way glass. I shuddered, just thinking about it. Ry was going to be exposed to all of that.

"I'm making desserts," I said, shaking my head at him.

"Reah, I may not be in a good mood when I come home tomorrow night," he said.

"Do you want me to fix something for you?"

"Just bring something to the apartment. That'll be good enough," he said. "That way if I'm not hungry, I won't insult your good cooking by not eating it."

"I will," I nodded, rubbing his back.

Ry and I leaned into each other as we took the elevator to the fifth floor inside the main building. At least the loud, thumping music didn't penetrate that far up. "Thank the stars; quiet," Ry sighed in appreciation and settled me on a sofa in the small sitting area. We had a single, large bedroom, a small sitting area, the equally small kitchen and a nice bath with a tub and shower. Ry had brought our bags over when he'd first come up so at least we had clothing and toiletries.

"Let's sleep late tomorrow," Ry said. *Do you want me to sleep on the sofa?*

*No, Ry. The bed's big enough. We have enough room. You only snore a little.* I smiled at him. *Besides, the sofa's not long enough.* It wasn't; Ry was six-three, in old Earth measurements, anyway. The bed was huge. As big as one of the beds I'd slept on at Teeg's or any of the others. "All right," I nodded to his spoken question.

"Good. I'm going to clean up," Ry stretched and headed for the bathroom.

"I'll wait until the morning," I called. Ry flung up a hand and closed the bathroom door behind him. I didn't want to, but I pulled all my clothes from the case and hung them up, then placed underwear and other things inside drawers. I did the same for Ry's things—we shared one walk-in closet. His things were on one side, mine on the other, with shoes on the floor beneath. I then stowed both cases in a corner of the closet. We'd have to bring more clothing if this took a while. I shed my suit and wriggled into comfortable pajamas, sliding into bed. I had books loaded on the comp-vid I'd gotten from Pripps, so I was reading when Ry came out of the bathroom smelling freshly clean.

"What are you reading?" he asked.

"A mystery," I said, turning the comp-vid so he could see.

"Any good advice in there?" he asked, scooting beneath the covers on his side. "At least the bed's comfortable."

"No good advice yet, and I'm done for tonight," I said, marking my place on the comp-vid and setting it aside. I'd leave it in the room, using the one supplied by Galedaro's while I worked.

"Goodnight, baby," Ry turned out his light, leaving us in darkness.

# CHAPTER 7

"Reah, time to wake," Ry's arm was draped over me and he kissed my bare shoulder, whispering against it.

"Ry," I moaned, unwilling to open my eyes. I'd been sleeping so well.

"Come on, I have to get up too," he said.

"Yeah." I slapped a hand over my eyes. "I'll get cleaned up. Do we have time for breakfast?"

"Sure. I have to get to work earlier than you, though."

"All right. I'm going. Now. Soon." I wriggled toward the edge of the bed, with my eyes closed still.

"Poor baby." Ry came around to my side and pulled me up. "Here." He removed the stretchy band that held my braid and loosened my hair, letting it fall around my shoulders. "That's better," he said and leaned down to give me a quick peck.

"Thanks," I patted his shoulder and stumbled toward the bathroom.

"I'll get groceries from somewhere, to stock the kitchen so we won't have to leave to get breakfast," I said a little later. Ry had gone to buy breakfast sandwiches; they were waiting when I got out of the shower.

I left when Ry did so I could get a head start on the ice cream, fruit puree and sauces I'd need for the cakes and pastries.

~

"She's here now," Perdil spoke discreetly into his communicator as he watched Reah from across the kitchen. "She came in early to make up the sauces and start the ice cream."

"I'll be there shortly," Zen replied and cut off the communication.

~

"Do you have anything for a midmorning meeting?" Zendeval Rjjn was inside the kitchen, asking for personal service and disturbing my work. I looked up at him after pouring raspberry puree into a squeeze bottle.

"Do you want cakes, tarts or pastry?" I asked, masking my annoyance.

"Can you do all three?"

"Yes." I wanted to heave an impatient sigh, but I didn't. I filled three orders quickly before turning to what Zendeval wanted. Rude, just as I thought. He could have mentioned a midmorning meeting the day before, but he didn't. Instead, he was here while I was trying to prepare for my shift. I wasn't officially on duty for another half-click.

"This is a sponge cake; it goes well with this sauce," I held up the container. "These pastries are best if they're slightly warm, do you have a zap oven at the site?" I looked at him. He blinked at me. "The tarts are good with fresh fruit," I went on. "And coffee or tea," I added.

"Can you come with me and serve it?" he asked.

"Yes." Stifling a sigh, I pulled out a tray, piled everything on it and lifted it to rest on my shoulder. "Lead the way," I said, preparing to follow Zendeval Rjjn to a meeting.

We rode up the elevator in silence. I wanted to glare at him but didn't. Instead, I kept my eyes straight ahead and watched the numbered floors light up until we reached the top suite. The elevator opened in Zendeval's private suite. Six men sat around his wide kitchen island, waiting for his arrival. Teeg had better inside his palace, but then he was Teeg San Gerxon. All six of the men looked as if they could have been Zendeval's brothers. All had dark hair and black eyes; I'd decided they were definitely black. I'm sure they could pick up any one of the young women cavorting in the bar downstairs if they had a mind to.

"We have cake, tarts or pastry," I offered, bringing my mind back to the task at hand, grabbing the kettle for tea and putting coffee on to brew in Zendeval's kitchen. At least he had those things there so they could be served fresh. I plated up some of each dessert I'd brought, along with freshly made coffee and tea. I'd found napkins and nice silver inside drawers, figuring that someone else came to clean up for Mr. Rude Rjjn.

"This is very good," one of the men complimented the cake. The others were too busy eating to say anything.

"Thank you," I nodded to the one who spoke while freshening his coffee. "Would you like cream or sugar?"

"No, this is good as it is," he said, taking another bite.

"Mr. Rjjn, will that be all?" I asked. "I need to get back to my prep work."

"That's all, Reah." I nodded, fuming that he'd used my first name, as if we knew one another. We didn't. And he was still rude, on top of everything else.

"Did Reah say anything when she came back down?" Zendeval asked Perdil later when Perdil went outside the kitchen to take a break.

"She didn't say a word, just came back and went to work. She makes a stair-step cake for special occasions; a couple arrived who'd just gotten married and they wanted something different. She cut the cake into little steps, iced it and then poured a redberry sauce that flowed down, garnished it with oxberries and mint sprigs and backed it all up with roses and edible lilies. The dessert was beautiful and the couple ate the whole thing, so it must have been good."

"Jerves says she invited him to dinner some night when she's off," Zendeval said. "Have you seen her husband? Jerves says that Inkle couldn't take his eyes off the man."

"Inkle would know if anyone would whether he's attractive or not."

"I'd like it better if she were unattached."

"Multiple mates are recognized by the Alliance."

"I don't share well, Perdil."

"Ah."

"And if our guests tonight ask for the cooks, I expect you and Master Cook Crade to go out. I don't want Reah near the two of them."

"For obvious reasons."

"Yes. For obvious reasons." Zendeval agreed with a sigh and walked away.

"It's such a treat to have all my sons here with me for dinner," Kaldill stood and raised a glass to Naldill, Faldill, Reldill and Lendill. Lendill watched his father's eyes as he toyed absently with his glass of thousand-year wine. "And I wish to make an announcement," Kaldill added.

*Here it comes*, Lendill thought. He wasn't wrong. "I will select my heir at the winter solstice," Kaldill made each son's glass rise in the air and come to him. He poured a bit of his wine into each glass, symbolically saying that he considered each of them equally. Lendill wanted to snort at the gesture. He was only half-elven and didn't have a chance against the others. His three brothers were pure-bloods and it was likely that Naldill, as the firstborn, would be selected. Lendill knew that if he still lived when Naldill took the kingship, he would never come to the Elven lands again.

"You have decided already?" Naldill asked as Kaldill sent the glasses back to all his sons.

"I think so," Kaldill gave his first son a beaming smile.

"Good." Naldill drained his glass. Lendill watched all of them carefully. Reldill would support Naldill without question, no matter what Naldill asked of him. Faldill might go along most of the time, but if Naldill asked something of him that went against his conscience, he imagined that Faldill would simply disappear, much like Lendill planned to do.

Lendill knew quite well that Naldill held humans in contempt and often wondered why Kaldill failed to see it. Naldill and Reldill certainly hadn't held back from torturing their youngest (and powerless at the time) half-human brother. That was why Lendill held back his burgeoning power now. It answered readily to him whenever he needed it, but he seldom employed it, worrying that his father might learn of it, making him a target for his two oldest brothers again.

Lendill had no idea what the extent of their power was and had no desire to discover it. The announcement was barely three months away on Wyyld. The human population always held a big celebration on Wyyld at the winter solstice. Lendill figured the Elven celebration would be well-hidden in the shadow of the human one.

"What do you plan to do after the announcement?" Lendill raised his glass to his father, who still hadn't taken a drink.

"I'm going to rest and make plans for my Prince-Heir." Kaldill smiled and drank.

"To you, then, father." Lendill drained his glass as well. "I have to get back; I have pirate attacks to deal with."

"I'll take you," Faldill rose from his seat after emptying his glass. Lendill nodded at the youngest of his pure-blood brothers. Faldill wasted no time folding Lendill to Ildevar Wyyld's palace.

"You think he'll select Naldill, don't you?" Faldill paced restlessly inside Lendill's office. Faldill, like his brothers, resembled Kaldill, their father, with shoulder-length golden hair, pointed ears and eyes the color of new leaves in the spring. All three had the glow of the Elven race about them. Lendill knew it was from the power they held.

"He's firstborn," Lendill gave a brief nod that, if he'd known it,

closely resembled one of his father's gestures. "And think about it,"
Lendill went on. "If he'd nodded at Reldill, then Naldill would be
plotting even now."

"You're right. Reldill might not live past the next few days if that
happened. Not without the power of Gaelar N'Seith behind him—he'd
likely be destroyed. Do you think Father will do the Alim'deru
immediately after the announcement?"

"It would only be prudent to do so, to prevent any thought of
attack," Lendill said. Faldill was referring to a transfer of power, which
tapped into and held Gaelar N'Seith, the Elven lands. It made (and
kept) Kaldill Schaff King of the Elves. The Prince-Heir would be able
to draw upon that power, too, should it be required.

"Brother, I'm sorry if I ever participated in any of the torture
Naldill put you through when you were young," Faldill sighed, raking
hair back from his face and revealing the delicately pointed tip of his
right ear. "You deserved more from brothers who were old enough to
understand and know better." Faldill disappeared in front of Lendill's
eyes.

"Apology accepted," Lendill murmured to empty air.

"You seem morose, my dear." Erland brushed Wylend's temple with
gentle fingers.

"I am, am I not?" Wylend looked up at Erland Morphis, his devoted
lover through six millennia or more.

"You seem so, beloved King."

"I know. And am I beloved? Truly?"

"To me. Always."

"Even when I do stupid things?"

"We all do stupid things."

"What was the last stupid thing you did, Erland? You can't
remember, can you?"

"I'm sure there are many things, it's just that I'm surrounded by those who either love me too much or are too nice to point them out," Erland replied.

"How is my great-grandchild?"

"Which one? You have four."

"Your son, Erland. Don't play cat and mouse with me."

"My son is fine, although he's gone off on a special assignment for the ASD. That's his idea of having a vacation."

"It wouldn't be the same assignment Reah is on, now would it?"

"How did you hear about that? And yes, it is."

"I have my ways," Wylend grumbled, standing and stretching. He and Erland had dealt with a full day at court and were about to share a glass of wine before retiring for the night. Erland uncorked the bottle and poured two glasses, handing one to Wylend, who sipped thoughtfully.

"Did you ever have a toy in your youth, Erland, that you didn't know quite what it was, or how it worked? Did you crush it with your clumsiness, only to find out later what a rare and precious thing it was and that you should have asked for advice before playing with it? Did you?"

"I recall destroying many toys in my youth," Erland sat down and sipped his wine. "I think I blew my entire room apart, once, when I was first discovering my power."

"I remember. Your father took your abilities away for months."

"He did."

"He was my father's devoted love, just as you are mine," Wylend said.

"I am not your only one."

"But Corolan seems distant at times. My fault, I know. I did so many things wrong, Erland. Wyatt's death was punishment. As is Reah's estrangement. She will never return to me. My son finally told me, after I pressed him mercilessly about it."

Erland didn't say anything, but he harbored a resentment against Griffin, Wylend's son. Lissa would barely tolerate Griffin, her father; he'd brought so much emotional harm to Erland's female mate. If Griffin hadn't interfered long ago with a kidnapping, substituting

Roff's son, Toff, for Wyatt to prevent his abduction as an infant, then Wyatt might still be alive. So many things had hinged on that one action. Erland at times figured that event had altered the timeline in some way, although he'd never said it aloud.

"I should have told you about the letter before I sent it. I should have known better than to strike out at Reah, who'd just suffered the loss of a child through miscarriage, before she was injured protecting Corolan. I felt slighted and I wanted to hit back, just like a child. Now I have no heir and I have no Queen. Will some conspire against me, as they did my father? Take me down, leaving Karathia in chaos? Erland, tell me what to do," Wylend moaned.

"Stop fretting, my King." Erland took the glass from Wylend's hand and set it on the bedside table. "Come, I will hold you tonight." Wylend allowed his head to droop on Erland's chest.

Rylend Morphis was more than glad that the voyeur booths were soundproof. Mostly it was a bevy of single males inside, whooping, catcalling and drinking as they watched couples of all kinds having sex. They could hear very well and were laughing at the sounds. Ry wanted to shake his head as he observed, but kept his emotions tightly under control. He imagined that if it were only a single male inside the booth, that masturbation would be the response. With a fellow audience, it might not happen quite as often.

Three sets of booths had been inspected already, and Ry had sent messages saying that they needed to be cleaned more often. Spilled drinks, the scent of semen and other things were present in several. Each row of booths was set above ten rooms designed for sexual activities. Only one set remained to be inspected, and those were in the restricted area. Only the visitors who'd purchased upgraded packages were allowed inside.

Ry left the one he was in after making notes in his comp-vid, and then walked down the hall, past a human guard who checked his employee chip. The guard waved him through after scanning the chip necklace. Steeling himself, Ry opened the first door. What he found inside was a bit surprising, after the other booths he'd visited.

Only three men occupied this one, watching a particularly pretty young woman with a man Ry imagined was employed by Stellar Winds. He was very well endowed and looked to be trained in the art. The girl was tempted and teased, slowly and surely by her lover, making her beg for release.

Each of the three men held comp-vids in their hands. Ry couldn't see what was on the screens; they were keyed to privacy. Two of the men were tapping their screens occasionally. If they were there to watch, Ry couldn't imagine what would pull them away from the sex happening below. They were older, too, than those normally visiting Stellar Winds.

Ry left and went to the next booth. No one was inside this one; one woman was with two men in the room below. Ry only found three of the ten booths in the restricted section occupied, and only the one had more than two inside. All these booths were clean and well-maintained, so he gave them a clear pass and went on to his next assignment.

"That smells wonderful," Perdil breathed in the scent of the freshly-baked chocolate cake as I pulled it from the oven. The cake wouldn't be frosted, that would alter the taste and experience of the dessert. The ice cream was at the perfect temperature inside the freezer; I'd made enough to serve twenty if necessary. The oxberries were large, beautiful and sweet, the raspberries delicious and the sauce was perfect.

Everything was ready to be served in half a click, just as Zendeval Rjjn had requested. Perdil was hovering, watching my every move. I'd been listening to kitchen conversations all day, and learned that some of the assistants had plans to go to a brothel at the Lemon Sea, one of five resorts Zendeval managed.

"Plate up the dessert," Jerves almost ran into the kitchen. The important guests had gone through the meal Master Cook Crade prepared faster than anyone thought they might. I cut eight thin slices of cake, placed the berries and mint sprig, sprinkled that with gold flakes and then scooped the gishi fruit ice cream on last.

"Get it out and hurry," I ordered the four waiters who'd followed Jerves in.

~

"Here it is, our newest and most expensive dessert," Zendeval nodded at the four waiters as they placed dessert plates in front of each of their eight guests. Nedrizif, upon hearing the gishi fruit dessert would be served, included himself at the private dinner, which was something he seldom did.

"Very nice to look at, but does it taste—oh, yes." Dantel Schuul was nearly in raptures as he dipped up a bit of the cake and ice cream and placed it in his mouth.

"Daddy, is this gishi fruit ice cream?" Darletta had only taken a small bite. She wouldn't eat any dessert unless it was perfect. She dipped up a bigger bite the second time.

"This is gishi fruit ice cream, served exclusively by Galedaro's," Zendeval announced proudly. "The recipe was developed by our pastry and dessert cook, and we will serve this for an additional charge of five hundred credits."

"Worth every bit of that," Nedrizif had eaten his ice cream first and was only now eating the cake with the berries. "Can we get more ice cream?"

"Of course," Zen jerked his head at a waiter, who rushed back to the kitchen. Master Pastry Cook Perdil came out with the second servings of ice cream. "Master Perdil was your dessert cook for the evening," Zen said.

"This dessert will be a status symbol," Dantel Schuul declared. "Perhaps we should offer a shirt or some other memento as well, telling the Alliance that the one wearing it was able to afford the most expensive dessert available."

"I agree," another of the owners said. "I think we should call this sex by dessert and slap that logo onto the shirt."

"It's certainly better than the last sex I had," another member of the party laughed. "Add it to the menu immediately, and we'll get our ad people on it."

"I will," Zen nodded obediently.

"How was your day?" Ry had a headache, I could tell right away, but he was asking me how my day had gone. Sitting on one of only two barstools, he had his head in his hands.

"It was fine." I pulled his head against my chest when I walked into the kitchen, rubbing his forehead lightly with my fingers. I didn't tell him what I suspected—that Perdil was taking credit for the expensive dessert—but then I didn't want to face Darletta Schuul or her father. The rumor was that both of them were among the important guests. It made sense that Darletta's wealthy father had a hidden finger in this particular pie. My job was to find the insects in said pie.

"That feels good," Ry mumbled, slipping an arm around my waist.

"Want some painkill? I think they have some in the shop downstairs."

"Along with plenty of hangover remedies. Come here." He pulled me closer. "Your heartbeat is the best thing for me right now." His forehead was between my breasts. My fingers went through his black hair. There isn't anything wrong with any part of Rylend Morphis. Except he couldn't fix his own headaches, apparently.

"I brought fish stew," I told him gently. "I made it for the pastry kitchen staff before I left. I have some fresh bread, too, if you're hungry."

"I'll eat in a minute. Just let me sit like this for a while."

"All right, honey."

"Taste this." Perdil held out a small bowl of fish stew to Zendeval.

"You know I'm not fond of seafood stew."

"Taste it anyway. With the bread." Perdil pushed a small plate of fresh bread toward his supervisor. Zendeval frowned as he dipped up a spoonful of the fish stew and ate it. Then dipped a piece of the bread in it and ate that.

"Outstanding," Zendeval muttered around a mouthful of food.

"Reah made this for the staff before she left for the evening," Perdil grunted. "None of the other cooks even think about doing that."

"That includes you, you know," Zen snickered at Perdil before eating more of the stew.

"There's usually enough dessert left for them to get what they want, but I've threatened them over the gishi fruit ice cream. Except that our guests ate all of it," Perdil grumbled.

"We'll drop by Mrs. Windle's now, and tell her we need enough on hand for at least sixty servings every day," Zen ate the last of his fish stew and scraped up the remaining broth with the last of his bread. "You should have saved more for me," he said. "I didn't get dinner, you know."

"I know. I just didn't think you'd eat all of it," Perdil replied, following Zendeval out of the kitchen.

I'd just set a bowl of fish stew in front of Ry when the guest bell rang. "I'll get it," I patted Ry's back and went to the door. Zendeval Rjjn and Perdil the Dwarf pastry cook stood outside.

"Is there a problem?" I asked as they invited themselves inside.

"I just wanted to tell you that we'll need enough gishi fruit ice cream on hand for sixty servings each day," Zendeval Rjjn didn't even bother with a hello. Perdil's thick brows were pulling together in a frown. Ry, from his place at the table, was also frowning—at both our uninvited guests. "Is that more fish stew?" Zendeval walked toward the table. I did the frowning, now.

"Yes, it's more fish stew. Would you like some?" I went to get the container holding my dinner.

"Yes," Zendeval Rjjn pulled out the other chair and sat. I served the fish stew to him, with a generous portion of fresh bread. "This wine is best with it," I poured a glass for my employer, wanting to toss him out the window instead. I imagined that he might scream on his way down, and that was more than fine with me. Ry glanced at Zendeval briefly before going back to his own meal.

"We could sell this, Perdil," Zendeval said after he'd eaten nearly the entire portion of stew.

"I was trying to tell you that earlier," Perdil said dryly.

"Tell Master Cook Crade how to make this tomorrow," Zendeval said, stuffing the last of the bread into his mouth.

"No," I said.

"What did you just say to me?" Zendeval rose from the table.

"I checked the contract over carefully and removed the wording that says all recipes prepared here belong to the ownership," I said. "I have a dated copy in my comp-vid. Feel free to review it," I said. "I don't give away my recipes."

"I can fire you."

"Go ahead. I can find work elsewhere."

"As can I," Ry rose to stare at Zendeval.

"Please, let us not be in haste, here," Perdil held out his hands in a placating gesture. "Shall we draw up a new contract that says any recipes developed on premises belong to the management?"

"That excludes the gishi fruit ice-cream dessert," I said. "I've been making that for several years."

"Then we need to keep our pastry cook happy, it seems," Zendeval nodded.

～

"Did you mean to be rude?" Perdil asked as he and Zen walked toward the elevator after leaving Mrs. Windle's apartment.

"She's the one who altered the standard contract. I'll be having words with Jerves over that."

"That isn't what I meant," Perdil pointed a finger at Zen. "You ate her evening meal. Do you have your head that far up your ass all the time?"

"I made a mistake?"

"You made a big mistake."

~

I wasn't speaking to anyone when I arrived in the kitchens the following day, putting gishi fruit ice cream together first thing. He wanted sixty servings on hand, we were about to have sixty servings on hand. Two assistants I'd fed the night before came over and silently began peeling fruit beside me.

~

"She's not speaking to anyone," Perdil replied to Zen's communication. Again, he'd moved to the far side of the regular kitchen to communicate with Zen.

"I'll think of something," Zendeval sighed. "Why didn't you tell me I was blundering about?"

"Don't you know anything about women? Anyone should know not to steal someone else's food, regardless. I thought you had enough sense for that, at least."

"I do, Perdil. What do you take me for? I have manners."

"Really? I thought you were trying to impress her. Lure her away from her mate, perhaps. She doesn't have weight to spare, lummox, and you take her food."

"I made a mistake. Leave it, Perdil."

"Now that you've made this mistake, though, it won't be such a stretch if you show up for dinner with Jerves when he's invited."

"I could do that. Perdil, you're a genius. I'll tell Jerves that he has to take me with him."

"I'd go too, if I thought I could get away with it," Perdil grumped and terminated the call.

❧

"I want you to take off your apron and come with me," Zendeval Rjjn was standing on the other side of my prep table as I was plating up an oxberry tart with fresh cream.

"Where are we going?" I wasn't planning to go anywhere with him if I didn't know what the destination was beforehand.

"I wish to go to Chrestin's and speak with the pastry cook. I want you to tell him what is wrong with his desserts. I get more complaints from there than any of my other restaurants."

"I don't think he'll appreciate the words coming from me," I pointed out. "I gave the information to you on the two desserts I sampled. I haven't tried everything he makes."

"Then we'll ask for a good sampling. We'll try a cross-section of his desserts and you'll tell me what the problem is."

"I don't see that this will help you in the least," I snapped, still angry that he'd eaten my fish stew the night before. I'd had a cold cheese sandwich for dinner instead after he and Perdil left the apartment. "Why don't you just tell him the dessert menu needs to be improved or you'll look for someone else?"

"I will, unless you think he has the capability to improve." Zendeval's black eyes searched my face before traveling lower. I was covered by a cook's jacket to keep from ruining a good blouse and pants. At least he wasn't rewarded by a view of tight clothing. I had no desire to reveal anything to Zendeval Rjjn. I was angry, too, that Perdil had gone out six times during the day to speak to customers, posing as the one who'd created the sex by dessert confection.

Yes, they were listing it as sex by dessert, and were printing shirts with the new logo on it, depicting a large-breasted woman with a scoop of ice cream in the valley between her breasts. I wanted to scream over the whole thing as Zendeval's eyes slowly rose toward mine. At least I was covered up and hoped Zendeval didn't have a good imagination. He was a cretin, in my estimation.

"Come, we will go to Chrestin's. Take off that terrible jacket and wear your hair loose." I stared at him as I removed the coat and took my hair out of its usual braid, promising myself that Zendeval Rjjn and I would have a lengthy talk after my job was finished here. After I tossed him through a wall or something equally as sturdy, first.

# CHAPTER 8

"Just keep folding and rolling the pastry like this," I demonstrated for the poor cook who looked flustered that Zendeval Rjjn was there and watching. "The layers are what make it flaky and crisp. Don't leave it too thick, now. Your recipe is good, it just needs a little more physical labor to make it great." I stepped aside and let poor Welt work a while.

"See, that's enough right there. Now, take your berry mixture here," we poured some of it out and folded dough over it, running the tool over the edges to seal the tart. "All you have to do is bake it now and you'll have something to be proud of." We worked on a mousse after that, plus a few other things before tasting.

"This is very good." We'd cooked a bit of the pastry in a shell and added the mousse, topping it with cream and fresh berries.

"It is good," Zendeval was eating a little of everything we made.

"Are you really serving gishi fruit ice cream at Galedaro's?" Welt ventured to ask.

"Yes. We are," Zendeval's tone warned Welt not to ask any other questions. He didn't.

"This has been most helpful," Welt gave me a smile instead. He meant well, I just couldn't imagine that someone had trained him so poorly.

"I want you to contact Reah if you have difficulty preparing other desserts," Zendeval grumbled at Welt. "Come, Reah, we will go back, now. Do you want something else to eat before you go home?" We'd worked past the time for me to leave the kitchens at Galedaro's.

"I feel a little ill from eating too many sweets," I put a hand to my stomach. "Thank you for the offer, but no."

"But I have to make up for taking your dinner last night," he said. "Perdil was quite shocked that I didn't realize it at the time."

"It's rude not to offer food or refreshments to your guests," I muttered.

"Yes. You are correct. I will remember that next time." I blinked up at him. He was managing five of the highest rated resorts in the Reth Alliance, and was forgetting his manners? I wanted to shake my head and didn't. "Where do you get your hair dyed?" he asked, fingering a few strands of my hair. I didn't like anyone touching my hair that I didn't know well.

"I don't. This is my natural color," I said, trying to move away from him.

"You were born with this?" He lifted the strands to his nose and sniffed.

"I imagine it smells like cake and pastry now," I said tartly. Likely it did—I'd been baking most of the day. "Can I have my hair back?" I almost jerked it from Zendeval's hand.

"You make me forget my manners, Reah. I have business to attend to. Perhaps I will see you tomorrow." We were at the bank of elevators and he stepped onto the one that would carry him to the penthouse. I watched as the doors closed on him, fuming silently. Of all the cursed luck, to get someone like him for an employer.

"Come on, you need protein," Ry placed a plate of chicken in front of me. He'd gone to get it downstairs. I told him I'd tasted too many desserts at Chrestin's, so this was his solution. "Just a couple of bites. Come on," he coaxed softly. "Then we'll put you to bed." I ate three bites and that was all I could stand. Heaving sounded good right then. Ry did put me in the bed after helping me undress, then dampened a towel in warm water and laid it across my belly.

"There. We'll get rid of that ache," he crooned.

He no longer remembered his name. At times, that bothered him. Now, he lifted and loaded, lifted and loaded. That was what they'd told him to do. When he slept—the few hours he was allowed—he dreamt of strange things. Wondrous, at times. Imagined that he was capable of things most people couldn't envision. But those were only dreams that evaporated upon waking, when someone kicked him and he rose again, to stand in the long lines to receive a small meal that wasn't fit for animals to consume. Then he'd be led to another waiting ship. There, he'd do his duty, unloading and carrying, sometimes for clicks without a break.

Some of his companions dropped while they worked, mostly from lack of water. Some of them were revived. Others were killed where they lay, begging for something to drink with their last breath. He paid them no mind; he was instructed to do so. Nothing mattered any longer, not even the absence of his name.

"I thought I would heave afterward, I tasted so many desserts. I do not wish to repeat that," I told Perdil the following day as I worked in the kitchen. No food looked good to me at the moment, and I'd barely been able to stomach a cup of weak tea at breakfast. Ry suggested that I call and say I was ill, but I dragged myself to work anyway. The gishi fruit ice cream had to be made and I was the only one who knew how to make it. That recipe wasn't leaving my head and I was careful that nobody saw the entire making of it.

"Tomorrow is Eight-Day and I will be off," Perdil reminded me. "You'll have the pastry kitchen to yourself."

"Of course, Master Cook Perdil," I nodded and continued with my work. I hadn't had a chance to speak with Ry for the past two days about Stellar Winds and ask whether he'd found anything or not. Hesitating to bother him with mindspeech at the moment, I concentrated on my work and hoped that Zendeval Rjjn would stay away from the kitchens and leave me in peace.

"What do you make of this?" Lendill and Norian sat in Norian's spacious office in Ildevar Wyyld's palace, reviewing images from the many microscopic cameras that Lendill had given to Ry. They saw three men inside the voyeur booth, all holding comp-vids in their hands while graphic sexual activity went on in the room below.

"I think we should get identification on the girl and then watch what happens to her," Norian muttered, using the controls at his desk to zoom in on her image.

"Already done—Ry has the information in this. He shipped it to me using a bit of that power he has. I may have to try my hand at the same thing." Lendill held up the comp-vid that Pripps Electronics had given to Ry. "The girl went home to Hraede yesterday and I've already got an agent keeping tabs on her there."

"I wonder if Lissa's busy," Norian sighed as he watched the sex.

"Norian, we don't have these men in any of our databases," Lendill attempted to bring Norian back to the business at hand.

"What? None of them?" Now Norian was staring at Lendill instead of the vid-screen.

"None of them. I've run their images through everything we have and unless they've all altered their appearances, they're ghosts or from outside either Alliance. I checked Teeg's databases, too."

"We're on the same page, then," Norian agreed. "I think they're bidding on that girl, and the one with the winning bid wins the prize."

"Yeah. But Ry thinks there's a lot more going on than that, he just hasn't put his finger on it, yet."

"What does Reah say?"

"I haven't heard from Reah. Just as the rest of her mates haven't. I think she's angry with all of us at the moment, and Ry tells me through mindspeech that he thinks the one who runs the five best resorts is sniffing after her, now. Ry says that Zendeval Rjjn is rude and contemptible and Reah may punch him through a wall before the investigation is over."

"Good for her. She can work off some of that suppressed anger and aggression," Norian nodded.

I had Darletta Schuul in my sights. She and her father were still on Stellar Winds, apparently; I'd caught sight of them at the bar when I'd gone out to get a bottle of wine to carry upstairs. I wanted to wind down with Ry for a little while and talk a few things over regarding the evidence (or lack thereof) in the case so far. But Darletta and her father, sitting at the bar with Faldin Bierla forced a change of plans.

Dantel had a lovely young girl at his side, likely drunk or drugged, I imagined. Her eyes were glassy and she giggled at everything Dantel said to her. I watched as they left the bar and walked toward the exit leading to the voyeur booths next door. Sending hasty mindspeech to Ry, he acknowledged it and said he'd find something for dinner while I tracked my quarry. I fended off hands that reached for me as I passed a knot of young ones cavorting on the dance floor.

Dantel and Darletta were aiming for the voyeur booths, all right, but I wasn't expecting them to all go into the same suite. Not to watch the ones below—others were going to watch *them*. I slipped inside the voyeur booth overhead. One other came inside with me. He looked very much like Zendeval Rjjn in my estimation, with black eyes and dark hair. The light wasn't the best inside the booth, but I took a seat at the window and watched what I thought to be one of the most perverted things I'd ever seen.

Darletta and the girl were having sex with Faldin and Dantel Schuul. I wanted to gag. I'd been beaten by my father when I was small, and he'd broken many bones. He'd never done this, though. The man sitting across the booth from me hauled out a comp-vid and pressed several keys before putting it back in his pocket. The privacy screen was on, but I was too far away to have seen anything anyway. When Darletta went to her father and put her mouth on him, I stood and walked out.

*Ry, that was the sickest thing I've ever seen.* I sent mindspeech while sitting in a warm tub of water with a damp cloth draped over my eyes. Ry was kneeling by the tub, running a gentle knuckle over my cheek and swirling the water now and then with his hand, keeping the water at the right temperature with power. I wish I could do that. Ry's father, Erland Morphis, finally told me one day that a warlock's power worked around me as long as it wasn't meant to harm.

"I don't know how High Demon physiology knows how to sort out the helpful from the harmful," he'd given me the smile that Ry had inherited from him. "Yet it does," he'd added. Ry had inherited more from Erland Morphis than merely his handsome face.

"I have a shield up, so we won't be heard," Ry whispered. "Reah, do you know how beautiful you are?" he added softly, a thumb caressing my mouth. His mouth replaced the thumb. "Do you remember the first time we met?" he asked.

I did. I'd sneaked into his mother's palace kitchen to fix something to eat. I was recuperating from injuries and wasn't supposed to be out of bed. Ry and Tory had both appeared, having just completed a special assignment for the ASD. I'd cooked for them and for Lissa's Falchani twins who'd also shown up. "I remember," I said. I'd thought those times were difficult. I hadn't known difficult, back then.

"Reah, I used to lust after Jhase and Jehri, Jayd and Glinda's twins," he said. "But that was just lust. I think somewhere in my mind, I knew that I'd find the right one for me someday. The right woman. I found her one night in my mother's kitchen. But I took a step back, because Tory's eyes were filled with stars when he saw you. I didn't want to stand in my brother's way. And then I took another step back when Great-Grandfather declared that you were his. When Gavril disappeared, then showed up later as Teeg San Gerxon with his ring on your finger, I took another step away. My heart hurts, Reah. For you. Aches. For you. There hasn't been another who held me or my heart. Not that I've been celibate. I tried to push your image away, anytime I went to bed with someone else. But it was always there. I'm tired of stepping back, Reah."

The cloth had slipped from my eyes and I was staring, openmouthed and perhaps for the first time, truly, at Rylend Morphis. "You were the one who said I'd be the King Karathia deserved. Do you know what that did to me, Reah? That you had faith in me, when everybody else saw me as the child conceived by artificial means? Do you know that many on Karathia saw me as an unnatural aberration?"

"Ry, honey, don't ever think that." I pulled his head toward mine and bumped my forehead to his. "Those people are backward and don't know any better."

"Reah, you said you loved me. Do you really love me? In the way a woman might love a man?" Ry kissed me, the kiss becoming more than just a peck. He wanted something from me. Wanted a response of a certain kind. I gave it to him. His kisses were demanding after that. I was lifted out of the tub and my skin dried with power. Ry's fingers might as well have been charged with electricity, they were sending tingles everywhere. And when he laid me on the bathroom floor and buried his head between my thighs, I shrieked with pleasure.

"Reah was right." Garde stared across Jaydevik Rath's desk at his brother, the King of Kifirin.

"About?"

"About the shipments. The nanna shipment was taken by pirates, when we labeled it as gishi fruit. The gishi fruit we labeled as nannas was left alone."

"Unbelievable. Have you informed Lendill Schaff?"

"First thing," Garde nodded. "Lissa told Norian, since he was spending the night."

"Then there are people providing information on the ground or on the ships," Jayd blew a smoky breath. "How much did that lost shipment cost us?"

"That was only half the harvest from the southern grove. The second half got through and we're labeling half the western grove shipment as wheat," Garde grinned. "The wheat harvest is going on, as you know. We'll just have to be creative to label the other shipments. So we only lost about an eighth of our profits. If we get the rest of the shipments through, we won't get hurt that much. I hear that some of the gishi fruit growers on Avendor have been devastated by the losses of this year's crop."

"Reah was right to work our harvests around theirs so we supply when they can't. It means a steady flow of fruit, instead of waiting for the proper seasons on Avendor."

"Reah was right about all of it, brother. With the cost of gishi fruit going up due to the pirate attacks, we'll be able to pay off the debt by the end of the year if our remaining shipments go through," Garde said.

"You know all those trees—the seedlings that created the groves? Do you know who paid for those?" Jayd watched his oldest brother carefully.

"What about them? That was twenty-five years ago."

"Who paid for those?"

"I don't know. Didn't the Crown pay that expense?"

"No. There isn't a single record that the Crown paid for anything regarding those seeds or seedlings. In fact, I don't even know which it was. When Reah mentioned it, I almost laughed in her face and told her that if she wanted to grow gishi fruit on Kifirin, she was welcome to waste her time."

"Reah paid for it."

"Yes. Whether she bought fruit and planted seeds or managed to get seedlings from Avendor, I have no idea. But she did. We don't officially own those trees, brother. Reah does."

"She'll never push it. She won't call us out on it. She hasn't yet. We're her family." Garde looked out the window that covered an entire side of Jayd's private study. The city of Veshtul spread out below the palace. The city was beautiful, laid out originally by the same vampire who'd designed the palace.

"No. She won't push it. She won't demand what is hers by right. Hasn't ever from us, has she? And yet we have the balls to insist that we're her family."

"Perhaps a terrible family, but still family," Garde insisted softly, rising to stand before the window. "Tory thinks his eldest are fourteen, now. Lissa and the Larentii are about to tell him that he has a second set of twins."

"How is he dealing with all this?"

"He's angry at first, because so many things have slipped away from his memory. I wish I knew what truly caused this," Garde's sigh was heavy and weighted with worry.

"As do I. The healers and the Larentii say they find nothing physically amiss."

"I think those Larentii know something and they're not saying. It's that damned rule they have of noninterference." Garde blew a cloud of smoke. "And I think Reah could help with Tory's memory loss, if she wasn't traipsing across the Alliance, somewhere, looking for that missing wizard."

"Do you look to Reah to solve all your problems, Gardevik?" Jayd said softly. "What will you do if she doesn't come back to us? If she doesn't return to Tory? We may have burned those bridges, brother. Think about that."

"I hate these things," Gavril muttered angrily as he walked through the tunnel connecting the San Gerxon Casino with his palace. Dee walked beside him. They were meeting with a section of Princes, Kings and Governors who were hardest hit by pirate attacks upon major exports.

Dee merely nodded in agreement. These meetings were extremely difficult. The potentates only wanted to shout about their losses, with none willing to sit down and talk reasonably about what measures might be taken to prevent the next wave of attacks. President Drix was among those gathering inside a meeting room at the San Gerxon. More than a third of the gishi fruit shipments from Avendor had been seized by pirates, in addition to crews and the ships hauling the fruit.

"Gavril?" Lissa appeared at her son's side.

"Mom, what are you doing here?" Gavril would always be young to his mother, although he was nearing a hundred years of age.

"Reah came up with a plan that worked for Kifirin, but if it works elsewhere, the less who know, the better. We pretty much have proof that somebody somewhere, either on the ground or on the ships, is passing information to the pirates," she was walking swiftly at her youngest son's side.

"What?" Gavril was certainly interested.

"Kifirin just shipped a load of gishi fruit in sealed containers that were labeled as nannas. The nannas were labeled as gishi fruit. Both were picked up at the same time and hauled on separate ships. The nannas labeled as gishi fruit were taken while the gishi fruit labeled as nannas went right through."

Gavril cursed. Stopped in the middle of the tunnel and cursed again. "Mom, this might work for a while, until the pirates figure out what's going on. And then we'll have to deal with it again."

"But at least some shipments might get through," Lissa pointed out. "I assume something is jamming all the locating beacons you slip into those shipments."

"Yeah. We can't get a handle on any of it. It's like the things go dead the moment the pirates hit."

"I'll come with you to your meeting, honey. Maybe we can work something out."

"If they stop yelling long enough," Gavril agreed. He already had a headache, and it was only going to get worse.

❧

"Jerves, would you like to come to dinner tomorrow evening? I'm off and Ry wants ox-roast for the evening meal." I was inviting Zendeval's assistant to dinner. I hoped he'd talk freely with us, especially after we served him a few glasses of wine with the meal.

"Yes. I'd love to come," Jerves usually vibrated in a restless sort of way, but he seemed happy, now.

"Good. Be there at eighteen bells and we'll start with drinks," I said.

"I will." Jerves trotted away happily to do Zendeval Rjjn's bidding.

❧

"Baby, if we hadn't invited Jerves for dinner, I'd lift you onto this table and love you senseless," Ry wiggled against me suggestively. He was my secret, now. And he could almost make me come just by smiling and placing his hands in certain spots. I don't know what kept us apart all those years, but he was certainly attempting to make up for lost time.

"Ry, I really do love you," I said against his mouth.

"I love you more," he said and kissed me.

I was pulling the ox-roast out of the oven when Jerves rang the guest bell. He then walked into the apartment, followed by Zendeval Rjjn and Perdil the Dwarf.

"I hope you prepared enough for two extras," Ry gave me a brief frown while his back was turned to all three of our dinner guests.

"I did," I sighed. So much for having leftovers on Second-Day. Ry got them seated in our tiny sitting area and offered all of them the rum and fruit drink I'd prepared earlier.

"You'll love this," Ry said as I laid plates of ox-roast covered in mushroom sauce and baked inside a pastry in front of our guests a short time later. "I think it's my favorite thing that Reah makes."

126

Perdil was in raptures after the first bite. Zendeval Rjjn was staring at me as he chewed. Jervis was busy eating as quickly as he could. I refilled drinks before sitting down to my own portion of food.

"Reah, I wish to be invited to dinner every time you serve this," Perdil demanded as he held his plate out for a second portion. I also laid salads by each plate, with a special dressing drizzled over the long leaves and tiny greens.

"I've never seen anyone cook as you do," Zendeval finally stopped stuffing himself long enough to say a few words.

"And you may never see it again," Ry said, holding up his glass to me.

"Thanks, hon," I smiled at him.

"This is a live feed?" Norian watched the dinner party with interest. Ry had hoped to get information from the assistant they'd invited to dinner. Instead, two others had shown up. Lendill had received mindspeech that those two were Zendeval Rjjn, the one who managed the five best resorts on Stellar Winds, and one of the other master cooks from Galedaro's kitchens.

"I've sent both images through the databases, and nothing comes up," Lendill said as he watched Zendeval Rjjn stare at Reah. He wanted to growl and fold there, just to kill the man. Zendeval had designs on Reah. Lendill recognized that predatory look.

"So, we've got Stellar Winds full of unknowns, likely from outside the Alliance," Norian paced as he watched the large vid-screen inside his office. "Are all of them involved in human trafficking?"

"It's possible, but we still need more evidence," Lendill concluded. "And you won't believe what Rylend told me through mindspeech."

"What was that?" Norian didn't take his eyes away from the image. Lendill proceeded to tell his oldest friend what Reah had seen from inside a voyeur booth.

"Norian, are you kidding me?" Lissa blinked at her lion snake shapeshifting mate.

"No. Ry says that Reah was almost ill over it."

"Has anyone ever looked into what happened to Darletta's mother?" Lissa thought to ask.

"No. But I will now," Norian hauled out his comp-vid.

~

"Six successful deliveries of gishi fruit," Dee whispered gleefully to Gavril as they walked through the pool area behind Gavril's palace.

"It's what Mom calls the old shell game. We used three separate shipments, all going out at the same time," Gavril smiled slightly. "Cotton, wheat and nannas. Only all those cartons held gishi fruit in special, cool boxes. The prices are already up, so the boxes weren't such a stretch to afford."

"It worked," Dee grinned. And for an old vampire, that grin was something to see.

"We'll have to be just as subtle about other things, Dee. And we'll have to send some normal shipments, or their suspicions will be raised."

"Already thought of that. I asked Drix to send the culls on a ship and label it as gishi fruit. It will be; it'll just be what he normally wouldn't sell off-world."

"Good idea. Perhaps we can do that with rejections from electronic plants and such as well."

"Potentially making their black-market customers angry, if they get substandard equipment and supplies," Dee's grin was wider.

"The shell game just became more complicated," Gavril slapped his surrogate father on the back—quite hard. As a vampire, Dee barely felt it.

~

"Thank goodness." I breathed a sigh after our guests, expected and unexpected, left for the evening. They'd stayed quite late, drinking, laughing and not saying one damned thing that we wanted to hear.

"Reah, it was a good effort. I just think that Zendeval Rjjn isn't going to let you out of his sight. He's got it bad, baby."

"Ry, he only knows lust," I said, lifting plates off the table and carrying them to the kitchen.

"I know lust, too," Ry took the plates from my hand and set them on the counter, and then lifted me up to sit there. "Big lust," he sighed against my mouth.

*Daddy Schuul left today, but his baby girl is still here and screwing Faldin and any other man she can pull inside one of those voyeur rooms,* Ry sent as soon as I walked inside the apartment on Second-Day.

*She's mortal; she has to do what she can while she can,* I quipped silently, causing Ry to laugh.

"Feel like going outside for a while?" Ry asked. Outside on Stellar Winds meant outside the vast complex of resorts and glassed-in tunnels and tubes that formed the city of Stellar Winds. There was plenty of planetoid left, but much of it was barren, not getting much rainfall. A small ocean bordered the city, and desalinated water from it supplied the needs of Stellar Winds. Hikers often went outside to climb nearby cliffs or explore canyons carved by eons of winds.

"If you go, I go," I smiled at Ry. The day hadn't been too bad, so I still had some energy left.

"After we walk, we can eat somewhere," Ry said.

"That sounds great. Just give me a minute to change," I said. Ry had already stepped into a more comfortable outfit, I saw.

"We'll go out the north gate," Ry said. The north gate led to the caverns and canyons. Ry had pulled a jacket from somewhere for me, too, saying it might be cool out. I nodded and slipped into it when we approached the gate roughly half a click later. It was quite the walk and we could have taken ground transportation but chose not to. Ry also held my hand as we walked. I couldn't recall the last time any of my mates had done that. I watched him covertly as we walked. Ry strode with purpose, his handsome face set. I wondered what worried him.

"I'm setting up a false signal for any sensors to pick up," he told me once we were half a click from the gate and well into one of the sandstone canyons. Blinking at him, I watched as he moved his hands gracefully, light forming around them. "It'll look like we're wandering around the canyon," he said, "in case anybody checks our employee chips. And I'll get a hit if anybody comes close." Ry took my hand again and folded me away from Stellar Winds.

❧

"Hello, Erland," I said, as Ry led me to a table inside the Star Gazer restaurant on Tulgalan. Ry's father was there waiting on us, which surprised me.

"Hello, Reah. I understand that this may be more than just a show," he tapped the ring on my finger. Lendill had passed rings to Ry and me before we left for Stellar Winds, since we were supposed to be married.

"I didn't realize he made an announcement," I worried my lower lip as I looked up at Ry.

"I told Dad a few hours ago that I wasn't coming to this meeting without you," Ry leaned down and kissed me. "We're together, Reah. What affects you affects me, and vice-versa."

"I got quite an extensive message from my child, here, over how he's loved you for a very long time," Erland gave me a small smile. "I'll inform his mother as soon as we're done here. But I'd like to get dinner for both of you tonight. I should have seen this long ago. I couldn't imagine why my son wouldn't spend more than a single night with any woman. Now I know."

"I can't believe you didn't feel the envy radiating off me when I watched her with my brothers or any one of the others," Ry said, accepting a glass of water from the waiter.

"We'll have a bottle of your best sparkling wine," Erland said. The waiter, a discreet man who looked to be sixty and in his prime for Tulgalan, nodded and went to fetch it for us.

"While you're here, Erland," I said, "I need to ask some questions."

"About?"

"About Radolf. I don't want any charges brought or anything, I just want them to walk away," I said. "He and Ilvan have been embezzling from Dees for years. I think it's time they managed on their own. I never officially married Radolf, but I don't know what the procedure might be for separating from him."

"You saw that, did you? Wylend finally admitted that he manipulated your relationship with Radolf, in order to keep Garek away from you." Erland's beautiful face looked troubled. Garek was Radolf's father, who'd stepped back in order to allow his son to become my mate.

"Why would he do that?" I asked, feeling hurt, even after all these years.

"He saw how much Corolan loved you, and worried that Garek would feel the same. Call it petty jealousy, if you will. Understand that he was in the first quarter of a female phase and that can happen. He knows now what that has cost him. And you."

"I won't ever go back to him."

"He knows that. His son, the Oracle, verified it."

"Oh, yes. I forgot about that one. The meddler." I thought of him that way—Lissa's father, that is. And Wyatt's. If he hadn't interfered at key junctures, Wyatt might still be alive.

"We all know what those things cost us." Erland couldn't read my thoughts any longer; none except the Larentii could. That shield was a gift from Nefrigar and I was more than thankful for it. Erland could read the expression on my face, however. He was adept at it, just as his son was. "As far as Radolf goes, why don't you let Lissa and me handle this one? Ilvan is still her cook, you know. I'll get into the records, determine the amount of damage they've done and then give them some choices."

"Only if it isn't too much trouble," I sighed. Suddenly, I'd gotten tired of being walked on or taken advantage of. There never seemed to be any profits from Dee's, although it was always busy. The books I'd been shown always accounted for each credit deposited. I didn't know how they'd managed to siphon away some of the income, but they had. And they were living in my house on Tulgalan while they did it. My uncle and my former lover, together, had done this to me.

Had they ever cared for me? I shook my head sadly at the thought. Our sparkling wine was served, with the rest of the bottle in an ice bucket next to the table. We ordered, I wanted fish. Nobody seemed to know how to make fish properly at Galedaro's. And I wasn't about to prepare it, in case Zendeval and Perdil showed up unexpectedly for dinner. I had the idea that Jerves had let it slip that he'd been invited, so Zendeval and Perdil came along, too. Erland answered some of Ry's questions about Tory's progress while we ate dinner.

"Tory now believes that Raedah and Tara are sixteen, and that Lara and Kara are fourteen. He was quite shocked when Lissa and the others brought out vid-photos of all of them. Now, we're working on Dara and Sara," Erland said, pushing his plate away with a sigh. "Lissa thinks that she might bend time a little when he comes to terms with all of it, just so he can see all of his babies when they were small. Kyler says that her father was taken back to the time of her birth, and it meant a lot to him that he was allowed to hold his daughter."

"Like Tory would care." A stream of smoke curled from my nostrils. That only happened when I was extremely angry or upset over something.

"Reah, he's coming to terms with everything now," Ry attempted to coax me into a better mood.

"Ry, who has stood with me the past twenty-five years?" I looked into his beautiful, dark eyes. "I worked the groves during the day and then visited the palace in Veshtul at night, just so I could see my children. At times, I imagined that Garde and Jayd were holding them hostage. Don't think for a moment that they wouldn't have pulled them away from me if I'd complained."

"Fuck," Erland muttered. "Reah, this isn't why I asked Rylend to come and speak with me. I know things didn't go as they should have, and all of us should have been better and more watchful. Please, we'll sort all this out soon, I promise. I just had something to speak with Ry about that couldn't wait."

"What is it, Dad, that can't wait?" Ry wanted to get down to business, now. We'd been gone long enough from Stellar Winds as it was.

"It's your great-grandfather, Rylend. He's talking abdication. But only if he has a legitimate and named heir beforehand."

# CHAPTER 9

"Then who is he intending to name as heir? I gave up my citizenship," Ry cursed softly.

"You. Your citizenship was never revoked, son. Wylend never recorded it. I told him that you were on a mission at the moment, and he says he'll wait two eight-days but no longer. He's walking away from Karathia, Rylend, and you're the ideal candidate. We have all watched you operate on Teeg's behalf for the Campiaan Alliance. The transition into a fully functioning Alliance would never have been accomplished if you hadn't been there to smooth the way and arbitrate between this one and that. You have every skill required and more. You're the best diplomat in either Alliance, and you're more familiar with the laws of both than any ambassador anywhere. For most of the skills required of any ruler, you are much more qualified than Wylend ever was. He's beginning to realize this. And he's weary, son. Tired of all of it. In fact, he's planning to live with Griffin for a while, and intends to help with Griffin's search for Amara. Belen allowed her to hide from her former mate, but he hasn't given up looking for her."

Ry and I were both staring at Erland in shock. Ry had to accept—had to. He would be the King he should be. Was meant to be.

"Reah, you were meant to be Queen of Karathia. Now, it will come to pass." Ry turned to me, lifted my hand in his and kissed my fingers.

"Ry, are you sure? You know what Keetha said about me."

"Reah, I don't give a fuck what Keetha said. She's a prejudiced cow. We will do this. Together."

"You are allowed to form a personal group of advisers, but I was hoping to be included in that number," Erland bowed his head to Ry. I drew in a breath. Erland was formally recognizing his son as the heir.

"Dad, if you don't, I'll get on my knees and beg," Ry said. "Is Wylend taking anyone with him?"

"I don't know that yet, son. If he abdicates, the choice will be theirs and not his any longer."

"If Corolan and Garek stay behind, I'd be happy to have them with me."

"If that is their choice, my Prince."

"Wylend already named him heir, he just had to accept. Didn't he?" I glanced shrewdly at Erland.

"True." The smile was blinding.

"Ry, maybe you should go now."

"No. But I will leave in a week. I'll tell them I have a family emergency."

"And that will be the truth," I agreed. "Although I was getting used to having a man in my bed." I gripped his fingers under the table.

"You won't miss me for long. Get that mess sorted out, Reah. I'll do as much as I can, but it could take a little while. We both know there's something going on."

"Yeah. We both know that," I sighed. "And we should get back."

"Yeah. Dad, thanks for telling me." Ry rose from the table, pulling me up with him. "Your majesties," Erland grinned hugely as he dipped his head. And then ruined it by hauling his son into an embrace and kissing his cheek. "Stay safe son. I'll see you in a week."

"Will do, Dad." Ry and I went to a discreet spot to fold away.

∼

"Here are the records, and I had to use quite a spell to get them." Erland flopped the comp-vid onto Lissa's desk inside her private study.

"I take it our son will be King?"

"And Reah will be Queen."

"Why didn't we see it? Why? I *Looked*, Erland. He's loved her since the beginning."

"Stepped aside for his brothers and his great-grandfather. Only now, one of those relationships is gone forever and another one is rocky, at the very least."

"What are we looking at?" Lissa lifted the comp-vid.

"Records of embezzlement," Erland replied. "Your cook and Radolf have been embezzling from Reah for years. And living in her home on Tulgalan while doing it."

"If he's guilty," Lissa hissed, her eyes going red.

"Oh, there's no doubt. They've got six accounts set up. I wonder if they thought they'd get away with it forever." Erland tapped the comp-vid screen and brought up the first set of records.

"Honey, I hate to bother you so late, but Erland got this information at Reah's request, and I want you to look at it, since your money paid for this restaurant in the first place." Lissa handed the comp-vid to Gavril. Dee sat on a nearby chair inside Gavril's private study; the other employees had left for the evening.

"What is this?" Gavril lifted an eyebrow as he went through record after record of deposits in Radolf and Ilvan's names. "They don't make enough to justify these amounts," Gavril huffed, his eyes going red.

"They're embezzling. If Reah had even half that money during the past twenty-five years, she wouldn't have been destitute."

"I thought she wasn't," Gavril muttered, scrolling through more and more records. "I thought Dee's was turning a nice profit for her. She should never have allowed either of them to keep the books."

"She was overworked as it was, son." Gavin appeared at Lissa's side.

Dee stood and nodded at Gavril's natural father. "She made the mistake of trusting her uncle and one of her mates. I can't understand how either of them could take advantage like this."

"What are we going to do about it?" Gavril's eyes were red and fangs were threatening. That didn't happen often with him.

"Reah doesn't want imprisonment, but I think we have to go to these two as quickly as possible and tell them if they quietly disappear and never bother Reah again, we'll not press charges. If they even think about retaliation of any kind, I'll have them on Evensun so fast their heads will swim. And we won't go through the normal process to get them there. Ilvan apparently has more of his father in him than we suspected."

"I'll see to it that they won't ever work in the Campiaan Alliance," Gavril growled.

"Son, that's a bit drastic. Just make sure they're watched. If they step out of line again, then drop the hammer. I think that's what Reah would want. I think we should let them leave with enough to settle elsewhere. Lendill will keep watch from our side. You can do what you want from this side." Gavin was laying out what he thought best in the matter.

"All right, Dad. I wish Reah were here, though. I'd like to talk to her about this. And these assholes were living in the house I bought for her."

"I suggest we go immediately. I don't think I want them to enjoy another night at Teeg's expense. Do you?" Dee's eyes were red as well, and that was something that seldom happened.

"You've been paying the bills, haven't you?" Lissa looked at her youngest son.

"Yes. I've paid the fucking bills while they've cheated Reah out of millions. They're lucky Reah doesn't want harm to come to them."

"Then let's go, honey." Lissa was ready to toss her cook out the door and watch him bounce.

~

"If we offer to buy the house, Teeg may look into where the money came from. It's worth seven million," Ilvan pointed out. "That's why I said we couldn't afford it when she was at the restaurant not long ago. We don't need them looking in this direction." Ilvan handed a glass of wine to Radolf, along with a plate of sliced cheese and toasted bread.

"What will we do if they do look in our direction?" Radolf took the glass of wine and drank.

"Get the hell away. I already have tickets to Surnath hidden away. I think we can get jobs there easily. And we should get a heads-up if they look into the accounts. I've got a couple of people watching for any hits from the ASD or the local constabulary. The minute somebody looks into those records, we pull the money and run. Stop worrying. We've got enough to do us for a good, long while. Besides, Lendill is much too busy dealing with pirates right now. We have nothing to worry about."

"Not anymore." Gavril appeared in the kitchen, Lissa, Gavin and Dee right behind him. "You had humans keeping watch on your accounts. You didn't factor in stronger warlocks or vampires." Gavril held up the comp-vid. "Want to see what we found?" he asked.

"What I want to know," Lissa hissed in a low voice, "is how you could steal from Reah and her daughters. You," she poked Ilvan in the chest, "that's your niece. How could you do that to her? And you, Radolf, she loved you. What do you think should happen to you now?"

"No, we'll give the money back, I promise," Ilvan was backing away from Gavril, whose eyes were so dark a red they were nearly black. Radolf was backing away from Lissa, who held enough power to keep him from using his warlock ability.

"We'll leave you with enough to get the hell away from here and never trouble Reah again," Gavril snapped. "Reah didn't want either of you in jail. I think that was much too merciful of her. She worked eighteen-hour days and wore rags for the past twenty-five years, while you lived in this house and stole from her. I will have no mercy for either of you if you come near her or any of hers again, hear me?"

"Y-yes," Ilvan nodded, almost too frightened to speak.

"I am removing your power," Lissa glared at Radolf. "You won't harm anyone that way, either. I'll see to it myself." Light flew away from Radolf and he nearly collapsed on the floor. "Now, get your things together. If Surnath is where you want to go, I'll take you and all your belongings tonight. After we transfer funds into the accounts belonging to Reah's restaurant. Someone will hire new cooks for both of us. In the meantime, I think Fes will be happy to send someone over."

"Please, don't tell Fes," Ilvan whined. "Or Edan."

"I won't. I'll let Reah tell them herself."

"We thought you were taking care of her," Radolf moaned to Gavril.

"She never asked me for a damned thing. I would have given her whatever she wanted if she'd asked. I thought Dee's was doing well enough that she didn't have to ask."

"It was," Dee had seen the records for himself. "There was enough there to keep her in clothing and give her better housing, as well as many other things."

"Come. We will do transfers immediately, and send these on their way. And you will never do harm again." Compulsion was thick in Gavin's voice.

"Nice, Dad," Gavril nodded at his father.

"Will you see me to the space station?" Ry hefted one bag over his shoulder and pulled the other behind him.

"Do you think I wouldn't?" I bit my lip, trying not to cry. Ry had come to be an anchor for me, and now he was leaving.

"Baby, don't look like that," Ry moved to dump his bags on the floor.

"No, honey, you have to go or you'll miss the ship." We both knew he'd be folding away the moment he was locked inside his private compartment. I was still worried that anything and everything connected to Stellar Winds was bugged. Zendeval, too, had pretended sympathy when Ry turned in his notice, citing a family emergency on

Le-Ath Veronis. Supposedly, his terminally ill grandfather lived there. That's what the official records showed for Ry Windle, anyway.

*Watch out for Zendeval and anyone else*, Ry cautioned as we walked toward the elevator.

*I will*, I reached out and rubbed Ry's back. *I'm so happy for you. You'll be King, honey. Just as you should be.*

Lendill stared at the two who stood inside his office. He'd never seen Ildevar Wyyld's assistant, Willem Drifft, in the company of the Larentii Archivist, Nefrigar. "Is there something I can do for you?" Lendill dropped his briefcase onto the desk. He and Norian had met with several high-ranking officials from across the Alliance, discussing the problem with pirates and other difficulties.

"We were just looking at Reah's awards," Willem observed, studying one stating that Reah had been instrumental in destroying the Drakus seed trade nearly thirty years before.

"These seem so trivial, in exchange for the actual accomplishment," Nefrigar said. He was sitting on the corner of Lendill's desk; otherwise his head nearly brushed the ceiling.

"Reah hasn't ever received enough compensation for her work," Lendill agreed.

"Or for giving her life," Willem pointed out.

"She still doesn't know she was brought back from the dead by the Wise Ones, and I wish you wouldn't tell her, I think it would upset her," Lendill frowned at his uninvited guests.

"We know this," Nefrigar said stiffly.

"Yes. I should realize that the Larentii would know before anyone else." Lendill's voice was filled with irritation.

"You are angry because we cannot interfere with the difficulties you are experiencing." Nefrigar's voice was even and unruffled.

"Got it in one," Lendill pointed a finger at the Larentii.

"Lendill, do not upset yourself," Nefrigar placed a hand on Lendill's shoulder. "Things will go as they will. If you need some time, I can bring you to the Larentii homeworld and you may browse through the archives. Few besides Larentii have ever been invited there."

"I don't have time," Lendill grumped.

"I bend time just as well as any of my kind. I can bring you back before you left, if you wish it."

"You'd let me touch the records?"

"Many of them are voice activated, so touch would not be necessary. Everything else is placed in stasis, so your hands will do no harm."

"I'll think about it," Lendill sighed. "Right now, I have records of my own to get through."

"As you wish it," Nefrigar nodded and disappeared.

"Lendill, doesn't our race have something to say about missed opportunities?" Willem lifted an eyebrow at the Vice-Director of the ASD.

"I'll regret it, I know," Lendill grimaced and pulled out his comp-vid to check on the latest pirate attacks.

"Almost eight million credits." Erland handed the records to Ry, who was going through records of his own regarding Ilvan and Radolf's embezzlement. Wylend hadn't come himself to speak with Ry. Instead, he'd asked Erland to show Ry what was happening with Karathia at the moment. Records of every Karathian citizen working off-world littered Rylend's new desk, but Erland had chosen to show him the figures he and Lissa gleaned from six embezzled accounts.

Ry had been given Wyatt's old suite; it had only been cleaned and refurbished recently. Ry figured that someone would let him know if Wyatt's ghost inhabited it. Wyatt likely was happy to get away—he'd never wanted to be heir.

"They took so much from Reah," Ry blew out a breath at the figures on Erland's comp-vid.

"It's in the restaurant account now, and I had Grant and Heathe go through and make sure sufficient taxes are paid. Don't need the Alliance Tax Service breathing down Reah's neck."

"Especially since she didn't know how much they took."

"We left them enough to rent on Surnath, but everybody's watching them, now. They won't be able to squeak without Lendill knowing. We handed the information to him yesterday. He wanted to arrest them, but Lissa talked him out of it."

"Reah didn't want that," Ry agreed, sorting through paper documents. "Didn't Em-pah ever learn to use a comp-vid?"

"Doesn't like them, but he knows how," Erland said. "You have to realize he's been King for more than six thousand years. Comp-vids weren't always around, you know."

"And there'll be something different if I'm King that long," Ry agreed.

"Yes." Erland smiled.

~

"We're having difficulty getting gishi fruit," Perdil growled the moment he walked into the pastry kitchen.

"Why? The fruit should be in season now," I said. I would know; I figured the western grove on Kifirin was ready to be harvested.

"I'll look into the matter," Perdil stalked out of the kitchen. I had enough fruit to make two more batches of ice cream. Wanting to smile (the ruse was likely working—pirates didn't want nannas or wheat) I went about my business instead.

~

"Stop fretting. Did you get the errand done?"

"No," Perdil was in a growling mood and almost didn't bear talking to. "He managed to get away from both the guards."

"Doesn't matter, if he comes back, we'll have him then. Meanwhile, the way is clear, wouldn't you say?" Zendeval Rjjn sounded happy. Perdil was in the worst of moods.

"You won't be smiling if Ned demands ice cream; he eats more of it than should be allowed."

"Are you going to stop him?"

"Me? Not on your life."

"See? You complain to me, but you'll be as smooth as butter with anything my cousin wants."

"So would you," Perdil growled again.

"Yes, but things are looking particularly well for me at the moment. I may get what I want with little or no trouble."

"And I'm telling you now to learn manners and finesse. This one isn't like the others."

"Are you offering lessons?"

"Hmmph." Perdil walked out of Zendeval's office.

"Aunt Glinda, what was Great-Grandmother Belarok like?" Lara fingered the brooch that Glinda gave her. Glinda had given Lara and Kara jewelry owned by Queen Belarok for wedding presents. Glinda was glad Eldevik had settled down after the claiming. She'd been worried that Reah would come and fight with him over his treatment of Lara in the claiming.

"My mother was gentle and loving," Glinda smiled. "As was my father. They were so proud to have a daughter, I think, and I was a little spoiled while they still lived."

"Did they ever take you off-world?" Kara asked. Her gift had been a bracelet.

"Very few times. Father always had four High Demons around us if we traveled anywhere. Mother wasn't able to skip. She said something about it, once—said there was a reason that she couldn't really discuss. She wasn't happy with my father about it, either."

"Why? Why couldn't she skip?"

"She said something about the stupid suppressor, I think. Whatever that meant. She never went into detail, and I was too young to ask. I wasn't supposed to be able to skip when I was eight and nobody had bothered to train me. When the palace was attacked by my oldest brother, I got my trial by fire, skipping away because I was so frightened. I landed in a garbage heap somewhere in Veshtul, and a comesula business owner thought I was one of their children and shouted at me for getting my clothes dirty."

"You didn't run to one of them and tell them what was happening?"

"Kara, I was eight and I'd just seen the most horrible thing ever. My mother and my aunt were raped by High Demons and they died that way. They couldn't skip away because of whatever it was that stopped them. It ended up killing them, I think. The fact that I could skip at such a young age saved my life. I lived among the comesuli for several years until your grandfather came looking for me. He trained me after that. We still have little respect for one another."

"That is not true," Gardevik Rath walked into the room, giving each of his granddaughters a peck on the cheek.

"Do you know what it was that kept grandmother Belarok from skipping away when she was attacked?" Kara looked at Garde.

"That." Garde's voice was flat.

"I don't know what it was," Glinda said. "I think mother called it a suppressor once. But she only said it once."

"They were designed by a now-dead race," Garde sighed. "As a means of control. Lendevik wanted a way to keep the females at home and under his thumb. He had one of those tiny gadgets shot into the collarbone," he pointed to his shoulder at the right spot. "It kept them from skipping away. Controls were available, too, for mindspeech and other things, but he never used them. Lord Nedevik refused outright to have one implanted in his mate. He and Lendevik seldom saw eye to eye on those things. Ned wanted to help the original Le-Ath Veronis. Lendevik didn't. Le-Ath Veronis fell, and we ended up with the comesuli and none of the vampires."

"An honored High Demon tradition. Take what you want and give nothing in return." Kara glared at her grandfather.

"What?" He stared at her, a puzzled frown on his face.

"Mom. I'm going home, Aunt Glinda." Kara skipped away.

"What happened to the world that made the suppressors?" Lara asked. Her grandfather said it was a dead world, now.

"Wars," Garde said. "Everybody trying to control everybody else. The suppressors were designed to be stronger and stronger through the years, controlling more and more things, until the various factions destroyed one another with them. There weren't enough left alive afterward to save the race. They are all dead, now."

"I hope that technology died with them," Lara shuddered.

"So, my father and alien technology killed my mother." Glinda stared at Garde.

"Glin, it's in the past. Do you think your father wouldn't regret that, if he were here?"

"I would hope so. My mother might have gotten away, only she couldn't."

"What was Kara talking about?" Garde asked.

"She misses Mom," Lara said.

"And she blames me for that."

"I didn't say that."

"You don't have to."

"Aunt Glinda, I'm going home." Lara skipped away.

"You didn't need a suppressor, did you, Garde? You had those girls."

"Is everybody out to beat me up?" Garde flung up a hand.

"You haven't talked to Lissa, have you?"

"No, why?"

"Radolf and Ilvan were embezzling from the restaurant. While living in Reah's house."

"That took testicles."

"You don't care that they were stealing from Reah. Mistreating her. Did you get what you wanted and now you don't care anymore, Garde? Is that it?"

"No! I wish you would all lay off. I didn't mean to hurt her. Truly. It just turned out that way."

"You wouldn't treat Lissa that way."

"Lissa is my mate."

"So, since Reah isn't your mate?"

"All right! I blame her for Tory's desertion. She cost me years without my son. Are you happy now?"

"Don't ever say that again within my presence." Kifirin was there, suddenly, smoke billowing from his nostrils. "None of that was Reah's fault. Someday, perhaps, you will know the full truth of this. For now, blame the King of Karathia and your son's sensitivity and quick anger. My daughter had nothing to do with this."

"She said he was too young."

"In private and to another. And she qualified that afterward, saying he was getting better. Only that wasn't passed on, was it? Your son is immortal. You have plenty of years to spend with him. Do not persecute Reah for this. She has suffered enough already, and my part in that is not small." Kifirin disappeared.

"Wylend's meddling did this, Garde. Tory would never have known otherwise. Do you guard every word that you speak to Lissa or do you speak your mind in private?" Glinda paced in front of Garde.

"What's going on?" Jayd walked into the room.

"Ask your brother, I'm going to look at the gishi fruit groves." Glinda skipped away.

I didn't like staying alone in the apartment. Ry had helped me handle being on Stellar Winds. Made me feel safer. I felt every one of the twenty-five years I'd been out of the ASD. I wanted to skip here and there to investigate this or that. Felt horribly restricted because I couldn't. Zendeval came by the kitchens at least twice a day, spoke to Perdil each time but watched me when he thought I wasn't looking.

I sent mindspeech to Lendill, now, since Ry wasn't here to do it. So many people had come to depend upon Rylend Morphis. Teeg sent him to take care of sensitive situations he didn't want to involve himself in. Lissa even asked him for help at times. So much weighed on his shoulders, but like his father, he managed all of it with a beautiful smile and a diplomatic word. Now, I hoped he was coming into everything he desired. He deserved that and more.

"Reah, we're having a rush tonight in the bar," Jerves was at my elbow and I hadn't even heard him walk up; I was too busy preparing plates of desserts. "Mr. Rjjn wants the employees to dress properly and be out on the floor to make sure everything goes smoothly."

"He wants an orgy to go smoothly?" I stared at Jerves in shock. That's what a rush was. I'd seen news programs that showed portions of a rush held in this bar or that on Stellar Winds. A rush was an event that drew certain types of crowds—the ones who enjoyed group sex.

"It will be recorded," Jerves admitted nervously. "We want it to go well, in case we wish to advertise with portions of it."

"And what does he expect me to do?"

"Dress appropriately and make sure it keeps to sex. No violence is allowed. Call the guards if anything looks to go in that direction."

"Dress appropriately?"

"Nicely. As if you belong in the crowd."

"Ah. Slutty. I left my slutty outfit at home."

"Reah, there are plenty of shops here. Go find something and be there at twenty-two bells. That's when it's scheduled to start."

"Right."

"Let your assistants handle the desserts. Go now." Jerves was beginning to fidget again. I figured Rude Rjjn ordered his assistant to come and tell me because he was too cowardly to do it himself. Forcibly preventing myself from blowing smoke, I tossed my apron aside and stalked out of the kitchen.

"She wasn't happy and said she didn't have anything appropriate to wear," Jerves almost had a nervous tic as he spoke to Zendeval moments later. "I told her to get something at one of the shops and be there at twenty-two bells."

"Keep the assistants in the kitchen. Perdil and Master Cook Dardell will be on the floor, helping."

"How many guards do we have?" Jerves was shifting from one foot to the other.

"Twelve. Not enough, but Nedrizif took away six of mine tonight for another project."

"Of course. If you need my assistance with anything else," Jerves sincerely hoped that wasn't the case.

"Get images of Reah tonight. Bring them to me only, do you hear?"

"Yes, sir."

The dress was nearly identical to the one Ry had bought for our visit to Starshine. I bought shoes that didn't have quite as high a heel. I had jewelry that was good enough to wear already, so I hauled my purchases up the elevator to change. I didn't have much time. By the time I got back to the bar, the music supervisor was already making the announcements for the rush. A crowd had gathered and most were drinking and likely taking drugs. I saw several who were already slipping out of their clothing. Feeling completely out of place, I went in search of Master Cook Perdil.

Perdil came to my shoulder, but I wasn't that tall. He hadn't gotten the instructions to dress appropriately, I noticed. He had on the slacks he normally wore, with a white shirt, the sleeves folded back a time or two. He wore his hair shorter than most dwarves I knew, and his eyebrows were trimmed.

Master Morwin, the Amterean Dwarf who'd tutored all of Lissa's children, wouldn't dream of trimming his eyebrows. Perdil wasn't Amterean. Likely he was from Liffel II, but I wasn't going to mention it to him. Most Liffelithi were too interested in crime and amassing fortunes to even think about cooking. Perdil was unusual as a dwarf, and he and Master Cook Dardell were standing together when I found them. Dardell appeared ready to participate in the rush, in my estimation.

"We're short on guards tonight," Perdil informed me over the noise of thumping music. Strobe lights were beginning to search out participants. Employees ran through, tossing thin mats onto the floor. The ads I'd seen had people on the floor, the chairs, standing, against the walls, on the bar, everywhere.

I'd also seen images of the bartenders pouring alcohol in a participant's mouth as they were having sex. Of course, the ads made much of a single male getting attention from two or more females. I shook my head in disbelief as the first couple disrobed to the music and dropped to the floor. That opened the gates, with screaming, shouting and frantic searching for a partner.

Perdil jerked his head toward the western edge of the floor. I skirted frenzied bodies as best I could and took up a position so I could guard against violence.

I discovered my thoughts about Master Cook Dardell were correct; he grabbed a young woman who was already disrobed, lifted her onto a stool at the bar and buried his head between her legs.

"It's something, isn't it?" Zendeval had found his way to my side.

"I don't recall that this was part of my job description."

"It says other duties as required," Zendeval Rjjn pointed out.

"Then I'll delete that from my next application," I snapped, arms crossed tightly over my chest as I scanned the crowd.

"You look lovely," he almost shouted to be heard.

"Sure," I said, still keeping my eyes on the crowd. Was anyone expecting it? I wasn't, and I was watching. A young man was suddenly screaming as he leapt upon the bar, a knife in his hands. Zendeval ran, but I was faster. My foot barely hit the barstool as I used it as a steppingstone onto the bar, and I had the knife in my hand and the man's head whacked against the top of the bar before anyone else knew what was happening.

# CHAPTER 10

"My records show I was conscripted by the RAA." I was trying to explain myself to Mr. Rude Rjjn.

"I saw. I just hadn't realized that you were more than I imagined."

"All conscripts get the same training."

"I know that." He didn't, he was lying. I knew it. He just didn't know that I knew it. He had no idea what kind of training Regular Alliance Army got. "What did you do for the RAA?"

"It's in my records. I served as a cook." One of Lendill's rules was be as honest as you could. Always. That kept you from living more of a lie than necessary. According to my temporary records, I'd served as a cook for a military installation on Tulgalan. All six years. It listed my age as thirty-four.

"Why are you grilling her like a steak pulled from an ancient cow?" Perdil snapped at Zendeval. "Her records were available. It's your fault if you didn't read them." He was pacing behind me as I sat in a chair in front of Zendeval's desk. His private study was nicely furnished, but I was surprised there weren't any images of nude women on the walls. "And if you are short-handed and your guards are slow, be grateful that you had someone trained well enough to deal with that." Perdil meant the man with the knife. I had no idea how he'd gotten the weapon—it wasn't a kitchen knife; I knew that for certain.

"The guards are working on his identification," Zendeval snapped back at Perdil. "If he's a guest, then he'll be sent out on the next ship." Schooling my face, I watched Zendeval, wondering what might happen to the man if he wasn't a guest but an employee. I was afraid to dwell on that too long.

"I hear the rest of the rush went very well," Perdil sighed. "Zen, we are tired and it is late. Let us go to bed. You can laze about tomorrow if you want; Reah and I cannot."

"My apologies." Zendeval stood and dismissed Perdil and me. Gratefully I rose and walked unsteadily out of his office. "Perdil, a moment," Zendeval called. Perdil rolled his eyes and walked back inside, closing the door and leaving me alone in the hall outside Zendeval's suite. Shrugging, I walked toward the elevator.

"That was one of our employees who went crazy," Perdil confirmed as Zendeval sat down again. "You know we get one occasionally that cannot be controlled."

"Then the guards should be discreet."

"They will be. Do not fear."

"My plans were interrupted because of this. I do not wish for this to happen again."

"Calm yourself. The full moon is coming. I believe you can achieve your goals then, no?" Perdil stalked out of Zendeval's suite.

"My King, here are the images." Mordis handed a comp-vid to Nedrizif.

"This is the little cook Zendeval is hiding from me?" Ned thumbed through the vid, watching the woman as she leapt to the top of the bar and disarmed the rogue employee. "Moves quite well, too, in addition to being beautiful. Does she visit the voyeur rooms?"

"No, my King."

"Too bad. Rumor has it that Zendeval will send her in with the others. He plans to make his bid, I think. Make sure our other buyers get these images." Nedrizif handed the comp-vid back to Mordis. "I may make a bid myself."

"My information shows that she is the cook who prepares the ice cream you like so much."

"What? Perdil did not do this?" Nedrizif was standing in an instant, outrage apparent across his features.

"No, my King. The kitchen assistants were quite clear. Master Perdil did not do this. This one—Reah Windle—created this dessert."

"Then I will certainly bid against my cousin."

"Of course, sire."

"And I will increase the control I have over him," Nedrizif added.

"Of course, sire."

～

"Mom, how could this happen?" Tory rubbed his forehead with shaking fingers. He'd just met Raedah and Tara. Knew they were almost finished with their medical certificates. Met their mates, Philavik Weth and Rindavik Foth, even. Knew he had three sets of twins and their actual ages.

"Kifirin did this," Lissa said softly. "He gathered your seed and placed it while Reah was sleeping. Twice she woke to find him sitting on the edge of her bed, telling her that she was pregnant again."

"And that didn't sit well. I've been gone twenty-five fucking years, Mom. Darletta took those years and left me with nothing."

Lissa didn't tell Tory what she was learning from Norian about Darletta. Perhaps Tory had known about her perversions and blocked them, creating holes in his memory. Lissa shivered delicately as she sat beside Tory, gripping one of his large hands in both of hers.

"Honey, you're back, now. That's all we care about. What did you think of your oldest girls?"

"Mom, they don't know me, and they should. I missed so much. They're grown, now. And I haven't done one damn thing in the father department for them. Reah must resent the hell out of me."

"I hope she'll sit and talk with all of us sometime soon, honey. We have to convince her that you can't remember much of the past twenty-five years. That it isn't your fault that you weren't there to help raise the girls."

"It wasn't fair. To any of us," Tory moaned.

Darletta was still in residence; I saw her a time or two with Faldin and perhaps one or two other men. She had a sexual appetite, all right. She always ordered sex by dessert every time she came into Galedaro's. Meanwhile, Jerves was getting more fidgety for some reason, and I couldn't figure that out.

"Jerves, do I need to take you to the bar and get you a drink?" I asked at one point, when he came to check our supply of gishi fruit. We'd received a few crates, but were running low on it. It was the same with oxberries, I noticed. I knew where to order those if nobody else did.

"No," he denied, shaking his head. He was terrified we'd run out of essential supplies, I could tell.

Off-day was coming, too, which coincided with the full moon. I wanted to do more exploring on that day. I hadn't had much opportunity, and I wanted to find out what had happened with the knife-wielding young man. None of the news vids carried any information. The vid-screens carried only basic news services, and I couldn't get anything on my comp-vid. When I wasn't too tired, I worried about that.

"Open that one!" The angry one was shouting. Again. He opened the crate the angry one pointed to. Fruit was inside, but it was the wrong kind. "Open all of them," the angry one shouted. He moved as quickly as he could to obey.

The court was full. Rylend waited behind richly carved double doors, but he peered through a small crack between them, seeing all of Karathia's nobility gathered there. Most of them knew what was about to happen. Ry hoped he and his father could control the crowd if they became angry when Wylend stepped down.

Griffin had also come. Ry recalled that Reah had called him the meddler. Ry hadn't seen Griffin since Wyatt's funeral. He'd changed. He looked old. As if the weight of the worlds had settled onto his shoulders. And, as an immortal, that shouldn't be. Most Karathians were nearly immortal but not wholly so, much like some of the Wizard Houses. Grey House was one of those. Ry, and Erland, through Lissa, were immortal, unless someone found a way to kill them. Lissa's power had seen to it. Now, Ry hoped that he and his father lived through the day.

"I abdicate my throne, in favor of my grandson and heir, Rylend Morphis," Wylend's voice boomed throughout the round hall.

"That's our cue, son," Erland said softly and ushered Ry through the heavy doors when Wylend's power opened them.

Greta and Alphine sat close by, recording the meeting that Teeg San Gerxon and Dee were holding with six leaders from the Campiaan Alliance. "The plans are working," President Drix from Avendor smiled widely as Greta and Alphine stood, raised laser pistols and fired into the gathered dignitaries.

"Teeg lifted both their heads." Dee paced outside a hospital surgery ward, waiting to see if President Drix and two others survived the shootings. Teeg was even now attempting to explain to families of the wounded that his assistants had gone berserk and started shooting. Dee, speaking to Lissa and Tory in the hallway, had no explanation for the actions of Greta and Alphine. Both bodies were inside the morgue of Campiaa City's hospital.

"Strange things are happening, Dee." Lissa patted his arm.

"Like those murders on Surnath." Tory nodded his head.

"Tory, are you remembering something?"

"I think so, it's kind of cloudy, though. Something about someone in a legal firm shooting other employees?" Tory was searching for corroboration.

"I remember that. Happened a while back, didn't it?" Lissa said. "Nobody knew the reason. And then another killing at an electronics manufacturer, after that."

"Getting too close," Tory said.

"What? Honey, what did you just say?"

"Huh? Mom, did I say something?" Tory gave Lissa a blank stare.

"It's gone," Lissa tossed up a hand in frustration.

"They meant to kill Teeg first," Dee sighed. "But he went to mist before they could fire the weapons, so they went after the others. I wasn't important enough to be a target, and had no time to do anything except knock their hands away before Teeg killed them. Then I had to place compulsion on the others, who were uninjured."

"This is such a confusing mess," Lissa said.

"It is most certainly that."

I hid behind a plant. Darletta might not recognize me, but Faldin certainly would. Ry and I had questioned him before coming to Stellar Winds. I wondered what he'd do if he found me here. He and Darletta were arguing about something as I watched from behind the foliage.

"Missed him, I tell you," Darletta hissed. "I want you to go back to

Surnath now and figure out exactly what went wrong. We can't afford more fuck-ups like this."

"We have enough, Darletta. It won't matter in the least if a few go astray."

"I don't care, Fal. Do this or you'll regret it, I promise."

"Darletta, there's no need to get pissy."

"Just go. There's a ship leaving in half a click. Be on it. Get Daddy to help figure this out."

"All right. I wanted to be here for the full moon, though."

"Tough. Do your job, Faldin. If you expect to be at my side when it's all over, then do this. For me."

"I will, honey cakes."

I wanted to gag. Faldin was calling Daddy-fucking Darletta honey cakes? I watched him walk toward the shuttle stop on the west side. Darletta went in the opposite direction, likely heading toward her suite, which was located on Galedaro's top hotel floor. She had the entire floor to herself if my guess was correct. Sighing, I walked toward the bar.

"There you are. I've been searching for you." Zendeval Rjjn was beside me suddenly.

"Just out for a walk. It's my day off," I pointed out.

"Other duties as required," Zendeval said. "Come with me. I need your assistance with a delicate matter."

"It won't involve half-crazed men with knives?" I lifted an eyebrow at Zendeval Rjjn.

"No knives, I promise." He smiled. I didn't trust that smile. I followed him anyway, as he walked past the elevators toward another door labeled as a service entrance. "We have a problem; one of our maintenance workers dropped a tool in a very small space and his hands are too large to reach it. We need smaller hands and fingers to get it out," Zendeval said, once he'd gotten close enough for his employee chip to allow him entrance.

"I'm afraid it's quite a way through the tunnel to get to the spot, but I think we'll get what we need," he said. Yes, he was lying, and I was prepared to fight him if it became necessary. He didn't look to have any weapons on him, and I imagined that my smaller Thifilatha would be more than sufficient to subdue him should the need arise. At least he shut up after a while as we walked a very lengthy tunnel, coming to another door after a quarter click. His chip got him through that one as well, and another long corridor stretched beyond that.

"We'll get there," he murmured, walking beside me. I saw his hands clench when I glanced downward quickly, and then pretended I hadn't seen the gesture. Something was happening, I just hadn't figured out what it was. Not yet, anyway.

"This is the list of dissidents," Corolan handed the comp-vid to Ry. Cory had decided to stay; Garek went with Wylend. Erland was there with his son, of course. "Will Reah truly visit, when she is done with her assignment?" Ry glanced up at Corolan's question. He had such hope in his voice.

"She will. I think I can guarantee that," Ry nodded. "Reah will be Queen, just as soon as we can get everything settled down."

"You will be a great King, just as she predicted," Corolan sighed.

"We have to eliminate these problems before I can be great at anything," Ry pointed out, tapping the comp-vid.

"As you say, my King."

"You're our real dad." Dara glared at Tory from across the small visitor's room. Lissa and Garde had brought Tory to the small, private college to introduce him to his youngest daughters. Sara wasn't saying anything, she just stared at Tory, who sat between Garde and Lissa.

"Yes. I didn't know I had more than two daughters until recently."

"Mom told you."

"She did, but I missed the communications, somehow."

"All we had was old vid-images to look at. Gram showed us," Sara finally spoke, jerking her head toward Lissa.

"I know. I'm not asking for anything right now. Except a little time. Get to know me first, before deciding how you feel about me. That's only fair."

"Where were you all this time? Mom said Surnath, but I don't know whether to believe that or not." Dara, again.

"I was on Surnath, but I don't remember much about it."

"Dara, I explained this to you," Lissa said.

"Gram, how do we know what to believe? I didn't think he'd ever show up. And then suddenly he's here, announcing that he's our dad. What are we supposed to do about that? And where's Mom? Lara says she hasn't seen her since the claiming night."

"Your mother went on a special assignment for Uncle Lendill, honey."

"So, Mom disappears and Dad appears? Doesn't that sound funny to you?"

"I saw her before she left," Tory offered. "She wasn't very nice, but then she had a right to be."

"Sounds like Mom, all right." Sara snorted softly.

"We just wanted you to meet your father," Lissa said. "We need to get back, and you need to go back to class. If you want to talk, send a message." Lissa rose and hugged both girls. Garde hugged them after Lissa let them go. Both of them eyed Tory before moving toward the door.

"They don't know what to do, Mom." Tory sounded lost.

"I know, honey. They'll get used to the idea, and winter break is coming. Maybe you can take them somewhere, or spend time with them."

"Yeah." Tory raked fingers through his hair.

Zendeval pulled a comp-vid from his pocket and punched the screen a time or two just before we went through the third door. I heard noise beyond the door, as if there were a work crew there. I followed Zendeval through. Someone grabbed my arm and shot something into the back of my neck. It hurt and I whirled to see Perdil standing there, a needle gun in his hand.

"We can control her after this," two large guards had walked over to stand next to Zendeval, but his words made them back away. "Reah, we've placed a controller in the back of your neck. I won't activate it fully unless you struggle against us, do you understand?" Shocked, I gazed into Zendeval's black eyes. I'd been shot like this once before, in my memory. Only Teeg had placed whatever it was in my collarbone to keep me from using mindspeech or skipping away.

This was how they were controlling the girls they abducted. If I wanted to get to the root of all of it and find out where the victims were being taken, I'd have to play along. I now knew why Nefrigar had placed what he had in my collarbone. Zendeval's controller had absolutely no effect on me. Nefrigar's future technology was disrupting it, somehow. My choice was made, however, when I slowly nodded at Zendeval Rjjn. I made a promise to him, though. Silently, of course. I would kill him if he harmed me in any way.

"See, she is docile," Zendeval gripped my arm and pulled me along, Perdil walking behind. Perdil wasn't just a cook. He was Liffelithi, through and through. If he wasn't a partner in the exclusive slave trade, then he was in the higher echelon.

"Reah, I promise you'll cook again; I'll see to it," Perdil said as I was led through what looked to be the largest underground warehouse I'd ever seen. I blinked as I was eventually led past cage after cage, each holding a young woman. The cages looked as if they might be transported in some way. I was placed in a cage just like theirs; it was the first empty one Perdil and Zendeval found.

"Bring water," Zendeval snapped to a waiting guard. "No one touches this one without my consent."

"Yes, Master Rjjn," the guard agreed, walking to a spigot and filling a pitcher with water.

"Food will be brought, Reah. Sit down and make yourself comfortable. You won't be moved to the loading dock for a little while." I blinked at Zendeval and sat down as ordered. The pitcher of water was slipped through the bars and set down beside me.

"A portipp will be brought if you need it," Perdil said. I wouldn't need it; I was immortal and didn't need a portable commode. I wasn't going to tell them that. I nodded slightly instead.

"I don't like this," Zendeval sighed.

"You can order her to speak," Perdil suggested.

"No. Do you think I'm that foolish?"

"You've never brought one. This is your first time. Come, we have arrangements to make." I watched both of them walk away before sending mindspeech to Lendill.

"You're joking? They zapped her with something they called a controller? I've never heard of that," Norian said.

"Think about it, Nori. She said they planted the thing in the back of her neck and Rjjn fiddled with his comp-vid. Somehow, the two are connected. We need to talk to Ry and see if he can shed any light on this."

"That might be difficult at the moment; he's got his hands full of dissidents who think he's an unnatural aberration and can't serve as King of Karathia. He and Erland are doing their best to quell an uprising."

"I want to throw Wylend Arden through a wall. Once again, his timing sucks." Lendill fumed over what seemed to be a conspiracy of some sort.

"Do we know where Reah is?"

"Yes. She says an underground warehouse on Stellar Winds. She told me that they plan to move the cages to a loading dock somewhere, so they're shipping them away from there to be sold, most likely. She and I agree that we need to have a location before we move on this. I've already got a dozen ships in that sector, ready to go on our command."

"Why didn't we give her the microcameras?" Norian whined.

"I can send some," Lendill stood as the idea hit him. "I can," he insisted at Norian's blank look. "I have enough power to get them to Reah; I can do it by focusing on the credit chip implant she has."

"Then do it. Tell her they're coming and get them in there." Norian was all business, now.

~

*Reah, I'm sending microcameras,* Lendill sent. *They'll settle on your skin, cheah-mul. Whatever you do, don't scratch while they're attaching themselves to you.*

*Fine,* I sent. I was beginning to feel grumpy; two clicks had passed and nobody had come to move the cages. My skin felt irritated as four microcameras burrowed into the skin of my neck, just below my ears. They were invisible, and how Lendill managed to send them, I had no idea. I resisted the urge to scratch.

*Someone's coming,* I sent to Lendill. I heard the noise of the vehicles needed to move cages.

*I can see where you are, breah-mul,* Lendill sent. *Just stay calm. We'll see what they're doing.*

*All right.* Lendill would have someone monitoring the cameras at all times. I could sleep if I wanted. I think I was too frightened to consider sleeping.

Six loaders came and lifted cages to haul them away. They were taking the ones behind me first. I watched while girls placidly observed as their cages were lifted into the air and transported. Some were tilted precariously, knocking the inhabitants against the bars. That caused a bit of shrieking and brought shouting from someone supervising the removal.

They couldn't control everything, it seemed. The fear reflex must have been stronger than the controller was. I tucked that knowledge away and concentrated on counting captives. I counted sixty-seven cages, mine being the last. They'd waited to lure me in, I noticed. I think some of the others had been there for several days at the least. My cage was jerked up by the lifting mechanism on the vehicle and swung slightly as it was driven away. The other cages had been hauled around a corner and out of my sight, so I had no idea where I was going. I learned quickly, once we rounded the corner.

A long, wide hall had been hollowed out, and it led toward a huge dock roughly a quarter click away. I could see a bit of daylight at the end of the hall, and what looked to be the side dock of a freighter ship beyond that. *Are you getting this?* I sent to Lendill.

*We see it,* Lendill replied. *Just stay calm, we've got ships in the area, ready to go. We'll be following discreetly, so hang on, all right?*

*Remind me to say the same thing to you if you're ever swinging inside a cage,* I returned. *Don't worry, I don't want any more women kidnapped and sold into who knows what,* I added. *I'll do my duty. Just remember you owe me.*

*I'll remember.* Lendill cut off communication.

I was transported to the edge of the loading dock and dropped off there, waiting for another vehicle to load my cage onto the waiting ship. Men were everywhere, checking the cages and the women inside them, lifting comp-vids and checking numbers by pointing the device at the backs of captives' necks. Some of the women were fondled, too. One was kissed through the bars of her cage. That one shrank back afterward, whimpering. Once again, fear was playing a part. Fear was a strong emotion and one of the most basic. Fear kept people alive. I was beginning to think that the controllers couldn't fully prevent any strong emotion.

"No touching this one." A man came up beside my cage and watched while my controller device was scanned by comp-vid.

"Information says so in the comp-vid," the scanner replied. "Not that I don't want to," he leaned down and leered at me. Stopping myself from reaching through the bars and grabbing his neck to squeeze it, I settled for blinking at him, instead. I'd remained in my sitting position, so I hadn't gotten knocked around like some of the others during the move. "Must be something special, mustn't we?" He was still leering when Perdil walked up.

"If you had half the intelligence this one has, I might think you were a genius," Perdil snapped. "Get away." I turned my head to blink at Perdil. He knelt down to my level. "We're moving you to the small moon nearby," he said conversationally, as if I weren't locked inside a cage and presumably controlled by a device in my neck. "The full moon is tonight, and Zen and the rest of his kind will go crazy if they don't have women available. It's either sex or destruction with them on a full moon, Reah. I promise it will be over in a few ticks. We have physicians standing by, can't have any of the merchandise damaged permanently before the sale, can we?" I drew in a breath. Perdil stood and walked away.

∽

Lendill cursed, long and hard. His father, a master at the art of cursing, might have been proud of his son at that moment. *Reah, Reah, baby, we have to get them. We have to get all of them. Fuck, I'm sorry, Reah. We have to get them.*

∽

I was cold. Very, very cold. It was a scheduled rape. Whatever Zendeval Rjjn was, he was something affected by the full moon. Werewolves, shapeshifters of many kinds and High Demons were all affected by the full moon. What was Zendeval Rjjn? And Perdil had said the rest of his kind. How many were there? My cage was lifted and hauled aboard the ship.

The tiny moon had no atmosphere, so we were unloaded inside an airlock later, and hauled belowground to a sealed warehouse. I saw crates and boxes stacked against one wall, much like the ones I'd seen inside the warehouse on Stellar Winds as my cage had been moved. Once all the cages were lined up inside the warehouse, several workers came through, offering small plates of food. I didn't feel like eating, but it had been a long time since I'd had food. I ate a bit of the sandwich, although it was dry and had likely been transported from Stellar Winds, just as I and my fellow prisoners had.

"Moon's rising, get ready!" Someone shouted. Another ship landed above us; I felt the thump of it through the bars of my cage. Plates and water pitchers were hastily collected from cages and piled off to the side.

I was frightened out of my wits, now. I have no idea how many men walked in, but I watched in horror as the first cages were reached, doors were flung open and seemingly humanoid men turned into the blackest of creatures. Short tusks and small, spiked horns appeared on jaws and foreheads as women were jerked from their confining cages. I heard screams as they were taken, right on the cold floor of the warehouse.

Lendill was shouting mindspeech, telling me to ignore what was happening around me. I whimpered—women were being brutalized all about me, but this wasn't the end of it. They'd be sold afterward, elsewhere. Lendill, Norian and the ASD needed to know where that was, in case Stellar Winds wasn't the only source of slaves for their market. I wanted to weep anyway, and to shut my eyes and cover my ears at the sight and sound of such a brutal attack.

"Back! Get back!" Perdil suddenly appeared beside my cage, a shock baton in his hand. He'd hit two of the black-scaled creatures and they'd turned away, howling, before finding another cage and jerking the imprisoned woman out of it. Zendeval arrived, then. He hadn't turned yet, but was about to—his eyes had gone feral and he stared longingly in my direction.

"If you want a bed instead of the cold floor, then come." Perdil jerked my cage door open, gesturing for me to step outside.

Shuddering at what was happening around us and terrified of what Perdil and Zendeval had planned for me, I briefly considered turning Thifilatha. I didn't think anyone there could stand against me in my largest form. That would only ruin any hopes we had of finding where the slaves were taken and sold, and it would all be for nothing. At least I kept telling myself that as waves of horror and revulsion tore through me while women screamed in pain and fear all around. Swallowing my fright, I followed Perdil while Zendeval Rjjn came out of his clothing beside me and became what his fellows were.

The room we entered was small, held only a bed and small table and had handcuffs bolted to the wall on either side of the headboard.

"It will go easier if you don't struggle," Perdil said, grasping one of the handcuffs. I didn't want that at all. I'd never done anything of that sort, even playing around with my mates. Zendeval stood by, barely holding on, I figured, his body already excited. He came forward and sniffed my hair and shoulder. I flinched away from him.

"Reah, do not fight. It will go faster and easier," Perdil warned. "Undress. Quickly."

Shaking, I disrobed as commanded. Perdil snapped a cuff around my right wrist. "Now, the other one," he pulled the other cuff over and snapped it shut. I made a promise to myself then, silently, of course, that Perdil might be the second one I killed. He grunted his satisfaction before shoving me onto the bed. "Now, you can use this or not," he drew a bottle of lubricant from the bedside table and tossed it to me. My chains rattled as I caught it. Zendeval growled.

"Hurry, he only has so much control," Perdil warned. "It'll be over quickly," he added. Zendeval was inching toward me, even as Perdil pointed the shock baton at him. Zendeval snarled at the dwarf but stayed away. I whimpered—Perdil made no move to leave the room. Was he planning to watch my rape? That was horror upon horror.

With trembling hands, I applied lubricant. Perdil lowered the baton and stepped back. I screamed as Zendeval lunged at me. I expected rape immediately, but his teeth sank into my shoulder, his enlarged canines capturing my collarbone and biting deep. The saliva felt like acid as it entered my body and I shrieked in agony. I might have fainted from the pain and impending rape, except *she* came.

Shining too brightly to look upon, she growled and batted Zendeval away from me as easily as a ball of fluff. He cowered and whined in her presence before leaping up and running out the door. Perdil huddled in a corner of the room, his hands covering his eyes. "There will be no rape of this one," the woman's voice was low and angry. She disappeared as quickly as she'd appeared, leaving me stunned and in terrible pain.

What do you think of, while you are subjected to this? It had happened once before, when Tory claimed me. Zendeval Rjjn had bitten me, and it felt exactly as it had when Tory placed his claiming marks. The other girls hadn't had a guardian who'd stopped their attacks. I wept—for them and for myself, knowing all of us were suffering. I hadn't been raped, but I was the only one. Was I grateful? No. I was angry, and at the moment, felt powerless, violated and humiliated.

Briefly, I thought of Lendill, who'd gotten full view of everything. I'm sure Perdil was correct and it only lasted a short time. To me, the bite lasted an eternity before my salvation appeared in the form of a shining woman. I had no idea where Zendeval's monster had fled, and at the moment, I didn't care. More than likely, I should have held my tongue. I didn't.

"One day, Zendeval Rjjn," I spat, "you will know how lucky you were at this moment." Perdil, who'd recovered from his fear and stupor, now stood beside the bed and blinked at me in shock.

# CHAPTER 11

"You are lucky to get this." Perdil was angry, I could tell, as he handed me a bucket of warm water, soap and a towel. I was quivering all over after my ordeal while Lendill sent mindspeech repeatedly, attempting to calm me. I finally told him to shut the hell up and leave me alone.

I had the privacy of the room in which to clean my wound, if you didn't count Perdil's watchful gaze, that is. I had no idea what the others were getting. As soon as I was finished wiping blood away from my shoulder I dressed, my hands shaking the whole time. I was ordered out of the room and down another hall. I ached all over from Zendeval's bite. The area around the bite was beginning to bruise, too —he hadn't been gentle.

"Sit. A physician will tend to you soon," Perdil pointed to an empty spot at the end of a long bench against a wall. Some of the other women were there as well, many of them weeping and still naked, all showing evidence of a brutal rape. None had been bitten as deeply as I'd been, however. I was quite shocked when Neeki and Teeki came to sit on either side of me.

"No, they cannot see us," Neeki said as I stared at him in surprise.

"And we would attempt to heal you, but that would be obvious. We shielded the baby, however. He still lives inside your womb. We are grateful the Mighty One arrived to stop the rape."

"Baby?" I whispered. The shaking became worse.

"Yes. Pregnant, by the one you call, oh, Teeg. Yes. His son," Neeki declared.

"No. Please, no," I buried my head in my hands. It must have happened the night Teeg came to my tiny house on Kifirin. "Please, don't make the night any more traumatic than it already is," I moaned.

"We were sent to help. We cannot interfere," Teeki spoke for the first time.

I blinked at him in shock. He couldn't interfere, but someone else had. He'd called her the Mighty One. I had no idea what that meant, and I wasn't sure how grateful I was to her—she hadn't prevented the bite. I turned to Teeki while smoke curled from my nostrils. "Then get out. You're not helping now."

"We're keeping you from screaming," Neeki stated. "The pain below would be quite bad, otherwise. A bite from one of these affects both areas."

"What?"

"We're removing most of pain below. You would be screaming if we did not."

"Is it going to come back?"

"Some. When you can bear it. A fever will come, too. It happens sometimes."

"How good are these physicians?" Now I was terrified, in pain, shivering and worried for a baby I hadn't known existed.

"They are good enough."

"I can't believe they're working here."

"Some will do almost anything."

I knew that. Jes had done it. He'd been dropped off on Evensun for his crimes. I had no idea whether he was still alive or not. "We're keeping the baby shielded. He must not be harmed."

"Sure. Take care of Teeg's baby, why don't you," I muttered sarcastically.

"We will. If you do not suffer some, the others will get suspicious."

"Great. Why don't you go help some of those other poor girls?"

"They are luckier than most who go through this. You are here with them."

"Like that's such a wonderful thing and all." I couldn't help it, tears were falling, now. Reaction was setting in. If I lived long enough, Zendeval Rjjn might get the worst of all possible deaths at my hands.

"What do we have here?" A physician knelt before me and unbuttoned my top, revealing the bite and bruises. "I'll have to do a pelvic, too, so why don't you lean on me on the way to the exam room?"

Jerking my elbow out of his hands, I stumbled along beside him as he pointed out a tiny cubicle down a dimly lit hall. My clothing was removed and the physician cursed in a language I didn't understand when he did the pelvic exam. He then administered a mistjection against my inner thigh and set about cleaning the bite.

"You may run a fever over the next few days," the physician said as I gathered my clothing in shaking fingers and dressed myself. "If they allow you to speak, tell them to ask for Geldis," he said and sent me out the door. Perdil was waiting. I shouldn't have been surprised.

"This way," he said. I followed Perdil, thinking that my Thifilatha could burn him to cinders in two blinks. "What did the physician say?" Perdil asked as he closed the cage door behind me. "You have permission to speak this time only."

"He said I was likely to run a fever, and to ask for him if there was any trouble. His name is Geldis."

Perdil cursed. "A fever is uncommon, but it happens at times. Lie down, I'll see about getting a mat for your cage floor."

Zendeval Rjjn stalked through the tunnels beneath the surface of Stellar Winds' moon, growling and snapping at any others he encountered. Inside him, somewhere, a small voice kept repeating *protect, protect, protect,* but he ignored it. On a full moon, he usually selected one of the paid prostitutes on Stellar Winds; one of those who preferred extremely rough sex.

His father always said that Zen's mother died in a Reaving. He'd never talked about her much; it upset him, somehow. Zen's father always said that females of their kind were to be protected above all costs, but Zen's mother had died anyway, and only the males had survived. Now, less than a hundred males lived, and they'd come to this. Zendeval kicked at the wall, sending brick flying.

"She's feverish," Geldis the physician glanced up at Zendeval Rjjn as he examined Reah inside her cage the following afternoon. She was shivering on the small mat, her body in a fetal position. Zendeval was back to himself and dressed impeccably in a dark suit. Perdil stood nearby, watching Zen and the physician.

"How feverish?" Zen crossed arms over his chest.

"Very. We shouldn't let her temperature climb any higher."

"Then what do you suggest?"

"Medication, sedation and cool baths to bring the fever down," Geldis said. "And keep her warm in between. We have one other suffering just the same. We've already treated her, at Nedrizif's request."

"Then do everything you can for this one," Zen sighed. "And keep me advised."

"They don't get ill often," Perdil pointed out as he and Zen walked away.

"I don't know what to do. How much ice cream do we have in the freezer?"

"Only enough for two more days. I was hoping to have her back in the kitchen between now and the sale in two weeks."

"How long does it usually take to get them back on their feet if they become ill?" Zen wanted to kick something.

"At times, they are still weak and sick when we put them up for bid." The sales were always held two weeks after moonrush. Girls were picked up sometimes months after potential bidders expressed interest, and the bidders were notified when the cargo was safely on Stellar Winds.

"Then I suggest you figure out how to make those desserts or take it off the menu," Zen growled. "And Nedrizif will not be pleased."

"Then we'll take the desserts off the menu now and hold all the ice cream back for him," Perdil suggested.

"Do it. And make sure Reah is cared for. Once she belongs to us, then she'll be back in the kitchen and spending her nights with me."

"It's a fair bargain. I get days, you get the nights," Perdil snickered.

"One of our better investments," Zen agreed.

"Absolutely."

Jerves knew. He knew everything. He picked at an eyebrow nervously as he spoke with a cook's assistant. Reah had been taken and subjected to who knew what. Jerves had a controller, too, only Zendeval allowed him free rein over most things. Completely controlled meant you couldn't think or make any reasonable decisions. The one controlling you made those. Jerves had to have some measure of autonomy. That meant he could feel anger. He felt it now. White-hot anger.

Reah had been nothing but kind to him, and he should have warned her. Now, she was likely suffering after moonrush. Jerves laughed hysterically for a moment. Moonrush. It sounded so benign. Except that it wasn't. He'd only seen it once, when Perdil forced him to help with some of the girls. Reah would be sold in two weeks, only Jerves suspected that Zen and Perdil were planning to bid on the pretty cook in order to keep her in Galedaro's kitchens.

"What is it, Master Jerves?" the assistant asked.

"Nothing. Keep working. Just get those orders sent to Ms. Schuul's suite as requested."

"We will." The assistant turned away.

~

"There are no messages from her husband." Perdil tossed Reah's comp-vid onto Zendeval's desk.

"Good. We don't have to answer if there aren't any." Zendeval ignored the comp-vid.

"But that concerns me. There should be something, don't you think?"

"He left because of family matters; perhaps she doesn't want to bother him."

"Perhaps. But let me know if you get any communication from him. We'll have to answer until we get her away from here."

"True. We don't need the ASD or some such sniffing around Stellar Winds."

"Have you gone back to check on her?" Perdil had been quite busy in the kitchens after his return.

"No. I have communication from the physician, however. If you'd like to read it," Zen pushed his comp-vid toward Perdil. Perdil lifted the handheld and scanned the message.

"You're not concerned that her fever's still high?" Perdil handed the comp-vid back.

"I called—he says it happens at times. Some of the women become ill for inexplicable reasons. They are feverish for days and in pain, but eventually they recover fully."

"Does it worry you that you caused this?"

"Yes. I've never made a female ill before."

"Perhaps we should take her out of the cage and put her somewhere more comfortable."

"Do you think so?" Zen gave Perdil a quizzical look.

"The lack of females among your kind has not improved your intelligence," Perdil muttered. "Did you notice that this wasn't one of Schuul's comp-vids?" Perdil tapped Reah's portable device.

"It matters not—we have her and we've confiscated this one. The others like it will be useless soon enough."

"It doesn't worry you that there are some not controlled now?"

"Why should it worry me?" Zen blinked in confusion at Perdil.

"It's dark inside your ass, isn't it?" Perdil grumbled and stalked away.

"What did he mean by that?" Zen did a little grumbling of his own.

I was ill. I knew it. Likely Lendill knew it too, since he was seeing the doctor's worried face quite often. He sent mindspeech occasionally, but the words were garbled if I were conscious enough to hear them. I wanted to heave whenever food was offered. Baths were given in cold water several times throughout the day. Geldis, the physician, complained that the normal doses of painkill didn't alleviate the pain.

I might have laughed if I could have. Normal doses of most anything had no effect on me. He upped the dosage several times, finally concluding that three times what was normal helped a little. I needed Karzac or my Larentii. Both were far away. Nobody was here to care for me except a physician I didn't know.

I was still inside my cage, I knew that much, and every part of my body ached, lying on a thin mattress spread across the metal floor. I wondered, too, why the physician failed to report to Perdil or Zendeval that I was pregnant. Something prevented it, and I was too feverish and in pain to worry about it for long.

"Reah?" The voice came. I knew it from somewhere. I struggled toward consciousness. "Reah?" A hand touched my forehead. "Burning up. Get over here!" The voice shouted. "Get her into one of the private rooms. We need to clean her up and get this fever down. Where is that fucking physician?"

I hadn't heard Perdil use that word before. He was with me now; I saw him through a fevered haze. "I didn't move her; I wasn't informed that I could." Geldis arrived quickly. Perdil was cursing again, raving about everybody needing permission to fart. I didn't care, I wanted to be unconscious again and away from the pain.

"What part of take care of her needs did you not understand?" Perdil shouted. Likely, Geldis was cringing before the dwarf. I would be, too, if I were human. I wanted to laugh, I think, at my thoughts. The cage door was opened and I was lifted out of it. Usually a guard did that; Geldis didn't fetch and carry. Another cool tub of water followed, more drugs were administered by mistjection and then someone carried me into a shower and bathed me. I didn't realize it was Perdil until it was nearly over. The drugs were beginning to take effect.

"Three days and still no better off," he muttered as I was toweled off and carried to bed. It was a much better bed than the thin mat had been. Perdil was combing out my freshly washed hair when I slipped back into unconsciousness.

"Any better?" Zen slipped inside the private room. Perdil hadn't told him that Reah had been moved, and at first he was angry to find the cage empty. The guards directed him to Reah's new room. Perdil had sat next to the bed for several clicks, watching Reah sleep.

"The fever's down for the moment, but I have to keep after that fool of a physician or he just wanders away. I asked him if we needed an IV; he said probably and walked out."

"Why does she need an IV?" Zen gave Perdil a worried glance.

"Because she isn't getting better. She hasn't kept anything down, including water. She needs fluids—even I know that and I have no medical training at all." Perdil snorted at his own statement.

"Do we have the necessary supplies? We can go to the hospital on Stellar Winds and get them."

"I sent one of the other physicians already," Perdil sighed. "About a click ago. They should be here anytime." That was how Zendeval Rjjn, who'd never needed a physician for any trouble of his own, watched in fascination as an IV was inserted into Reah's hand and taped there, while a bag of fluid was attached and began to drip. Geldis attached another bag as well, which administered a steady flow of medication.

"Some develop infection of some kind," he said when Perdil asked about the treatment. "This drug treats a broad spectrum of infections, so I hope it has some effect. We'll know by tomorrow if it helps."

"And if she has a reaction?"

"We'll remove it right away. I'll have someone watching if I can't be here myself."

"See that you do." Perdil rose stiffly and walked out of Reah's room. Zen, unsure what to do, rose and followed Perdil, leaving the physician with Reah.

"You will not recall my presence," a tall, blue-skinned man appeared and lifted Reah up, holding her against him. Geldis nodded briefly before the gentle trilling noise the blue creature made had him falling asleep in his chair.

"If we tell Teeg about the baby, he'll show up and blast the place," Norian growled at Lendill. Lendill and Norian had seen Neeki and Teeki just as well as Reah had the night of the attack. They'd also seen a flash of bright light, and still couldn't explain the events surrounding that anomaly. They'd set that aside; Reah was pregnant with Teeg's child, and according to one of Kifirin's assistants, it was his son. Both knew Reah was very ill, too. Lendill had tried to contact Reah through mindspeech, but she hadn't been able to send a coherent reply.

They'd also seen the physician several times as he'd treated Reah. Then, Lendill had seen Nefrigar appear, telling the physician that he wouldn't remember the visit. Lendill had only seen a wide blue chest and listened to some very restful trilling for two clicks after that.

Ry, too, hadn't been told, and neither Lendill nor Norian wanted to tell Garde, Lissa or any of the others. "Norian, what if that were your child she was carrying?"

"Lendill, don't throw that in my face," Norian muttered angrily.

"What if she doesn't recover? What then? Teeg may come after us."

"I don't think that Larentii will allow his mate to die, do you?"

"But he was there last night and she's still sick," Lendill pointed out. If he were honest, he was scared witless that Reah couldn't even send mindspeech. And that thug who'd bitten her? Lendill had plans for that one. He still didn't know what Zendeval Rjjn was, but he wasn't really interested in anything other than Rjjn's death.

"Look, those two said they were shielding the baby, so he's not suffering, I think."

"No, Reah's the one suffering. We don't know what kind of pain she's in, she can't tell us." Lendill paced inside Norian's office. It wasn't Norian's mate caught up in the middle of this, it was Lendill's, and he was frightened. Reah was ill, pregnant and in the hands and care of the enemy. "Someday, Norian, come and talk to me if you find Lissa in this situation." Lendill folded out of Norian's office.

"Fuck," Norian cursed. "Fuck!"

~

"The girl is in here, Master Nedrizif," Geldis opened the door for Ned. "She has been very ill. We are making some progress, though. The fever is down somewhat."

Nedrizif walked to the bed and stared down at the little white-haired beauty. The color had drained from her cheeks as was usual if a girl became ill. "I want her treated as well as can be. I want her healthy for the sale, do you hear me?" Nedrizif snarled. "And why was I not informed that this one was as ill as she was?"

"I do not know, Master. I was only told to care for her."

"Then continue to do so. Spare no expense, and if it is needed, bring someone else in to help."

"Of course, Master. It will be as you say." Geldis bowed to Nedrizif.

"And do not speak of my visit to anyone," Nedrizif demanded before leaving the room.

"Of course, Master," Geldis muttered at Nedrizif's retreating back.

"Here's our pretty High Demon, back among the lucid," Teeki grinned as I opened my eyes.

"Why are you here?" I could barely get the words out, my mouth was so dry.

"We've been checking on you regularly, you just didn't know," Neeki's head popped up over his twin's shoulder. "And the baby is quite fine, we are proud of the job we have done," he grinned.

"Sure. Pat yourself on the back," I muttered.

"You are not happy with our work?" Teeki sounded hurt.

"With one of your patients, yes. The other, no."

"She is talking about herself," Neeki looked at his twin.

"I know. But we must do as Kifirin says. He says that we must hold back from helping you too much. He has some reason," Teeki informed me.

"You haven't helped me much at all," I grumped. "Go away."

"She keeps saying that to us. I do not think she likes us."

"You work with Kifirin. That's enough to ensure you're not welcome," I said wearily. The conversation was wearing me out.

"We will make sure food is brought," Neeki said. "Come, brother. We will do what we can." He and Teeki disappeared.

"Awake now and much better," Geldis said as he entered the room with a tray of food later. I noticed that I'd been handcuffed to the wall after Neeki and Teeki fled. I wasn't supposed to get away. Right then, I was too weak to get away. The food Geldis brought consisted of bland and tasteless, with bland winning.

"How much have we eaten?" Perdil walked in. I blinked at him.

"You have permission to speak," he added.

"This stuff is awful," I said, making a face and pushing weakly against the tray.

"Spoken like a true cook," Perdil chortled. "How weak is she?" He turned to Geldis.

"Weak. I don't think she can stand for longer than two ticks."

"How about sitting?"

"Not long."

"Long enough to put ice-cream ingredients together?" Perdil looked from Geldis to me. I grimaced and closed my eyes. I didn't know how long I'd been down, but likely they were out of gishi fruit ice cream.

"She could faint," Geldis warned. "Or be sick, since she just ate."

"We'll watch for that. You will come and keep her awake," Perdil jerked his head at Geldis. "I have a hoverchair coming. We'll float her to the dock and transport her to Stellar Winds."

"Reah, we're here." Perdil's voice woke me with a start. I was inside Galedaro's pastry kitchen, and ingredients were already laid out on the prep table. Three assistants were looking at me, all with pity in their eyes. I knew then that they all bore controllers.

The hoverchair was no help at all and it took every bit of strength I had to pull ingredients to me and dump them into the ice-cream maker. I never measured anything, basing amounts on the number and size of gishi fruits I had. Assistants peeled and chopped those for me while I watched. The rest I did, feeling dizzy while I did it. Perdil watched me closely the entire time, and I didn't lose what I'd eaten until I stumbled away from the prep table and ice-cream maker.

"I told you this might happen," Geldis said over my head as I huddled on my knees upon the floor, vomit splattered on my clothing, my hands and on the floor itself.

"Clean it up," Perdil snapped at the assistants. "We'll take her upstairs." I fainted twice on the way, after I'd been shoved into the hoverchair by someone. I thought they might be taking me to the apartment I'd shared with Ry. We didn't stop there. The top floor was our destination. The hoverchair moved past Zendeval Rjjn while he stared at my attendants as we came inside his apartment.

"You couldn't clean her up first?" Zendeval demanded.

"This happened in the kitchens. Do you suggest we do it there?" Perdil was angry with Zendeval for some reason. "Get her into the bathroom," Perdil ordered Geldis. Geldis was confused until Zendeval showed him where the bathroom was inside his master suite. I didn't want to be anywhere near Zendeval Rjjn. And the tear that dropped? I wanted to hide that, if I could.

Zendeval and Perdil both watched as Geldis lowered me into a tub of water. I sobbed, thinking about how Ry had kept the water warm for me when I'd bathed under his watchful eye. There wasn't a soul here who cared for me now; I was a job to do and money to be made. Otherwise, I likely wouldn't have gotten a bath.

Zen watched impassively as Reah was bathed, even as a voice in his mind screamed *protect, protect, protect*. He ignored it and stood his ground. The evidence of his bite was still upon her shoulder. She bore his marks. That should please him. His black eyes betrayed nothing. Perdil glanced at Zen a time or two, but turned back to Reah's bathing both times. Did Perdil want her as well? Perdil hadn't expressed interest in any female. Zen wondered briefly why that was.

"Pick her up," Perdil hissed after Geldis dried Reah's skin and hair. "Are you completely devoid of feeling?" Zen wondered where he'd been, mesmerized as he was by Geldis caring for Reah. "One arm around her torso, beneath her arms, the other under her little butt, do I have to show you everything?" Perdil grunted as he helped get Reah's limbs sorted out. Geldis stepped back and watched as Zen lifted Reah.

A warm mouth on mine. That's what woke me. "Ry?" I mumbled.

"No. Never again," a voice replied when the mouth was taken away.

I struggled. I knew that voice. It wasn't a voice I wanted anywhere near me.

"Reah, do not force me to activate the controller further," Perdil's voice was harsh. My body stilled in Zendeval's arms. That's where I was; Zendeval was holding me. Carrying me somewhere. I watched his chin as he carried me along, that's how close I was to him.

"Do not have sex with her for another eight-day at least; you will make her ill again," Geldis warned as Zendeval laid me on a bed. Standing back, he blinked down at me. I knew, then, whether he did or not, that he was being controlled just as I was supposed to be. I wanted to ask Perdil about that. The dwarf knew many things and he wasn't saying anything. Geldis' warning meant nothing to me—I was prepared to fight with Zendeval Rjjn if he even attempted sex. I still felt achy and out of sorts, my stomach wanted to heave again and I had a headache.

"Do not harm her," Perdil ordered. "You," he pointed to Geldis, "stay in the other room unless you are needed." He led Geldis away. I heard Zendeval's door closing shortly afterward. Perdil had left me alone with Zendeval Rjjn.

"Yes, I know there are still problems to be worked out," Faldin snapped. "I can't seem to separate what constitutes affection, and we're still experiencing difficulty with implanting instructions on how to escape or hide if they are implicated in a crime."

"It's only a matter of time before someone discovers the controllers," Dantel Schuul remarked, irritated that Faldin seemed to be wearing a hole in a very expensive Serendaan carpet. Dantel had asked Faldin to meet with him in Dantel's spacious, private study at the Schuul estate. Darletta was still amusing herself on Stellar Winds; Dantel had purchased the controlling interest in it for his only child once the opportunity to do so was presented to him.

"And you can't control fear," Dantel added to the list of the controller's shortcomings. "Although it was a stroke of genius to make them from this ancient technology. Who knew that these microscopic transmitters, combined with the tiniest of electronic chips, would prove to be practically invisible to medical technology? I commend you on your innovation, Faldin."

Faldin preened for Dantel Schuul, although the original idea hadn't been his. He wasn't about to tell Dantel that he'd borrowed anything to make the controllers possible. When he, Dantel, Darletta and the other six controlled both Alliances and what lay beyond them, Faldin expected to live beyond his wildest imaginings and have every sentient creature at his beck and call. All of it was within his grasp. Faldin flexed his hands and smiled at the thought. The last auction would be held, the last bit of their technology would be brought online and the universes would be theirs.

Faldin hadn't known when he was studying engineering that it would bring him to this. Who cared that his controllers couldn't command love? He and Darletta were made for one another. Neither cared that sex was obtained from others. It only titillated them. The controllers worked perfectly for commanding sex from any partner, including the unwilling ones.

I woke with warm arms around me. I still ached and moved slightly, trying to find a more comfortable position. "Don't move. I think better with you close like this." Zendeval's voice. I froze.

"There's no need to be frightened." A hand was placed between my bare breasts. He'd undressed me. I was naked against him. "Your heart needs to slow down." Lips caressed my ear and then my temple. I couldn't slow my heart any more than I could stop the planetoid from spinning; the organ was pounding in my chest. I whimpered without meaning to.

"Someday you will not be afraid of me." That wasn't going to happen. Someday, I intended to kill him. Then my heart might stop pounding like that. Zendeval's comp-vid beeped and he moved away to answer it. I huddled into a smaller ball on his bed.

"I must go." He stalked away. I blinked at his retreating back—he was just as naked as I. Sighing with relief that he was gone, I fell asleep again.

∼

"Wake, Reah." Perdil was back. Was it his personal mission to torture or aggravate as much as possible? I blinked at the dwarf. "We have food for you, and then you will be taken to the kitchens again. It is six days before the sale. You must get on your feet as quickly as possible. We cannot have a weak female stand for the bidding."

Geldis helped me off the bed; I almost fainted in the shower while I washed myself, almost lost what I ate for breakfast and then shivered when a strange guard carried me down the hall to the elevator.

"Tell us what to add," an assistant begged later as I attempted to put the cake batter together for the dessert. More gishi fruit ice cream had to be made as well; the dessert was more popular than anyone imagined, even with the exorbitant cost.

"No, more ground chocolate," I said, shivering slightly.

"She is still feverish," Geldis stepped forward to check my temperature.

"Reah, get the cake batter together and we'll put you back to bed," Perdil snapped. I told the assistant how much chocolate to add, then watched while he stirred everything together. "That looks good," I muttered weakly. The batter was poured into the pans and slipped into the oven. "Take her upstairs," Perdil jerked his head toward the kitchen door. "Carefully, that is an investment," he ordered.

That's what I was, now. An investment. Something to be sold for money, and then likely ordered to do Perdil's and Zendeval's bidding in the kitchens from then on. Except I didn't intend to let that happen. Lendill would be watching through the cameras embedded in my skin, and as soon as we arrived at the base of operations where the sales took place, all of them were going to get a surprise from me. Meanwhile, I had to rest as much as I could and build up my strength. I was going to need it, and I cursed Zendeval and his attack silently.

He'd inflicted this weakness upon me, with whatever it was he'd become at the full moon.

~

"There's some sort of microscopic device in the neck," Lendill indicated the spot on his own neck while Gavril watched.

"We looked," Gavril sighed. "But I beheaded both of them, and if there was anything there, it was destroyed." He spoke of his and Dee's assistants, Greta and Alphine. He and Lendill had gone through the records, and neither assistant had traveled to Stellar Winds, but that didn't mean that someone else who'd come in contact with them hadn't.

Lendill was beginning to have suspicions, and those suspicions were frightening. Ship's passengers and their baggage were checked at the point of origin, not the destination within the Alliance. Controlled guests could be sent away from Stellar Winds with anything in their possession and the controlled inspectors at the space station would allow it to pass right through.

"This is how they're getting weapons," Lendill muttered. "These two had unregistered weapons, those two killings on Surnath involved unregistered weapons and who knows how many others have them, too?"

"This is the worst possible scenario, isn't it?" Gavril sighed.

~

"If there was something there, it was removed," Karzac said after examining Tory's neck. "And it could have been small enough that a quick blast with a laser needle might have taken care of it, leaving no discernible wound. Easily disposed of, I think."

"But could that explain all this? The holes in his memory and everything? Norian says that people are being controlled." Lissa cast a worried glance at her healer mate.

"Yes. It could definitely explain it," Karzac agreed.

❧

"Reah, you will sit there quietly while the meeting takes place." Perdil was in Zendeval's suite again while he and Zendeval ordered waiters and kitchen employees to place this or that on Zendeval's kitchen island. It looked as if he were inviting at least seven or eight people.

"I do not want this," Zendeval muttered.

"I know that, but Nedrizif was quite adamant. And he knows about Reah. One of his spies, no doubt. He insisted that she be here so he can look, as will the others. When I told him her health was poor, he ignored me, saying he was bringing a physician with him to check her over." I watched as calmly as I could—they'd placed me in a hoverchair inside Zendeval's kitchen while people moved around me. All controlled, I think, except for Perdil. He still answered to the one he'd called Nedrizif; it looked as if they all did. Who else was coming? Would I see all the major players now? It worried me that Faldin might have returned. I truly hoped that wasn't the case, I didn't want to take all of them on as weak as I was.

Faldin wasn't with them, but Darletta was. Dantel was also missing. I suppose the little wrinkle hadn't been smoothed out yet. Two others I recognized—Matiss Meldrim and Gescht Prekisule. I was beginning to get the bigger picture now. Maris Krastel may have gone crazy because she was controlled. She'd been doing the basic legal work on the antitrust case for her firm. Perhaps she'd found out that there was something to all of it and Faldin had made sure it didn't go any farther. An elaborate scheme, but then there was collusion going on and billions of Alliance credits at stake if all of them were found out.

Dantel Schuul had likely set these two up as heads of Meldrim Enterprises and Prekisule and Co., when he actually owned all of it or at least controlling interests in all of it. And it helped with whatever the comp-vids had to do with the controllers, I'm sure. *Lendill, are you getting this?* I asked through mindspeech.

*I am. Breah-mul, this is getting more complicated by the moment. Do you know who that other one is? The one with the black hair that looks a little like a troll?*

*They call him Nedrizif, and they're all bowing and scraping to him,* I returned.

*He isn't in any of our databases, but then a lot of them aren't,* Lendill said. I had to cut off the mental conversation; Nedrizif was coming toward me.

"And here's the little cook," he announced. Another male followed him. He was older, with silver hair and gray eyes. Was still handsome and probably knew it. The silver-haired one put his hands on me, doing the examination. I suppose he was Nedrizif's physician.

"We're not doing her any good by having her out on display like this, she's frightened," the man leaned back after checking my pulse. "And likely weak as well; I spoke with Geldis."

"We need her to be stronger and better in five days," Nedrizif growled.

"Then put her to bed and make sure she eats," the physician said.

"Do it," Nedrizif growled at Zendeval, who lifted me from the chair, kissed me twice on the way to the bedroom, covered me up in his bed and walked out. The fact that he seemed more lucid whenever he held me made me wonder if some residual effect from the device Nefrigar planted in my collarbone was interfering with his controller from so close a distance. Worrying over it wearied me, so I closed my eyes and slept.

"This will help," the physician was back, slipping an IV needle into my hand and taping it down before hanging the bag of fluid on a pole beside the bed. "Now, be sure to eat the broth they're bringing for you. I told them under no circumstances are you to be forced to work before the sale."

Some physician he was. He didn't care that I was to be sold, he only cared about what I looked like during the sale.

"She won't be damaged permanently?" Nedrizif was right behind the physician, as was Zendeval and Perdil. "This one can make desserts that you only dreamt of before."

"If you let her rest. The infection that some of them get was quite virulent in this one. We will try to keep the damage to a minimum." I turned my head away, no longer willing to watch while the physician spoke as if I weren't in the room. I'm sure Lendill had already run his image through the available databases. If he held a license anywhere, Lendill would know it.

"Daddy may want to bid on her," Darletta walked in to see what was happening. Perdil's drawn breath was a hiss.

# CHAPTER 12

"It's bad enough that Nedrizif may bid," Perdil snapped when I woke the following morning. Food was waiting on a tray and Zendeval was glowering in a chair beside the bed. "But if Dantel Schuul starts bidding," Perdil didn't finish the thought.

I felt a little better physically; Geldis had come in twice during the night to check the IV and change bags, working around Zendeval's arms, which were wrapped tightly around me.

I wanted to tell Perdil that Dantel Schuul's head might be removed first thing if he attempted to place his hands on me, but I didn't. I wasn't supposed to speak unless I had permission. I'd read stories—old ones, of slavery before the Alliance was born. I hadn't gotten the full impact of their subjugation until now and I had to force myself not to snap at everyone present.

"First morning without fever," Geldis observed when he walked in with a fresh bag of fluid.

"You should have been doing this all along," Perdil grumbled. "But then Nedrizif holds your leash."

"I do as I am told," Geldis muttered, slipping the bag onto the hook.

"Reah, eat," Perdil sighed and walked out of the room. Zendeval sat on the chair, never moving, watching me place every shaking spoonful of bland, hot cereal in my mouth. I was wishing for a bit of fruit or brown sugar at first, but I couldn't eat much of the stuff anyway.

"A little more?" Zendeval urged with his hands.

"I can't," I said without thinking, my head falling back against the pillows on his bed.

"Reah, I can't think unless you are close," he was pulling me against him, making me whimper, he hugged so hard.

"Come now, the physician will bathe her. You must go to work," Perdil was back and herding Zendeval away. My hands shook but I bathed myself. I had four days to recover enough to deal with what was coming.

"I think father will make the announcement tonight, a little ahead of schedule," Lendill grumped. Norian, surprisingly, had been invited to dinner with Lendill in Gaelar N'Seith.

"Announcement?" Norian gave his oldest friend a puzzled frown.

"His heir. Who he'll name as Prince-Heir. Faldill and I figure it will be Naldill, and Reldill will be right there to kiss Naldill's ass. I think he asked you to come as support for me since Reah isn't available right now."

"You act as if naming his heir means he's handing everything over," Norian observed.

"The Prince-Heir is expected to rule with him, to prepare for the day when he takes Gaelar N'Seith. When that happens, and I hope it will be a long time from now, the King steps back and only offers advice, which the new King may or may not choose to heed." Lendill didn't like that fact at all, Norian noticed.

"You won't go back, will you, if your oldest brother is named Prince-Heir." Norian made it a statement. Lendill only nodded.

"We may be leaving early tonight. Naldill will be puffed up and insufferable when father names him Prince-Heir. There won't be any room in the Elven lands for a half-human younger brother."

"I see." Norian did understand. Lendill, the few times he'd spoken of his two older brothers, hinted that they'd tormented him during his childhood.

"I can always take you drinking afterward," Norian offered. "Or whatever you want to do. Get back to Reah's cameras, if you want." They'd left Drake and Drew behind to watch Reah's cameras—they weren't sure who else they might be able to trust.

"We'll do something," Lendill promised, folding both of them to Gaelar N'Seith, the Elven lands.

"Norian, good to see you again," Kaldill took Norian's offered hand. *Stay beside Lendill tonight, no matter what*, he sent in mindspeech. Norian, unruffled at the mindspeech, barely blinked at Kaldill Schaff's words. Was Kaldill expecting trouble? Norian nodded respectfully to Kaldill and stood beside Lendill at Kaldill's formal table.

Elves were all about the natural world. The table was piled with bowls filled with grapes, oranges, pears, nannas and even gishi fruit. Norian knew that this crop was likely from Avendor. Kifirin wouldn't have another crop ready for three months.

Kaldill's guests sat after Kaldill sat. He and Lendill's brothers were dressed richly in long, open robes over tight leggings, the brothers' robes embroidered in gold, silver and copper for first, second and third son. Kaldill's were embroidered in green and gold.

Lendill wore a suit and looked out of place against the finery of his father and brothers. If he'd dressed according to tradition, his robes would have resembled brass. Lendill had always felt out of place, though. Norian realized that Naldill and Reldill had seen to that, likely torturing Lendill when he was small because he didn't have power. Now he doubted any of them had noticed that this was no longer true.

"Try the rolls, I helped make them," Kaldill smiled at Norian and Lendill. Kaldill had become quite the cook as far as bread making was concerned.

"It's wonderful," Norian agreed after the first taste. Talk was sparse over the dinner table, with Kaldill making most of the conversation. He asked a few questions about the current problem with the pirates and such. Lendill, sending Norian mindspeech that it was all right to speak freely at Kaldill's table, offered the information.

"We're finding controllers in at least half the population, I think. We're not sure exactly what they're planning, but it doesn't look good."

"Fools," Kaldill muttered, lifting his wineglass.

～

"I've never seen this part of your father's home," Norian whispered as he followed Lendill, Lendill's brothers and Kaldill Schaff down a lengthy hall in Kaldill's palace after the meal was finished. Very little metal existed in his home, which was built mostly of wood, stone, marble and granite. Beautifully carved wood made up most of the furniture, with richly decorated and embroidered cushions. Norian wondered then that he'd never seen any of Lendill's brothers' mothers. He ventured to ask Kaldill about it.

"We mate for a thousand years, and may renew after that if we desire. Or, we go looking for another mate. It is the way it is, and presently I am unmated." Kaldill showed all of them into his private study where elves must have painted and decorated; the artwork and furniture was stunning.

"I wish I'd seen this before; it would take days just to examine everything in here," Norian sighed appreciatively.

"It has taken millennia to get it just the way I like it," Kaldill beamed at the compliment. "Please, sit down." Seats were set before the desk for all of them while Kaldill sat in the chair behind the wide desk.

"I know I said midwinter, but I am moving things up a little," Kaldill said, getting right to business. "My Prince-Heir will be named tonight, and the Alim'deru will be performed immediately after. There will be no struggle, one against the other. Do I make myself clear?" Faldill glanced at Lendill, who gave the slightest of nods to his brother. Lendill wouldn't return after tonight.

"Now," Kaldill continued, "I have watched all of you over the course of your lifetimes. I have to be sure that the one I select is prepared to lead. Truly. One who knows how to bring out the best in his people, even when it is painful to do so. One who can see the future unfolding and place his people so that the best possible outcome will be achieved." Lendill watched, his heart sinking as Naldill preened expectantly.

"Did you think I wouldn't notice," Kaldill went on, turning to Naldill, "when you removed Lendill's power at birth? You made sure you arrived at his mother's side before I could, and it was gone when I got there. But I knew. I could smell the signature of your power, Naldill. That is what the Alim'deru will do for my heir—provide that knowledge when needed." Naldill was now casting a stunned look at his father. Lendill, too, gasped aloud at his father's statement.

"And you, Reldill," Kaldill went on, "you were right behind Naldill, always. Supporting every twisted decision that he made. Did you think it sport to torture your youngest brother, who had no power against you?" Kaldill gave Reldill a hard stare. "Yet you think that Naldill will be generous enough to allow you to help in his rule. He will not. Naldill has room for only one in his heart, and that one is Naldill. Neither of you deserve to be King of Gaelar N'Seith. Now, to my other two sons," Kaldill turned to Faldill and Lendill.

"Father, I have not the strength to rule," Faldill hung his head.

"But you have the strength of honesty, my child. Keep it. It is very useful."

"Then who will be named Prince-Heir?" Naldill was standing and angry. "Faldill doesn't have the strength and Lendill is only half and has no power."

"Because you removed it, correct?" Kaldill gazed critically at his oldest son.

"Yes, I fucking removed it, but he would never have enough power to hold Gaelar N'Seith." Naldill was breathing hard in his anger.

"But he met Reah, child," Kaldill said, gesturing for Naldill to sit. There must have been power in the gesture; Naldill sat.

"What does a fucking High Demon have to do with anything?" Naldill snarled at his father.

"See, you do have insight, although it is truly rare," Kaldill smiled.

"Fucking Reah is exactly what happened. She is High Demon. No magic or power wielder has any ability to get past that natural shield she possesses. And when, as you succinctly put it, Lendill fucked her, that power removal spell you performed began to unravel. It is completely gone, now. Lendill has everything he was born with, and more. I name him my Prince-Heir. Lendill knows how to lead. Taking charge of Gaelar N'Seith will be nothing next to what he has done for the ASD through the years."

Lendill didn't know what to do. His mouth hung open until Norian sent mindspeech for him to close it. "Stand, Lendill Schaff, and the Alim'deru will be performed." Kaldill rose from his chair. Lendill struggled to his feet, still looking confused.

"No!" Naldill shouted, leveling a blast at Lendill. It melted away against an answering blast sent by Kaldill. "I am still King here," he thundered. "I will remove your power first, and then you will watch your brother take what might have been yours if you'd allowed your heart to rule instead of your greed and cruelty." Kaldill raised his arms and a flash of power blasted Naldill against the back wall of Kaldill's study, knocking several delicate paintings down and causing a few tiny glass sculptures to tinkle to the floor around Kaldill's firstborn.

"I give you chance after chance, year after weary year, to step up and act as a king should act. You have failed to do so at every turn. You, my oldest, would torture your people just the same as you tortured Lendill. Therefore, you have no power, now. I suggest you learn to live without it. Make yourself useful to your brother and it might be restored one day. Now," Kaldill straightened his clothing, "Kneel, Lendill Schaff, and the Alim'deru will be passed to you."

"But he doesn't have any power," Reldill whined. "Father, you have fucked up one time too many." Faldill drew in a breath at Reldill's insult against his father.

"You have permission to teach your older brother a lesson," Kaldill said gently to Lendill. Lendill looked down at his clenched fists— they'd gone that way the moment Reldill had leveled his insult. Opening his hands, Lendill held only one out. Light blasted from it, knocking Reldill against the wall next to Naldill, who was still slumped there, unconscious.

"Now, you see what your youngest brother can do, only one-handed?" Kaldill said with satisfaction. "Kneel, Lendill, and I will pass power to you." Lendill knelt, and with words in an ancient language Norian didn't understand and light glowing around Kaldill and Lendill, Lendill was made Prince-Heir of the Elves.

"I will keep watch over Gaelar N'Seith until the time comes when you weary of serving the Alliance," Kaldill slapped Lendill gently on the back later, after a thousand-year wine was served. Naldill had been carried out earlier by waiting elves and Reldill was revived and escorted away, leaving only Kaldill, Lendill, Norian and Faldill, who seemed too stunned to speak. Lendill, numb and feeling crowded with power he'd never held before, worked up the courage to embrace his father before folding away with Norian.

"So, Prince-Heir of the Elves, eh?" Norian slapped Lendill on the back much harder than Kaldill had. "Still feel like a drink, old friend?"

"Yes. Definitely a drink," Lendill said. "Yes."

"Are the shields going to hold?" Corolan was worried and it was coming out in his voice. He'd put everything he had into the shields around the palace. Six warlocks and three witches had spoken out against Rylend Morphis' selection as heir, and when Wylend handed the throne to him and left, they'd started their campaign immediately, saying Ry's birth wasn't natural, he wasn't a true Karathian and therefore was ineligible to hold the throne. Ry knew that if the palace fell, all nine dissidents and their followers would fight amongst themselves over who would sit upon the throne afterward, likely splitting Karathia into factions and sending it straight into civil war.

Gavril had already offered to send Regular Campiaan Army, but Ry had asked Gavril what he thought regular troops might accomplish against power wielders. Gavril had seen the sense in his brother's argument and offered to come himself, whispering a few well-placed words into Ry's mind. Ry had grinned at the suggestion and he and Gavril had started a mental planning session. Now, all they had to do was keep the shields up for just a bit longer.

~

"I'm doing interviews for an overseer for the groves," Garde threw out a hand when Jayd asked if anything had been done. "Only one or two have come forward who worked for Reah, the rest are demanding that we get Reah back. I have several from off-world, claiming experience and clamoring for the job. That doesn't include the complaints I'm getting from the disabled." Garde sat heavily on a chair beside Jayd's desk.

"The Council is demanding we do something soon—they're all worried the income will evaporate," Jayd remarked dryly.

"We have three months, maybe, before the next harvest," Garde sighed. "But in that time we apparently have to prune, weed, fertilize, plant and mulch. Whatever that means."

"If we had someone reliable, then Torevik's land could be planted," Jayd pointed out. "Since we no longer have to worry that his former wife might take any of it."

"We could. It will take five years for the trees to yield, and they have to be tended. We'll have to hire more people for that, obviously," Garde grumbled. He wasn't looking forward to more interviews, since he didn't really know the proper questions to ask.

"Find someone and soon, brother. We can't let this go much longer." Garde nodded at Jayd's words, staring at his hands instead of his brother.

~

"You are not progressing as well as we'd like; we think the pregnancy is holding you back," Teeki had returned with Neeki. "Therefore, we will do some healing. You must be strong when the move comes."

I stared at both of Kifirin's helpers. "Do you know where they'll move us?" I asked, including all the other girls who would be put up for sale in my question.

"We cannot say," Neeki replied, placing hands on my body. "You would send mindspeech to your mate who helps run the ASD, and he will have troops waiting. That is too much interference. We cannot involve ourselves in that."

"Goodness, no," I muttered as Teeki began to help. I had four hands running over my body, paying special attention to my abdomen—they seemed fascinated with the baby for some reason.

"We cannot reproduce," Teeki said when I asked him about it. "So of course we find children fascinating."

"He is a bit obsessed," Neeki grinned.

"You wouldn't be if you'd gone through labor," I grumped.

"Why do females always grumble about that?" Teeki sighed as he made me feel better.

"Come see me when this one is born," I snapped back.

"Perhaps we will come; it will be a new experience," Neeki agreed. "In the meantime, this will help. You must be strong when the time comes."

"Sure. Be strong, he says. Have you ever been ill?" I stared at Neeki while his brother worked.

"No. It is not permitted."

"You have to have permission to be ill?" I found that disturbing.

"Just for the experience. We would have to beg."

"Trust me, once you're involved, you'd be begging to not be ill, I assure you."

"It seems somewhat tedious," Teeki said. "Waiting such a long time to conquer illness."

"You make it sound like a military campaign," I groused. "I can assure you, if I could fight this thing in a fair fight, it would be gone already."

"They'll move you soon. You should be ready. Do what must be done, child of Kifirin," Teeki drew his hands away, as did his brother.

"I don't claim Kifirin as a father. Not anymore," I said. "Don't ever say those words to me again." Teeki glanced nervously at Neeki before both disappeared.

∽

"We have to prepare the dessert for several in Miss Schuul's penthouse; she's having a private rush," Perdil and Zendeval woke me later. Wanting more than anything to berate both of them and then squeeze their throats until they choked, I made an annoyed sound in my throat as they helped me off the bed. I felt like slapping Zendeval's hands as he helped me dress, including underwear. I didn't like it when strange hands wanted to dress me in panties and a bra. Zendeval kissed my hipbones and my breasts as he worked. I wanted to heave. Perdil finally cleared his throat when the petting threatened to escalate.

The trip to the kitchens came next, and I was able to stand and get the ingredients put together for the cake and ice cream. The oxberry tart was also requested, so that came next. I worked as efficiently as I could, economizing my efforts so I wouldn't be weakened after Teeki and Neeki's healing. Perdil and Zendeval both watched as I worked, utilizing the kitchen assistants as much as possible.

Finally, the desserts were finished and hefted onto a tray, bound for Darletta Schuul's suite. I cursed her, her father and all the other sick, sadistic and twisted persons involved in the entire mess. I vowed, too, that many of them wouldn't live past the next few days if I had anything to say about it.

It no longer mattered whether Lendill and Norian wanted to question any of them. I intended to kill, plain and simple. They were placing my life, my child's life and the lives of countless others in jeopardy, and there was no telling how many they'd raped or killed already. I could only guess at that. I wanted to berate Perdil and Zendeval Rjjn, too, before anything else happened to them and I missed the opportunity.

"We'll be leaving tomorrow evening for the sale," Perdil informed me as we rode up the elevator. Lendill was likely watching and listening, so he was getting the information he wanted, we just didn't know where the sale would be held. He'd be tracking me, though, so wherever we went, he could have ships in the area quickly. Unless Dantel and Faldin had some final, engineering miracle in reserve. With the way things were going, I wouldn't be surprised at all.

"They'll be shipping the cargo off Stellar Winds tomorrow evening, if my source is correct," Lendill paced in front of a room filled with ASD starship commanders. "I want your troops ready for anything, since we don't know yet where we're going or what we'll face when we get there. It's likely that they're well equipped, wherever they are, so we may have a battle on our hands before we can even get to the site. Once there, we have captives to worry about. These are kidnapped women, bound for the slave trade. Most of you have been briefed that we are dealing with slavers. As you know, you were examined, too, when you walked into this room. The few who were shunted aside, well, let's just say they're having a bit of impromptu surgery to rid them of a device known as a controller." Lendill snapped the remote in his hand, pulling up images on a screen behind him. Those images illustrated what the controllers looked like and where they were placed—in the neck at the base of the brain.

"Some of us have been controlled, and unless we stop the ones responsible now, it's very likely that in only a few moon turns, all will be under the control of a few masterminds. We cannot let this happen, and our physicians and scientists are working feverishly to produce a tiny disruptor that can be injected into the body, likely in the collarbone, which will negate the effectiveness of the controllers. Each of you will have one of these before you leave tonight to board your ships. We are using every one of the prototypes developed in the last few days, and your troops are now getting them as well. Only they think they are being immunized against a chemical agent."

"These people likely have the latest weaponry, chemicals and forbidden technology, as you can see in the illustrations," Norian took over. "They are the pirates we have struggled to track, and with the aid of these controllers and compromised chips in comp-vids, they have access to almost everything. We would not have this information now, but we sent a special agent out to search for another who has been missing. The agent is currently working undercover, at great risk, to get this information to us. Let us hope that our agent, along with the captives and every person in the Alliance, is safe after tomorrow night. Good luck and good hunting," Norian said.

Physicians waited at the doors into the meeting room at ASD headquarters, armed with injectors, ready to give each commander the necessary disruptor. It was their hope to keep these men under the control of the ASD instead of Dantel Schuul and his small band of masterminds, who were bent on controlling both Alliances.

"Bro, it won't be the greatest loss," Gavril reminded Rylend. "They're out there, killing your loyal subjects without asking questions or considering the matter. It's either do them in now, and in the worst possible way to get the others to back off, or it will be civil war for who knows how long. You know I can do this. And, since the regular army can't handle this, well, I'm the commander in chief. It's my job."

"Then get Aklus and Chimbl first; they're killing everybody, including children. We've beaten them back a little, but they still have murder in their hearts. They want to cleanse the entire planet of any Karathian who might oppose their rule, and unfortunately, that's just about everybody," Ry raked a hand through his hair. Erland and Corolan stood nearby, impassively listening to the exchange between brothers.

Gavril had warned Ry that it might come to this. He held the ability—because he was who he was and his parents were who they were. Gavril could go undetected if he wanted, and that was ideal for this situation. If Aklus and Chimbl fell, the others would likely fall to their knees and ask for clemency. Gavril didn't like messy, but he could do it. After all, his mother had done it before him, just under different circumstances.

Ry had sent images of children to Gavril, their bodies tossed carelessly onto the streets of Karathia, in Aklus' bid for power. He'd done that to terrorize the population. Chimbl wasn't any better. He'd committed heinous acts of his own. Now, Gavril and Ry were about to show them what Lissa's children were capable of doing. Tory, too, was due any moment. He was the wild card. As a High Demon, no warlock or wizard could hurl spells that might harm him.

"I'm here." Tory skipped in, ready to skip again at Ry's command.

"Get us here," Ry pointed to the spot on the vid-image map. "It's Aklus' stronghold. He and Chimbl are holed up in Wylend's old summer palace. He hasn't used it in centuries, so it's a good place for them to hide."

"I'll get you there," Tory nodded to Gavril and Ry. "And I'll turn as soon as we arrive. Gavril, I assume you'll go in as mist and keep me mist as well?" The plan was that Tory would stay beside Ry—as mist, while Ry looked to be immune to any power thrown at him. Gavril could force anyone to remain mist, once he turned them if he so chose. Gavril would then proceed to lop off a few heads, making it appear as if Ry were effortlessly killing his enemies while they hurled their worst at him.

"Yep. They'll never know we're there," Gavril nodded.

"Take me as well," Erland stepped forward. "Corolan can disguise himself to look as I do. I want in on this, son. This is ours to do. We will succeed or fall, together."

"Dad," Ry almost begged his father to stay behind and then thought better of it. "All right, we'll do this. All of us," he nodded at Gavril and Tory. Gavril turned all of them to mist and Tory skipped them away.

"What are these?" Zendeval had finally seen my claiming marks. "Answer me," he demanded. I blinked at him.

"Scars," I replied. "I was bitten. By an animal."

"I'm surprised you lived over it," he muttered. "Get dressed. I'm taking you to dinner before we leave."

I didn't want to wear anything he wanted me to wear. He chose the black dress I'd bought for the rush in the bar downstairs, with the heels and jewelry I'd worn with it that night.

"I planned to convince you to come to bed with me—before moonrush," he wrapped his arms around me after I was dressed and ready to go. "I think so much more clearly when I hold you," he kissed the side of my neck. "And if I point out your scars during the sale, it might lower your price or convince some of the others not to bid." He was worried, I could tell. "I have never said this to any woman. I found them beneath me—was taught by Nedrizif and Perdil to consider them as such. Reah, I love you. If we are separated after tonight, I want you to remember that. That you were loved. Before moonrush. Come, we will have dinner."

I followed obediently behind him as we made our way to the elevator, and then down to the lower level. I saw Perdil going toward the kitchen—he was on duty for the evening. I wondered how he lived with himself—if he found solace making desserts while lives shattered around him.

Barely casting a glance in his direction, I continued to follow behind Zendeval. That might have been my place if I'd been ordinary. I wasn't. I was something larger than that. I intended for Zendeval, Perdil and the others to see how large I could become. Neeki and Teeki had finally given me good service—I felt better. I was determined to eat as well—I needed as much strength as I could muster for the coming clicks. As for Zendeval Rjjn—af te Jufaleh.

"What do you think of the steak? You have permission to speak," Zendeval said later after our food was delivered. He'd ordered for both of us. I hated that.

"The marinade needs work," I said, cutting a small piece off and chewing.

"I was too impatient, hiring Crade," he sighed. "But Nedrizif was pressuring me to hire, because the others were coming for a meeting. They were planning the final stages of the takeover, and wanted something extraordinary for the meal. They didn't get it with the main course—they got it instead with the dessert. All the tourists are talking about the dessert, Reah. You have vindicated me in the eyes of my cousin the King."

I didn't get permission to speak, so I wasn't able to tell him that he wasn't getting any support from me and I didn't give a damn about Nedrizif, King or not. I had enough monarchy in my life—some good, some not. I wondered how Ry was faring and resolved not to send mindspeech. I didn't want him to know what my present situation was and idly considered taking Zendeval Rjjn by the throat and choking him as after-dinner entertainment.

If he expected me to believe him when he said the word love, then he needed to think again. I had an entire herd of mates who said it all the time and then followed it with practically no substance at all. Instead, I dutifully got up when Zendeval was finished with his meal and followed him back to his penthouse suite.

"So, the pretender King has come to bow down to us, my friend." Aklus smiled at Chimbl, who stood next to him, and then the twenty-seven witches and warlocks who'd sided with them at their backs. Ry and Erland stood before them, seemingly defenseless against so many.

"Go ahead, show Karathia what you can do," Rylend said, standing firmly before the worst that Karathia had to offer. He recognized the warlocks and witches behind Aklus—Wylend had searched for some of them for years. Yet here they were, like a flock of crows come to pick at the spoils Aklus offered. Chimbl was nothing more than an empty-headed thug, willing to lick Aklus' boots in order to gain a place in his kingdom.

Ry was certainly hoping it wouldn't come to that. He'd practiced diplomacy through the years, in addition to perfecting a very good poker face. If his mother knew what he was doing at the moment, she'd likely have a fit. But this was his war to fight—he was lucky that he had brothers—and a talented father—to help him fight it.

"Surrender now and I will spare your lives," Ry said calmly. "I give you ten ticks to decide."

"So little time?" Aklus laughed. Ry knew what Aklus was doing—he, Chimbl and the others behind them were pooling their strength to hurl it in a single blast at Ry and Erland.

Erland, more than six thousand years a warlock, neither blinked nor twitched. He was prepared to live or die at his son's side. Rylend was his son and a dream he'd had for a very long time—a child who would make a difference to Karathia. He would stand firm and offer his support at this pivotal moment. If they lived, Karathia was likely theirs—to rule as justly as they could. If they fell, Karathia would have to be dealt with.

Erland had already contacted Connegar, asking him to place a shield around the planet if it fell into the wrong hands. Karathia gone rogue could destroy both Alliances. Connegar had already received permission from the Larentii Council to place the shield. The Larentii homeworld stood to suffer if Karathia fell, as Karathia stood on the border between light and dark worlds. Few knew it, but the Larentii homeworld had once stood guard between the dark worlds and the light. For millennia, the Larentii kept their world hidden from all and had no desire to deal with Karathia gone rogue.

"Here's our answer," Aklus grinned and blasted the gathered power at Rylend Morphis and his father. The expended power, when it hit, could be seen light-years away, it was so bright and destructive in its force.

"Reah, come," Zendeval sighed. It was time, I suppose. I followed him to the elevator again and we rode it in silence. The door that we'd traveled through before, marked as a service entrance but coded to Zendeval, Perdil and few others, was our destination inside Galedaro's. Perdil waited outside that entrance, and walked with us down the long, narrow hall lined with electrical wiring and comp-boxes that ran lights, air-conditioning and such.

I kept my eyes on the floor beneath my feet—it was stone of some kind, kept clean and polished by those controlled slaves who worked like ants in the bowels of Stellar Winds. Lendill was speaking in my mind. I ignored him. His words were the same ones I'd heard many times before; instructions on what to do in this situation or that. I had my own plans. Lendill could do what he wanted with me afterward. If there was an afterward. I kept walking, Zendeval before me, Perdil behind.

Another cage waited for me, just as there'd been before. At least the full moon was another two eight-days in coming. I hoped Zendeval and his race didn't turn often outside the full moon, else I'd have my hands full, Thifilatha or no.

"Reah, we are prepared to offer millions, but Nedrizif has greater resources," Perdil muttered as the cage door was shut, locking me inside. "If Dantel Schuul bids, he can pay more than Nedrizif. We will find a way to deal with that, should it happen." Perdil walked away, Zendeval close behind.

I gazed around me, at all the others inside cages. They were controlled and had no idea they should be frightened. I did. The lift hooked onto the first cage with a metallic clang, pulling the small prison with its inhabitant up and rolling toward the dock of a waiting transport. It had begun. I clenched my hands around bars and counted prisoners again.

# CHAPTER 13

"Are you getting the feed?" Norian and Lendill were both aboard the command ship. The captain had led their forces away from the binary system that included an older star and a white dwarf in the same sector as Stellar Winds. They'd been moving behind it; the energy given out masking their gathering force.

"Yes," Norian said. He and Lendill were in the map room, watching Reah's camera feeds on one vid while another showed the dot indicating the ship carrying the human cargo.

"Where are they going?" The captain grimaced at the image. He couldn't think of any viable planets or planetoids in the rogue ship's direction.

"This is why we couldn't find them before—they're heading toward mostly empty space. What's there?" Norian barked at an ensign, who scurried to check the comp, pulling up the area the rogue ship targeted.

"Nothing, Director," the Ensign muttered. "There's no life anywhere there. A couple of dead planets, that's it."

"Which dead planets?" Lendill did the barking this time.

"Cloudsong and Thiskil, sir," the ensign replied.

"Both killed by Zellar," Norian cursed.

"We've checked them in the past—they're still empty," the captain offered.

"But they may not be empty tonight. Tell me, you were looking for life-forms, weren't you?" The light was coming on for Lendill.

"Yes. We found nothing. There was no need to search further—the planet is only home to old or ancient technology, now. Why would we need to look for that?" the captain scoffed.

"Because new technology may have been added to it," Norian felt ghostly hands move up his spine. He was on the same wavelength as Lendill, now. They'd both heard Zendeval Rjjn talk of a takeover. Technology was available to force the Alliance satellites and main comp systems to succumb to its commands. It wasn't legal in either Alliance, but these people were smarter than he'd imagined—setting new technology among the old, knowing that with so much of it there, a few additional items would go unremarked.

"They're going to do it tonight," Lendill whispered. "They'll not only take over the people, but every information system in both Alliances. Bro," he turned to Norian, "we're screwed."

"Every ship on manual, break away from ASD comps now!" Norian shouted. The ensign rushed to obey, as every system shut down on the ship and darkness fell.

Two clicks at hyperspeed. That's how long it took. My fingers itched to hold a comp-vid and calculate which systems might be reached from Stellar Winds during that time. My cage and sixty-six others were in a cargo hold with no windows or comforts available. Controlled slaves dressed in little more than rags walked among the cages, watching for distress, fainting or illness. Some people don't do well at hyperspeed; it disorients them. It's much like traveling upon an ocean in a boat, for some reason. Buckets and cleaning cloths were provided to the few who became ill, while a physician tended to two who fainted. I watched all of it dispassionately, waiting for our landing.

~

"So, you think that little cook is going to be yours, do you? I heard dessert isn't all she can do." Dantel Schuul grinned and slapped Zendeval on the back. Perdil grimaced at the one who'd provided all the comp components to construct the brain machines, set to take over every information system in both Alliances. With controllers injected into so many, now, it was easy to set things up for the takeover.

Perdil, however, was one of the few who wasn't controlled. Regretted now that he'd allowed Zen to be controlled by Nedrizif. Wished more than once that he'd removed the damn thing himself. That way he would be assured of having one ally when he killed Dantel Schuul and the others. They were human scum.

Nedrizif, well, he and Perdil had been allied for a while. They understood one another. Zen's streak of fairness had been quelled—and his life taken over—by a controller developed by Schuul Enterprises. Perdil sighed and turned away from Dantel Schuul. The opportunity would come, and Perdil still had a winning card to play. He would employ that option only if necessary.

"We have arrived," the commander announced to the gathered dignitaries. Yes, they would be exactly that, Dantel smirked. Dignitaries. Honored leaders. He would be held in reverence one day, much as Ildevar Wyyld was now. As the founder of the new, Combined Alliance, Dantel had plans to rule all of it, and with his controllers, there would be no crime unless he commanded it. He was looking forward to playing with lives. He already did that, but this would be on the grandest scale imaginable. Dantel's fingers twitched, just thinking about it.

~

I felt the ship lurch when we landed. The ship was a modified freighter, no doubt with luxury cabins added. Those cabins would be equipped with the most expensive shock systems available, to cushion

Zendeval and his cronies from the inconvenience of the landing jolts. The caged slaves received no such comforts and some had to be tended a second time. I looked at eyes around me—mostly blank stares met my gaze. A few clutched the bars of their cages, feeling a bit of fear. At least that much was left to them.

Slaves didn't live long, usually. Their owners tired of them or used them for their sick perversities until they either died or were sold into heavy labor. I held little hope that those who'd come before had been treated well after their sale. They were likely dead or well on their way.

The loader was powered up and the first cage was lifted. I stared through the opening hatch at the sunlight outside. This section of the planet had its face turned toward the sun. All the better. I recognized it, too. I'd been here before, to heal the core. Cloudsong greeted us as the bay door yawned wide.

*Lendill, do you see this?* I sent mindspeech.

*Little busy here, Reah. See what?* Lendill returned.

*Cloudsong,* I said. *We're on Cloudsong.*

Lendill and Norian had spent the better part of two clicks folding from ship to ship, punching in private codes and taking each vessel offline from the ASD mainframe. Then they employed other, private codes to power it up again as an autonomous ship. It could be done; it just took time. Lendill and Norian put their cursing skills to the test, too. They were behind—far behind, and had no idea where they were going. Until Reah sent mindspeech.

Lendill hadn't contacted her—didn't want to worry her with the fact that help might not be swift in coming, if at all. And he'd doubted that Reah would even be allowed to know which world they'd landed upon, until he'd gotten mindspeech from her. Reah recognized Cloudsong, all right. She'd healed the core. The planet still appeared dead; Zellar had drained it more thoroughly than any other world. A dead world was now the perfect place for pirates and slavers.

"Set everything manually to get to Cloudsong," Lendill shouted into the aud-comp. "Best possible speed," he added. It would take another click to reach their destination, and anything might happen during that time. Lendill didn't remember ever being this frightened.

"Cloudsong," Norian came in from resetting the last ship on manual, slumping onto a chair beside Lendill's with a sigh. "Fucking Cloudsong. Why didn't we see it before?"

∼

The old palace in Song City was our destination. Yes, it was in disrepair, with the roof caving in places, allowing sunlight to filter onto the stone floors beneath. So much the better. I and the other captives were shunted into an anteroom, just off the central grand hall of the palace. We traveled through the grand hall on our way to the smaller chamber, where a crowd was already gathered. Caged women were scrutinized by prospective buyers as they passed by.

Someone had to place an initial bid on a girl I'm sure, before the effort was made to collect. Then, if another buyer failed to bid against the first bidder (who'd likely viewed the girl from a voyeur room at Stellar Winds), he could claim her by default at the initial price. I didn't think many would be sold in that way.

I saw businessmen, criminals, professional slavers, brothel owners and sadists—all there to claim what they wanted. Those girls should have been weeping and screaming. Instead, because of a tiny controller shot into the base of their brains, they were eerily silent as our cages rattled past those who'd come to buy. Several bidders reached out to finger my hair as I was hauled in.

"It's natural," I heard Dantel say. He'd joined the others. I wanted to burst out of my cage immediately, killing him first. That would wait. Other things had to be dealt with before that could happen. I saw the long row of large, round metallic brains lined up against one wall in the grand hall. At one time, I imagine a throne once sat against that wall.

Those days were gone—a different ruler had taken up residence.

One with electronic chips designed to control every information system inside both Alliances. And, if my guess was correct, a smaller version had already been activated—against the ASD's systems. My help, if it came, might be slow in getting there. It didn't matter—I was prepared to strike out on my own.

"I'll bid on that," someone leered at me as I was hauled past.

"Place my cage near the door," I hissed at a slave who was shoving cages inside the anteroom. Instructed to obey only, he followed my directions, motioning for the lift to drop my cage near the entrance. From that spot, I could see the crowd in the grand hall clearly, in addition to the long row of large, globe-shaped comp-brains. I smiled for the first time in days.

"Is that all you have?" Rylend smiled a blinding smile at Aklus and Chimbl. Their power, combined with twenty-seven others, should have obliterated even the two most powerful warlocks anywhere. Instead, Rylend Morphis and his father, Erland, stood upon a tiny island of stone—all that remained of Wylend's expensive Ooklaran marble courtyard.

"I grow bored," Erland turned to his son. "Shall we show them what we have, now?"

"I think so, father. We might be late for lunch, otherwise." Erland and Ry turned to Aklus and Chimbl, raising their arms and preparing a spell.

*Reah, we'll be there in a click. Just hold on until then. Surely they can't sell so many girls in that amount of time,* Lendill sent mindspeech. *Your cameras aren't working,* he added, *so we can't see anything where you are.*

*Don't worry, everything is under control,* I sent back, almost in a soothing tone. Dantel Schuul had decided to give a speech. It made me sad that Lendill couldn't see any of it—Dantel's speech revealed just what kind of megalomaniac he actually was. He was talking about complete domination over all the worlds, starting with both Alliances.

The criminal element clapped and cheered when he told them they'd share in all of that. I wanted to snort at the statement—they'd share until a controller was shot into their necks and they stumbled along meekly at Dantel's heels, just like the others. Instead, I busied myself with other plans. Turning to my smaller Thifilatha, I bent the bars of my cage and stepped out of it. I then lifted my head upward toward Cloudsong's sun and coaxed its energy to me.

No epic blast came from Rylend and his father, such as Aklus and Chimbl had funneled from willing witches and warlocks. No. This was a concentrated attack. The first heads that exploded were Aklus and Chimbl's; their brain matter spattering those behind them, who shrieked and ducked away from the bloody rain. Many thought to fold away, but power held them rooted to their spots, even as more heads exploded. The screaming began immediately as head after head became bits of blood and mist, the body subsequently dropping to what remained of the courtyard.

Cloudsong's sun smiled upon me again, welcoming me like an old friend. I felt its warmth through my body as I pulled more and more energy from it. Dantel was still prattling on, standing upon a makeshift stage while Darletta and Faldin stood behind him.

Darletta's arms were wrapped around Faldin's forearm; she listened raptly to her father's words as if he spewed the most beautiful, poetic verse. What they actually held was nothing less than complete annihilation. Of everything.

Turning my eyes that now shown as golden as the sun I'd pulled energy from, I lifted arms and aimed all my gathered energy at Dantel's brains. Not those he held inside his head—he truly wasn't using those for much of anything. I targeted his metallic monstrosities instead, and released my power.

Only three warlocks remained of all that Aklus had gathered. Ry smiled at those three. "Want to die?" he asked pleasantly. All three shook their heads violently. "Good. Your power is removed," Ry casually flung out a hand, stripping all three of what they had left. "Now, why don't you clean up this mess?" The King of Karathia stared with disgust at the messy courtyard. "And I'll have you rebuild the courtyard after that. Complain and I'll remove your tongues." Ry nodded to his father, who folded them back to the palace.

"Bro, that may have been the coolest thing I've ever seen," Tory slapped Ry on the back. Gavril was brushing imaginary blood and bits of bone off his shirt. He'd done the executions, Tory had provided the shield and Ry had provided the wizardry.

"I made sure that every warlock and witch was tuned in to that little confrontation," Erland grinned at his son before hauling him into a tight hug. "Corolan's getting oaths of fealty, even as we speak."

"That's perfect, Dad," Ry clapped his father on the back. "Thanks, Gav. Thanks, Tory," he nodded to his brothers.

"Not a problem. You've been there for us, every time," Gavril hugged Ry next. "It's always good to have the King of Karathia at your back, don't you think?" Gavril grinned.

A disturbed anthill might describe how Dantel and his audience reacted to the first brain exploding, sending bits of metal and electronic chips flying everywhere. Then the second exploded, making the girls around me scream. I became my larger Thifilatha, bursting through the anteroom doorway with little effort and causing a third brain to explode.

"Weapons!" I heard the faint shout as I stomped into the throne room. Laser rifles were fired at me. They had no effect. I was filled with the power of Cloudsong's sun and laughed at their puny efforts to bring me down. I stood between them and the women in cages as well—I had no intention of allowing them near those women again. I'd had to hold back when they were attacked before; now I allowed my anger and frustration to boil over. Another brain exploded and I laughed in exultation.

*Norian, the power just went out across both Alliances,* Lissa sent mindspeech to her mate. If anyone knew what was at the bottom of this, he would. *Nobody can access anything. Vehicles are stopped in the streets. Transportation and informational systems are blocked everywhere. The hospitals are on backup solar power, but this could be disastrous. Norian, what's going on?* Lissa's voice held panic and Norian wasn't used to hearing that.

*We're working on it, all right. I'll contact you when we have a handle on this. In the meantime, if you or any of those others that you know can help us out, I'd appreciate it.* Norian cut off the communication. The command ship was entering Cloudsong's airspace.

Dantel would never dream of attacking anyone or anything. His power lay in ordering others about. Nedrizif, too, was now marshaling his forces. I watched as at least seventy of Zendeval Rjjn's race became darker creatures and rushed toward me, even as others continued to fire laser pistols and rifles that had little effect. One thought to attack me with a sword. He was now ash at my feet.

Nedrizif should have learned from that example. Seventy black-scaled creatures thought to attack me with fists, teeth and claws. They burned just as the first one had, winking out of existence as their flesh was incinerated in an instant. I briefly wondered how that might feel, their lives winking out so quickly.

I turned my attention to the last two brains as Dantel Schuul screamed at those around him. I'm sure he was watching all his dreams blown to bits before his eyes. Meanwhile, the buyers had learned their lesson—they were running from Cloudsong's old palace. Nedrizif, in an ill-advised and final effort, shouted for his controlled slaves to attack me.

~

"If it isn't female or looks like this," Norian pointed out the vid-image of Reah in Thifilatha, "then shoot first and ask questions later," he ordered as the ship's door opened to allow his troops to disembark. "You all know what Dantel Schuul looks like. Spare him if you can, I want to speak with him first. Go." Norian nodded and the first ship sent its soldiers onto Cloudsong's soil.

~

Filled as I was with solar power, I made Nedrizif's Ranos launcher disintegrate before he could lift it to fire. Nedrizif was blasted away immediately after. His slaves were still rushing me—they must have been brought by the hundreds. They died just as easily as the rest. They were innocents, though, and I wept scalding tears as their lives were snuffed out.

I had no idea where Zendeval and Perdil had gone—I was only seeing and dealing with the mindless slaves Dantel was now sending against me. And then I saw them—Dantel had ordered Zen to attack me; Perdil struggled to pull him back. For a moment, I negated my ability to burn and slapped them away, before restoring my burning talent as a new wave of controlled slaves attacked. I wept again as they screamed and died.

~

Faldin and Darletta were cowering in a corner, hoping to escape my notice after the last slave perished, when Norian, Lendill and the ASD army they'd brought with them blasted their way into the palace.

I sat heavily on the dusty, stone floor, suddenly feeling weary as Dantel and his cronies gave up easily. I overheard Dantel assuring Darletta that his lawyers would get them out of this. Lendill came to stand before me. I looked down at him, wiping away another scalding tear so it wouldn't fall on him. He knew better than to touch any part of me at that moment.

"Reah?" That's all he said. One word that held reams of questions. I didn't answer a single one of them. I skipped away, instead.

Three days. Three of the longest days ever felt in either Alliance. Nothing was recorded, nothing announced, nothing built, copied, manufactured, researched. No government conducted business. Everything was at a standstill. Constabulary everywhere were hard pressed to keep some elements of the population under control—they were looting. Not just food and other necessities, but anything else they could lay their hands on. Surprisingly, no comp-based devices were taken—they weren't working anyway.

During that time, anyone who could fold space shunted work crews here and there, removing the remnants of the controlling devices placed inside informational systems and bringing them back online after three difficult and grueling days. Ildevar Wyyld and Teeg San Gerxon took to the vid waves immediately after, reassuring both Alliances that everything was now under control. They explained how the pirates had managed to take control, albeit briefly, but now, steps would be taken so that no system might be taken over like that again.

"Think you convinced 'em, bro?" Tory cast a worried glance at Gavril. The two-click announcement, followed by a brief press conference, had worn him out. Still, there was no word on Reah. Gavril had even attempted to contact Nefrigar, but the Larentii wasn't answering his mental pleas for help.

"There's a lot to do and many will not understand how we let this happen," Gavril raked fingers through his hair. "I don't understand how we let this happen. We were trying to treat the various symptoms, and not seeing clearly the underlying cancer. I understand Wylend's timing, now."

"Wylend? What does he have to do with this?"

"I think Griffin warned him that something terrible might come, and he wouldn't be prepared to handle it. Not without Ry at his side. I think those rogue warlocks were in league with these other fucks. This went farther than most people imagined." Gavril paced inside his private study. Dee was in his office, fielding calls and making reassurances across the Campiaan Alliance. Others were doing the same for Ildevar Wyyld and the Grand Alliance Council.

"Meanwhile, Reah is still missing."

"Yeah. I have no idea where to look for her, and frankly, we all have our hands full here. There's no time or resources to search for her now."

"What do you think really happened? On Cloudsong? Norian and Lendill say the ASD swooped in and saved the day. We both know Reah was there. What happened, bro?"

"I don't think Lendill and Norian know the whole of it," Ry folded in. "Dad's watching over the flocks," he held up a hand. "We need to find Reah. You know she and I," he tapped his chest.

"Yeah, Lendill told us," Tory grumbled.

"Now you know," Ry said.

"How did you deal with that, all those years?" Gavril offered Ry a pointed look.

"Kept my mouth shut and my eyes looking elsewhere," Ry replied readily. "When Great-Grampa was out of the picture, that made it easier, but I had to wait for the right opportunity. After watching live sex shows on Stellar Winds, I couldn't help myself."

Tory ducked his head to hide the snicker. Gavril and Ry heard it anyway.

"How much of that were you exposed to?" Gavril turned a knowing glance on Tory.

"Plenty, I think," Tory shook his head, as if attempting to clear it. "My memory of the past twenty-five years is a little spotty, bro. I have bits and pieces. Darletta made me watch. Lots of times. I don't know how I managed to not turn and go after her."

"Controllers," Gavril gave the one-word reply.

"Others may have been involved, but that information died with Nedrizif," Norian muttered angrily. He paced inside Lendill's office on Le-Ath Veronis. Lissa had accused Norian of being a bear instead of a lion snake and thrown him out of her study moments earlier. Norian was more than frustrated. He wanted all these criminals in his hand, so he could clench his fist and squeeze the life from their bodies.

Reah, too, was still missing, so no information could be had from her. She likely didn't know the names either—she'd had minimal contact with Nedrizif and Zendeval Rjjn was little more than a drone. The controller had been removed from his neck and he'd blinked in shock at Norian and Lendill afterward. His memories of recent events were just as bad as Tory's had been. No useful information had come from him or Perdil, the Liffelithi Dwarf.

Dantel Schuul and his daughter, Darletta, sang like birds, however, once the vampires placed compulsion. Those two, plus Faldin Bierla, Zendeval Rjjn, Perdil, Matiss Meldrim and Gescht Prekisule, cooled their heels in Lissa's dungeon. They wouldn't be walking out with their lives—Norian had provided information to journalists, telling both Alliances that the ones responsible had been killed in the ASD raid on Cloudsong. Ildevar had been advised, as had Gavril. Both had given their blessings.

"How did the controllers do against vampires?" Lendill thought to ask.

"Only the youngest of them experienced any effects at all," Norian sighed. "Those less than a hundred years of age. I think it has to do with the immunity they build against compulsion, except by an older vampire," he added. "I've been afraid to talk to Lissa about that; she's mad enough to spit over the fact that somebody got to a few of her people as it is. Most of those were former comesuli, so that made it worse. They're vampire children, in her eyes. I think Dantel Schuul and that thing he calls an engineer are lucky to still be among the living at this point."

"Faldin Bierla. We don't have any official records past twenty years ago; the ones we found in the system are forged. He's managed to conceal his past successfully, and he's the only prisoner that vampire compulsion doesn't work on. Unfortunate for us, I know, but I don't think he knows any more than Dantel does, and we got everything from Schuul that we could." Lendill shook his head in confusion.

"Lissa says that any man who isn't susceptible to compulsion will make a King Vampire if he's turned. Can you imagine that thing as a vampire?" Norian flung up a hand. "That was his technology. Dantel admitted it. Faldin Bierla brought the idea to Dantel, and he envisioned controlling everything with it. Un-fucking-believable," Norian cursed.

"I imagine that those not under the control of Schuul and his associates would have become small, renegade islands, constantly threatened by Schuul and his technology," Nefrigar folded in and sat leisurely on a corner of Lendill's desk. "I have placed new records in the archives concerning this near-catastrophe. We have been quite busy, lately, my sons and I, getting all of it sorted and cataloged. Had you visited the archives when invited, we might have pointed you toward the section containing information on this forbidden technology."

"Fuck," Lendill mumbled tiredly, rubbing his forehead. "Where is Reah?"

"Safe. On Tulgalan. Did anyone think to check her home there? Her uncle Fes has been taking meals to her. You didn't think to contact him, either. Did you? He is a kindly soul, more so now that his father is out of the picture. Fes was always frightened that Addah and Marzi would harm his mother and the others, so he bent under

Addah's commands for a very long while. Now, he is his own man and runs a very good restaurant. He hasn't forgotten what Reah did for him, either. He is repaying a little of that debt. Reah is not feeling the best, as you might imagine. I have visited her several times. She allows my touch, but barely. Being bitten and made ill during an attempted rape, witnessing mass rape, and then the events upon Cloudsong have taken a terrible toll."

"The attack, followed by the illness and the attempted takeover," Norian nodded. "We may have to offer help."

"She may refuse it, out of hand," Nefrigar sighed. "But the need is there. I will not deny it. I would advise all who know her to tread carefully in the next few days."

"We need a report from her," Lendill grumped. "I'll go chase her down."

"Do not chase. Approach. Cautiously," Nefrigar warned.

"Fine." Lendill stood and lifted his jacket. Winter had come to Tulgalan. Again.

~

"No, I want this cut," I was about to become impatient with the butcher. Again. Was I invisible? Did he think I wouldn't recognize the best cuts of meat? Was he looking to sell inferior stock to one who likely didn't know the difference?

"Sell her that one or Desh's will stop doing business with you," Fes was at my back, a hand on my shoulder, steadying me. "This is my niece, by the way, so when she returns to your shop, I expect the best to be laid out for her at the beginning."

"Thanks, Fes," I whispered, putting an arm around his waist and hugging him briefly. "What are you doing here?"

"We need a little extra for dinner tonight—we have a party coming in from off-planet. You wouldn't like to come and help me with that, would you?"

"Maybe." I felt numb, weak, and more than a little stressed, still. Memories crowded my mind often—of hundreds of innocents—all controlled by Nedrizif and Dantel Schuul, hurling fragile, emaciated and nearly naked bodies at my Thifilatha.

I'd watched them burn—countless numbers of them. They'd had no choice and neither had I. If I'd turned off that part of me for more than a tick, then the weapons the others fired at me might have harmed me or my unborn child. I'd made a horrible choice; one I'd have to learn to live with. Still, their screams invaded my sleep at times and I woke, hyperventilating every time.

"Fes, how many are expected?" I asked.

"Just four, I think, but it's a special group. Come with me, now. I'll cook that for you," he nodded at the package the butcher packed up and handed to me, "and then we'll plot out our meals for the evening."

Fes did cook for me. Sliced the cut of beef thin, barely sautéed it and then covered it with a wonderful sauce, serving it up with pasta and a green salad. "Fes, this is so good," I sighed, pushing a nearly empty plate away. He knew I was pregnant with Teeg's child—I'd told him right away when I'd called to tell him I was in Targis, Tulgalan's capital city.

The house in Targis was empty—Erland and the others had made sure Ilvan and Radolf didn't make off with any of the furniture or collectibles. Fes had shown up there as soon as I'd contacted him, a covered plate of food in hand. He'd sat with me, too, while I told him about the baby and some of the other things. I didn't want to talk about the mass rape or most of the other stuff, but he did know I'd been held in a cage until we'd gotten to the sale site. He'd shaken his head and held me while I cried on his shoulder.

"Let's do some shellfish," I said. "With a bit of sauce, risotto and vegetables," I suggested. "And we can do steak—what you did for my lunch would be perfect," I smiled at Fes. I was happiest when I was cooking or planning meals.

"How about a pork dish, too?" Fes had a gleam in his eye.

"Yes. Definitely. Let's do a pork roast, and stuff it." We set to work right away, because the pork roast had to cook for several clicks. It was done perfectly and right on time for the guests to arrive.

"We'll be going in together, with the food," Fes said. "They want it served family style." Fes and I walked in behind the servers, carrying trays of food to set on the table. I should have known—Lissa, Gavin, Lendill and Norian had come.

"Nefrigar told us," Lendill pulled me down beside him. "We need a report, breah-mul. I know this may be hard, but we need it anyway. And if you want, Norian and I can send someone to talk with you."

"Q'and Ribalo? No thank you," I snapped. He was currently on tap for ASD agents and I didn't like it. Or him.

"Reah, we need the report. Ildevar is asking for it," Norian said.

"Then I'll do it, but only because Ildevar wants it," I said.

"Come home with me," Lendill begged softly when the meal was nearly over. Fes and I had sat down and eaten with Lendill and the others. Fes silently raised his glass to me halfway through—the food was excellent.

"I'm not ready for that," I said. "I'll get the report filed. When are you planning to do something with your prisoners?"

"In two days. Ildevar and four members of the Grand Alliance Council want to be there. As does Teeg. We want this finalized," Norian made the reply.

"Leave Zendeval and Perdil," I said. "I want to talk to them first."

"Then we'll do that. For you," Lendill agreed. "Come at two bells. That will give you some time before Ildevar comes in at three."

"Do you want me to come with you?" Fes was worried.

"No, Uncle. It's bad enough that I have to see them again," I said. "These people are terrible."

"You will not repeat anything about any of them," Gavin laid compulsion. Fes wouldn't have said anything anyway, but he nodded his understanding.

"Reah, do you want to spend the night with mother and me?" Fes asked after our guests left.

"No. Tell Farla thank you, but I need some time alone," I patted Fes' arm. "Do you want me to skip you home so you don't have to drive or take the bus?"

"That would be nice," Fes smiled. He didn't get skipped much, but he seemed to enjoy going from one place to another almost instantly. I skipped him home, gave him a peck on the cheek and waited for him to go inside the massive Desh complex before skipping to my own rather large and mostly empty home nearby.

"Reah, at least let me put my hands on our child." Teeg was waiting in the kitchen, somewhat impatiently. I didn't understand why he didn't join the others at dinner, but soon learned why that was. "We've been clobbered with frantic calls and angry messages," he said, rubbing his forehead. I knew he had a headache and sent a message to Nefrigar. My Larentii showed up immediately and removed Teeg's headache. At least he felt better afterward.

"Now, about the baby," Teeg said as soon as Nefrigar left us alone. Someone had told him—likely it was Lendill.

"Teeg, I didn't know I was pregnant until after I was bitten. Teeki and Neeki told me, when it was too late. Do you think I'd have let anyone put his hands on me if I'd known? Do you?" I had a headache, now. There was no way to tell what Zendeval's bite might have done to the baby, if Teeki and Neeki hadn't shielded it. Somehow, I had the idea that the baby might have been lost due to the ensuing illness. I intentionally didn't mention the fever and sickness I'd endured to Teeg.

"Reah, that's not why I'm here, and I would never blame you for that," Teeg grumbled. "So many things have happened while you were gone. Ry fought off a coup to keep his throne and Lendill was named Kaldill's heir. After removing Naldill's power, of course, since he was offended by Kaldill's choice. I hear Naldill and Reldill are missing from Gaelar N'Seith, now. That can't be good for Lendill. And that doesn't even touch what happened in both Alliances while we worked to restore power after the blackout."

"My troubles are insignificant to you?"

"Reah, we didn't know where you were."

"Did you send mindspeech?"

"No. We shouldn't have to."

"Get out, Teeg," I said as pleasantly as I could. "We'll talk about the baby some other time. I'm assured by Nefrigar that he's fine. Go home. Deal with all those things that are more important. Go on." I made shooing motions with my hands. Teeg, unsure what to do at that moment, folded away. I stared at the space he'd occupied for several minutes before I broke down and wept, dropping to the floor.

Was I expecting sympathy? I should have known better. All my mates likely knew where I was and none were there for me. Were they likely to be soiled by me after I'd been bitten by a monster? I had no idea what ran through their minds. I only knew that Nefrigar was the only one who'd offered support of any kind. He'd come if I asked, but I shouldn't have to ask. I shouldn't.

# CHAPTER 14

Two days later, I skipped to Le-Ath Veronis. Lissa was waiting for me inside her private study, Gavin and Flavio with her. I nodded and said hello to both of them. We walked down steep steps to the dungeons later, arriving at the part set aside for high-profile prisoners. Only certain members of the Palace Guard visited that section; it was off-limits to everyone else. I'm sure a large amount of compulsion surrounded it as well.

Drake, Drew and a handful of others were there, waiting for us. Lissa's twin Falchani mates were guarding Dantel and Darletta Schuul. I felt sorry for the twins immediately. Darletta's mouth was in a pout as she stared at Drake and Drew, hoping, I'm sure, to lure both handsome Falchani into granting her favors or other things. Neither were swayed by anything she had to offer. Dantel Schuul was shouting, occasionally gripping the bars inside Lissa's prison and threatening all of us with legal action when we walked in.

Gescht Prekisule was sullen, sitting on the small bed inside his cell and glaring in Dantel Schuul's direction often. Matiss Meldrim held his head in his hands and moaned. Faldin's bewildered expression let everyone know that he had no idea what had hit him. Several empty cells lay between Faldin's and the last two, which held Zendeval Rjjn and Perdil the Dwarf. They were the ones I'd come to question, as soon as I felt up to it. Not only were Drake and Drew in Queen Lissa's dungeon, but Tony, Rigo, Aryn and several other vampires were also present.

Dantel Schuul, who had no idea what sort of danger he was in, elected to shout at everyone as if that would solve his current dilemma. I was waiting for Lendill and Norian to arrive so they could witness anything I said or was said to me. Other visitors would arrive after that. At least that's what Lendill told me. I'd asked Lendill to bring Teeg with him, too. He and I were about to have a short chat.

"We're here, breah-mul," Lendill wanted to put an arm around me. I flung it away. No mate was welcome near me at the moment. "Reah?" Surely, he knew better than to turn that hurt look upon me.

"So, tell me what you are," I snapped at Zendeval Rjjn when I walked up to his cage.

"I will answer that for you," Kifirin appeared at my side. "He is the last of his kind now, since you killed his cousin and the others."

"Kifirin, state your business and leave," I said, turning to the god of the Dark Realm.

"Kifirin? Did you say Kifirin?" Zendeval was at the bars of his cage, and if there was such an emotion as crushed hope, he wore it.

"Yeah. Kifirin. The god of the Dark Realm and all that," I waved a hand loftily in mock grandeur. I didn't add that in my mind he was the god of everything that was wrong with my life.

"Where were you?" Zendeval slid to his knees. "My father asked and asked, but you never heard."

"I answered, you were just too deaf to hear," Kifirin blew smoke. "Every woman who became ill when they were bitten would have borne children to that particular Greater Demon. Yet you and your kind sold them. All of them."

"What?" Zendeval didn't understand. I was now staring at Kifirin in shock. He'd called Zendeval a Greater Demon. He was right, too, about the claiming. A claiming always made the female High Demon ill. For days. I'd been ill for days after Zendeval attacked me. I wanted to slap Kifirin.

"Reah became ill," Zendeval whispered.

"Reah is High Demon. Among that race, there are only seventeen females. Females have never been plentiful among the immortal Dark races. Did your father never tell you that? And yes, Reah could have borne your children. You might have convinced her, if you'd treated her better."

"My father only said that the females of our kind must be protected." Zendeval hung his head.

"The females who would have accepted your seed deserved your protection, too. How were they treated, son of the last Greater Demon King?"

"You already know the answer to that."

"I do."

"Reah?" Zendeval raised his eyes to me.

"You'll never touch me again," I said. "And thanks to you, none of my other mates might touch me either." I turned to Perdil's cell. Just as always, he was watching and listening. "What did you hope to gain out of all this?" I asked him.

"I? I wanted what all my kind wants. Wealth and power." Perdil's voice was a growl as he turned away from my steady gaze.

"Somehow, I don't believe that. But I'm past caring, I think."

"Reah, what is going on?" Teeg had come to stand behind me. Tory and Ry were right behind him. Lendill was watching me closely after I'd rebuffed him.

"She's pregnant with your child, according to those who would know," Lendill announced. "And dangerously ill after that filth bit her." He jerked his head in Zendeval's direction. I wanted to hit him for that. This was neither the time nor the place for that announcement. Now Zendeval and Perdil knew. I didn't want them to know. Didn't wish for them to have that knowledge—of how badly they'd hurt me. If it hadn't been for Teeki and Neeki, it was likely that Teeg's child would now be just a memory.

"Shut up," I hissed at Lendill.

"Reah, how ill were you? Are you sure the baby is all right? I want Karzac to do a full examination." Teeg cursed. At Zendeval Rjjn. At me. At Dantel Schuul and everyone else there, his eyes red. I was surprised we weren't getting the full blast of fangs, eyes and compulsion.

"Teeg, don't get self-righteous with me. This is all your fault."

"I had nothing to do with this," he hissed. Fangs were likely to pop out next, unless I missed my guess.

"Come here." I hauled him by the arm toward the other cells. "Tell me you don't recognize him," I jerked Teeg around to face Faldin Bierla.

One sniff told Teeg what he wanted to know. His nose was just as good as his mother's, I think. "Prin Ralnik?" Teeg was staring at Faldin.

"It took a while to figure it out, but you had to get that chip from somewhere, didn't you?" I poked Teeg in the chest. "The one to keep me from skipping or sending mindspeech. Only your little helper here took it a few steps further, and then sold the technology to Dantel Schuul. Your technology, Teeg, made it possible for the pirates to operate across both Alliances. Allowed the Schuuls and their partners to rape, kill, and sell into slavery anyone they wanted. They were well on their way to controlling everything. And it's your fault."

Teeg stood as if thunderstruck. "I didn't know the compulsion didn't work."

"Too bad, Teeg. It didn't. Forget about taking me to Campiaa while I'm pregnant. I won't go." I stalked away from him.

"I want to kill you, you little fucker," Teeg reached in to haul Faldin against the bars of his cell. "I hired you. Paid you well and handed over the schematics. And then thought I'd placed compulsion well enough that this would never see the light of day again. And what do you do with it?" Faldin gazed helplessly into eyes so deep a red they were almost black. I watched as wetness stained Faldin's trousers. I walked over to him after Teeg let him go.

"They'd have shot you with one of those things too, you stupid fuck," I hissed at him. "Go ahead. Ask Dantel. Lissa, will you tell Dantel to answer Faldin's questions honestly?" We both listened while Lissa laid compulsion for Dantel and Darletta to only speak the truth.

Faldin's voice quavered as he asked the question. "Would you have done that to me?" He stared at Darletta.

"You stupid little shit, you don't think I'd have kept you for anything other than the technology, do you?" Darletta's voice was sickly sweet. "Face it. You don't have anything in the looks department, and honestly, you're just—tiny."

"And now we learn the technology wasn't even yours," Dantel shouted. "Wait till my lawyers get their hands on you. This is all your fault." Faldin was weeping as soon as Darletta dropped her little bomb, so Dantel's words went unheeded. Dantel was unhinged, in my opinion. He wasn't expecting to ever see the inside of a jail cell. My thought was he wasn't going to see it for much longer. Teeg stepped back from Faldin's cage before turning a look of shock and sadness in my direction. Did he expect sympathy from me? I'd gotten none from him.

"I allowed this," Kifirin sighed, breaking the silence. "Reah, do not penalize Gavril overmuch for this. I allowed it. Made it happen. Should never have interfered in the way I did."

"That name is dead to me," I said. "Gavril was taken when he was seventeen. I haven't seen him since."

"Reah, what do you think should happen to these?" Lissa walked over, Thurlow at her side.

"I don't care."

"I will allow you to execute all of them, if that is your desire." Ildevar Wyyld appeared with four others that I recognized as members of the Grand Alliance Council.

"I don't want anything to do with that." I had to raise my voice; Dantel Schuul and his daughter were shouting their displeasure, now. Mostly that they had lawyers and would bring charges, but that meant nothing to me.

"These five, then, will die tonight," Ildevar said. "Lissa and Willem both say that you can be trusted, little High Demon. If you do not wish to watch because of your pregnancy, I will understand."

"I'll stay." I crossed arms over my chest. I had no idea what Ildevar planned, but I was going to watch. After all, I'd seen at least seventy of

Zendeval Rjjn's race die; they'd burned after coming in contact with my Thifilatha's skin. They'd screamed while they burned, too. After I'd seen them commit mass rape, it was the least they deserved. But then hundreds more—mindless, unsuspecting slaves—had been cremated instantly by my Thifilatha's scales. If for nothing else, Dantel Schuul needed to pay for that.

"Bring out that one first, so the others will see what awaits them," Ildevar pointed at Matiss Meldrim. He was hauled out by Gavin and Tony. He tried to run when they released their hold on him, but he didn't get far. One of the Grand Alliance members turned to Ra'Ak, and in one quick gulp, Matiss Meldrim was history.

Darletta was shrieking by that time and Dantel Schuul was about to swoon. Gescht Prekisule tried to put up a fight, but no mortal is a match for vampire strength. Faldin came after that, his body stiff and uncooperative as he was swallowed swiftly. Then it was Darletta's turn.

"It's too bad we can't give you the misery you've given others before you die," I said as she was led out of her cell. She tried to spit at me, but Kifirin sent an energy blast in her direction, knocking her to the floor. She was eaten quickly.

"Now, you are mine, Dantel Schuul," Ildevar Wyyld said pleasantly. Tory had come for the executions and stood by silently while the others died, including Darletta. He never blinked when Ildevar turned to Ra'Ak as his four companions did and devoured Dantel Schuul. Perdil, from his cell at the end, never said a word, either.

"Now, what shall we do with these two?" Ildevar walked down to Zendeval and Perdil's cages.

"Kifirin, what world did the Greater Demons inhabit?" I asked.

"Nrath," he said. "Only it is deserted, now."

"Good. Send them there. And shield the planet so nobody gets on or off for a thousand years. You owe me that much, I think."

"It will be done as you say, daughter."

"Daughter?" Perdil was interested, now.

"The daughter of my heart, only I abused her, much as her mortal father abused her when she was small," Kifirin sighed. "Did you know she is the mate of Kings? Surely you recognize the founder of the Campiaan Alliance? And the mate who came with her to Stellar Winds? He is the newly-crowned King of Karathia."

"And she is mated to me." Nefrigar appeared at my side. "My little one is feeling queasy. Make your statements quickly so I may attend to this matter."

"We harmed a Larentii's mate," Perdil sighed. "We would never have gotten away with that, would we?" He turned to Zendeval, who was staring at me.

"If I had my say, you'd be dead with the others," Teeg growled at Zendeval. Perdil only then realized he was talking to a vampire.

"Oh, I'd kill you, too, and not in any nice way," Lendill agreed. "I had cameras on Reah's skin, you bastard," he pointed at Zendeval. "I saw what you did to her. You were lucky, you know. Reah could have torn both of you apart. I begged her not to, so we could get the others and find their base of operation. That was before I learned she was pregnant. If I'd known that then, I'd have come to kill you myself."

"You were pregnant during moonrush." Zendeval heaved a weary sigh.

"I may still kill you, if Kifirin doesn't get you away from here soon." Ry appeared in a flash of light. He looked the part of a King. He was dressed so finely, I couldn't help but be proud of him.

"Reah, I am sorry," Zendeval sighed. "I know it is far too late to say it, but it is truth. If I had known—so many things. Yet I did not. I realize I was controlled, but I had a bit of will. I should have acted differently. Should have worked harder to do so. Never forget what I told you there at the last on Stellar Winds. It is the truth. Will always be the truth. You have no fond memories of me, but I have them of you." Zendeval turned away from me.

"I was willing to spend everything I had for you," Perdil muttered. "To save you from Dantel Schuul."

"Perdil, that does not absolve you," I said.

"I know."

"Reah, come," Nefrigar lifted me and folded away.

~

"This is Nrath. As you see, you will have to make your own way, Demon." Kifirin swept an arm out. They'd landed in a clearing, with trees surrounding them and mountains in the distance. It was nearing twilight, Zendeval saw.

"You thought to have the one you'd seen—the one who destroyed your cousins and left the throne to you, didn't you?" Kifirin stared at Perdil. "Only you intended to control her, like the others. Know you that Reah's request is the only reason you live now, Dwarf," Kifirin blew smoke as he stared at Perdil. "Lissa is the one you had your eye on. I saw you watching her in the dungeons. She is my mate, and I would have separated your atoms and you would never have been reborn had you attempted to take her." Kifirin disappeared.

"Now what?" Perdil sighed as he looked up at Zen.

"Do you know how to hunt?" Zen asked, staring at open fields and forest in the distance.

"No."

"Then you'd best learn, I think."

~

"Where do you think Nefrigar took her?" Tory asked.

"He can bend time; it could be anywhere and anywhen," Gavril grumbled. "And why wasn't I told about the illness? About how much danger my child was in?"

"I could say nearly the same thing," Tory grumbled. "I have six daughters, and none of them know me. I have no idea how they were raised or what their lives have been like these past years."

"I think a lot of flowers and some well thought-out gifts, along with kneeling and groveling are in order for Reah," Ry said, accepting a dish of ice cream from a Niff's employee. "And Reah knows how to make gishi fruit ice cream. If she wants to make a fortune, that's the way to do it, I think."

"You'll inherit all of Schuul Enterprises; the courts will make that decision when they learn you were controlled all that time," Thurlow appeared suddenly behind the brothers and placed his order at the counter. Gavril got his dish of ice cream, as did Tory.

"Really? What should I do with Stellar Winds?"

"You'd better sell it. I don't think Reah will be happy if you keep it."

"Yeah. Probably true."

~

"I wanted to see you," Ry held me against him, hard, making it difficult to tell him that I'd missed him. He'd sent mindspeech two days after Nefrigar took me away from the dungeons on Le-Ath Veronis. I'd met Ry at his palace on Karathia. It was pleasant to think that—Ry's palace. "We have almost everybody on board and convinced," he grinned as he held me away from him.

"Of course diplomacy, coupled with the most incredible power Karathia has ever seen hasn't hurt much either," Erland appeared at our side. "Reah, how are you? And this little bump here?" He patted my belly.

"The little bump is fine according to the Larentii. Nefrigar took me to Dee's last night. Fes sent someone over there to cook until I can find someone else. Thanks for sending Ilvan and Radolf on their way."

"We put the money they still had into the account for the restaurant," Erland said. "And made sure all the taxes and such had been paid. It's there if you need it." I thanked Erland again for the time and trouble he'd gone to just to do that for me.

"It was no problem," Erland assured me with a smile.

"Reah, Tory wants to talk to you," Ry pulled me into his arms again. "We all know why he had holes in his memory and stayed away for twenty-five years. Sweetheart, tell me you won't hold that against him."

"I'm trying to come to terms with it, but you can't turn off twenty-five years of feelings, Ry. I felt betrayed and abandoned. Tell me what I should do about it? And my daughters? They don't even know him."

"He knows that. Do you think he's not being tortured over it?

Reah, Tory wasn't the only one to ignore you all that time. Or treat you badly."

"I know." I stepped away from him and rubbed the ache between my eyes. I had no idea why my mates had ignored me and my circumstances all that time. My life was in upheaval, and it was all I could do to hold onto my sanity at the moment. I was trying—really hard—for Ry's sake. He'd always been the same with me, throughout those years. I couldn't fault him as I could the others.

"I was going to have lunch with Mom and Dad," Ry said, nodding toward Erland. "I think we can leave Karathia long enough for lunch. Come with me, baby."

"All right." Ry took my hand, gave me a dazzling smile and folded me to Le-Ath Veronis.

More people were there for lunch than Mom and Dad, I discovered. Tables were set out in Lissa's solarium on the light half of the planet. Tory was talking to Teeg next to a clump of potted palms. Farzi and Nenzi had come with Teeg. Astralan and Stellan were there to guard Teeg—as usual. Lendill folded in with Norian. Both went straight to Lissa, who was speaking with Amara. Somehow, Amara had been invited. I was shocked when Aurelius and Lok folded in from somewhere. I hadn't seen either of them for months. They went to talk with Teeg and Tory. Was I invisible? It seemed that way.

"I'm leaving," I told Ry, who still stood beside me.

"No, baby, stay with me," he pulled me against his side and lifted my hand to kiss it. "We have to plan our wedding sometime soon, sweetheart. I hear that my great-great-grandmother's crown is inside the treasury, waiting for you."

"Are you sure that's what you want?" I gazed up at him. He was such a beautiful man.

"More than anything. Reah, you will be the Queen Karathia deserves."

"Did you forget that you promised to come visit when you finished with your assignment?" Kaldill Schaff stood before me, a glass of wine in his hand. I wished I could have wine right then. None of my other mates had come to speak with me.

"The meal is ready," Cheedas walked in. Well, he'd been Lissa's cook before he was made vampire. It seemed he'd taken his old job back. Ry had informed me that Ilvan and Radolf were currently on Surnath, looking for work. I hoped they were happy, now. I was happy they were far away, to be honest. Ry pulled me toward the table and I was seated between him and Erland.

"Fruit juice," Ry grinned and handed the glass to me. *You know I'd be getting drunk right now if I could*, I sent to him, making him smile. *Stay with me, baby*, he replied.

"Sorry we're late," Ildevar Wyyld appeared with Willem Drifft. They took seats at the head of the table near Lissa, Gavin, Garde and several other mates. Teeg sat next to his father, Gavin, while Tory sat next to Garde. I had no parents at the table. Somehow, that felt like a blow.

Edan recognized me as his daughter, but he was always doing work somewhere, providing free medical assistance where it was most needed. I shouldn't feel envious of that, but I did. And my grandfather? Most of the time I had no idea where he was, either working as liaison for both Alliances or spending time with his wife, who was also my biological grandmother. I watched Lok, Lendill and Aurelius; they sat together on the opposite side of the table. Lok and Aurelius hadn't even bothered to let me know their assignments were over.

"Food may be served now." Kifirin appeared and sat at the end of the table opposite Lissa. He was the self-proclaimed King of Le-Ath Veronis, although he didn't show up often, according to Teeg and the others. I'd seen too much of him, in my opinion. And every time I saw him, it brought something new and nasty in my direction. Delicate bowls of soup were served by a bevy of servants. I fumed a little and felt queasy at the same time. I wasn't sure I could eat without losing whatever I'd eaten quickly.

"I'd like to propose a toast," Willem stood and raised his glass at the table. All eyes were on him, now. "I want to toast Reah, for throwing most of the known universes into total chaos," he said, holding his glass toward me. If he wanted to embarrass me, he'd succeeded. I'm sure many crimes were committed during the blackout. I just hadn't known what else to do to stop the Schuuls and their partners from controlling everything. And I wanted to skip away in the worst way possible. Is that why I was there? So people could point out the many flaws in my hastily formed plan? Ry gripped my fingers under the table.

"I'm not done, Reah," Willem went on. "If you hadn't done exactly what you did, we'd all be under the yoke of a few people who had nothing less on their minds than complete domination of everything. The worlds would have died, Reah. Just as another world with the same technology died long ago. The controllers could command war and anger. They could not control love. Their numbers became smaller and smaller, and the population became angrier and angrier until they killed each other or themselves. A day or three of chaos is worth the resulting command over our lives again. I honor you, Reah. You kept the Alliances alive, although you suffered to make it so. To Reah," he drank from his glass. Everyone else at the table did so as well. I wished the floor would open up and swallow me.

"I also have an announcement," Ildevar stood when Willem sat down. "I have approval from the Grand Alliance Council, and it has been duly recorded in the Alliance records that Thiskil now is the sole property of Reah Desh Nilvas. Thiskil has been granted membership in the Reth Alliance and is currently a member in good standing, with taxes paid for the next one hundred turns. Reah's name has been written in the records as Queen of Thiskil, and she may allot citizenship as she sees fit." Ildevar gave me a glowing smile. It wasn't anything close to what Ry could do but I gaped anyway.

"Uh, thank you," I said as politely as I could. Great. I was Queen of a nearly dead planet. I'd seen it myself not that long ago. Perhaps five years or so. It took a long while for a planet to come back from the dead, it seems. And I didn't have sufficient funds to do anything to said planet, even if there was anything there to work with. Ildevar took his seat.

"And I have a confession to make," Kifirin stood.

"And I wish to hear it," another being appeared, clothed in light so bright it hurt my eyes. I blinked as he dampened the light, appearing humanoid although he still glowed. "Go ahead, child, tell them. I am waiting."

"Of course, Father," Kifirin bowed respectfully to the other. I blinked again. Kifirin had a parent? Where had he been all this time? "I made a promise long ago that I wouldn't interfere with the Dark Realm," Kifirin sighed. "Only I have broken that promise time and again during Reah's lifetime. Mostly I meddled with her life only, but the promise was broken. So many things I did not intend occurred while I slept for many thousands of years. And, in an effort to bring those things back in line with the master plan without direct interference, I placed the burden upon one. She came through for me every time, although she should have walked away long ago. The daughter of my heart flung a few insults in my direction from time to time, but it was much less than I deserved. She then went to perform the duties I needed her to perform anyway, and never asked anything from me in exchange. But that is not the announcement I wished to make. I meddled in the worst way possible with her life, to get everything I wanted from her. I made her pregnant twice, without the benefit of lying with her mate. I did this to keep a promise I made to another. And then I did the worst thing of all." Kifirin hung his head.

"Tell her. She deserves to know," Kifirin's parent coaxed softly.

"I arranged to hand Reah's daughters to Jayd and Glinda, so they might save the High Demon race. I also muted the love and affection in all her mates," Kifirin muttered, "to keep her on Kifirin. I kept them away from her as much as I could. Made it seem as if that were the proper thing to do and the right way to treat her. I came today to take it back." Kifirin lifted dark eyes to me, and they were filled with stars. "I cannot control your fate from now on, little one. My precious one. You are taken away from me. I have been forbidden from interfering with you from this point forward. You will only speak with me if you desire it." Light formed around Kifirin then and blew outward toward all of us seated at the table.

"Thanks," I said, as every one of my mates now stared at me in shock, as if they were seeing me for the first time in a very long time.

As I suppose they were. "I'm leaving now." I skipped away as Ry reached out to stop me.

～

Gishi trees lined the dark soil on either side of a long row as I walked toward the small house I'd lived in for more than twenty years. Many of my things were still there—small things. Little gifts from my daughters when they were young, a few bits and pieces of jewelry and all my rings from my mates had been left behind when I'd gone on assignment.

I wasn't sure any of those rings would be worn after today, but that remained to be seen. I walked through the back door into the cooler interior of the house, getting quite a shock. A strange woman stood at the kitchen sink, preparing a meal with my dishes and tools. Those were the things I hadn't skimped on. They were the best I could afford, especially the knives. This one was using a filleting knife to slice gishi fruit.

"Can I help you?" she asked, not sounding friendly.

"I came to get my things," I said.

"What things? This house came furnished. Everything in it is mine to use."

"What about my clothing and jewelry?" A curl of smoke escaped my nostrils.

"The clothing and the rest of the junk is out on the trash heap," she pointed the knife at me. "I found no jewelry."

"There was jewelry here. Did Garde take it?" I knew she was lying; I just wasn't prepared to point it out yet.

"I have no idea who Garde is. I suggest you take this up with his majesty, King Jayd. There's nothing here that belongs to you."

"I bought that knife you're using," I nodded toward it. "It's a fine-edged filleting knife. It wasn't meant to be used to cut fruit. Where's the trash heap?"

"On the west side, over by the piles of trimmed brush. My husband is in charge of these groves, now, I'll have you know. He'll throw you out of here when he comes in for lunch."

"Your husband can try to throw me out," I snapped at her before skipping away.

~

They'd burned my things. Clothing, little gifts, everything they hadn't wanted or thought was valuable. Most of it was ash, lying in a heap beyond the cottage. I brushed tears away as I stared at the smoldering pile. Hunching my shoulders, I struggled to hold tears back before skipping to the palace in Veshtul. Jayd and Glinda were there, having lunch with my four oldest daughters and their husbands. I stood and gaped at them for several moments before the first sob came.

"Did Garde wait five minutes before he tossed out my things and gave away my jewelry?" I wept. "I found a woman using my knives in the kitchen and she said my rings weren't there when she moved in. She took them; she was lying to me. You took my daughters, didn't you? What else are you going to take from me?" My body shivered so hard it was difficult to remain standing.

Jayd was on his feet, now, a worried frown on his face. "Reah, we'll get them back," he said.

"And all the things my girls gave to me when they were small are in a trash heap and burned, Jayd. Can you give that back, too?" I couldn't stop the sobs. Raedah stood up, then.

"Mom? Are you all right?" I skipped away before I could hear any more lies.

~

"What the fuck just happened?" Jayd shouted inside his study. Lunch with his great-nieces had been interrupted in the worst way possible. Now, he had no way of finding Reah. He'd sent mindspeech to Garde the moment Reah had skipped away. Kifirin, Lissa and all of Reah's mates, except for Nefrigar, had come, many of them angry and willing to shout at just about anyone. Reah's daughters were all concerned, now. They'd seen their mother break down before their eyes.

"She said the woman lied about her rings," Glinda said. "And threw all her other belongings out that she didn't take. Garde, what did you do? What did you tell that woman when she moved in?"

"I told them the house was furnished," Garde muttered, flopping onto a chair beside Jayd's desk. "I didn't think about the things Reah left behind. Assumed there wasn't anything important there."

"You thick-brained lummox." Aurelius' eyes were red and his fangs were out. "We were forced to ignore her for twenty-five years by that dark bastard over there, and you give away all she had left of us? Do you know what those rings are worth? Do you? Gavril's is Tiralian crystal, you idiot. It's worth millions, by itself."

"If poison work against High Demons, we would bite," Farzi declared. He and Nenzi were very close to becoming lion snakes.

"I said I wasn't thinking," Garde snapped. "We'll get her things back."

"Only if you can bend time on some of them, brother," Jayd said. "And where is Reah?"

"I think you should all come, but be very quiet and not make sudden movements." Nefrigar appeared and he looked frightened. Larentii never looked frightened. He folded all of them to the Southern Continent.

"No," Garde whispered and began to walk forward. Aurelius gripped his shoulder and jerked the High Demon back. *Stay still,* Aurelius' voice hissed in Garde's mind. Reah was weeping, standing on the edge of Baetrah. If a High Demon wished to end their lives, they leapt into the fiery heart of the volcano while humanoid. It was the only way, unless they were overpowered and killed by another.

"I told you she was near the breaking point," Dee said softly to Gavril, who stood, petrified, by Dee's side. "I'm sure the attack and everything else during the assignment didn't improve matters any."

"Dee, she can't kill the baby," Gavril wiped his cheek. It was wet, somehow.

"Is that all you care about?" Dee turned dark eyes on his adopted son.

"No. God, no."

"Lara'Kayan?" Nefrigar held out his hand to Reah.

Nefrigar had come. I could barely see him through my tears and the sobs wouldn't stop. I couldn't stop them, somehow. Something was broken and I didn't know how to fix it. The blow had come, as it does in any fight, when you can't take the beating any longer and you fall to your knees, beaten and uncaring what happens to you after that. Glinda and Jayd had my daughters. Had them all along. I'd only been allowed to pretend I was their mother. Now, there wasn't any evidence that I'd even existed in their lives.

"Little one?" Nefrigar held out a large blue hand to me. I stared at it for moments. If I took it, it meant more pain. More betrayal. More people taking what was mine.

"Reah, no, child." Kifirin was there, too, and weeping.

"You said I didn't have to talk to you unless I wanted it."

"My father pointed out that I shouldn't make promises I cannot keep." His tears sizzled as they hit the dry and crusty earth on Baetrah's western edge. It was the one with the cliff hanging directly above the caldera. The heat from below was drying my tears almost as quickly as I wept them.

"Go away," I said, turning to look into Baetrah's flaming depths again.

"Reah, it wasn't meant to be like this. You have to believe me," Kifirin begged.

"I can't believe anything you say, Kifirin. Can I?" I wasn't even looking at him. The fire below was giving a promise of its own. Of peace and no pain.

"Reah, I only placed Baetrah here for those who'd lived so long they couldn't remember their births and life no longer held interest. Come back to me, little one, and things will be made better."

"How? You can't do it, Kifirin. It isn't within your power to fix this. My daughters were stolen from me long ago. They're Jayd and Glinda's, didn't you know? You took my mates away, you said so yourself. I don't have anything left. My own mate and uncle stole from me. Garde gave away all the sentimental things I had and a Greater Demon violated the sacredness of the act of love. Tell me what I have left now, Kifirin. What do I have left that you will likely take from me in the future?"

"Little one, come away." Nefrigar was still there, only now he stood between Kifirin and me. I blinked at him. He'd been the only one who'd come to visit, no matter what. "My love," he said, "think of the child, if not of yourself. Come away, little one. Take my hand, and I promise enough peace for you until these things might be dealt with. None of these are worth your life. Take my hand, love." He was closer, now. I gazed into the caldera. And then turned back to Nefrigar, who was now close enough to touch. "Take my hand, Reah. I will help you make this right. For you, as well as Garwin Wyatt."

"Garwin Wyatt?"

"Yes. That will be his name, if you take my hand."

"This is Wyatt, back again?" I looked up at Nefrigar's beautiful, blue face. Only now, it held worry and pain.

"Yes, love. He will live again, if you choose to live again. Will you give your hand to me, Lara'Kayan?"

"Lara'Kayan?"

"It is Forever Love in Neaborian. There will be no other for me, Reah. You are all I have." Two more tears fell and Nefrigar caught them with his fingers. "Come, little one. Come away from this death. It is not for you or for Wyatt." Another sob came, and another, before I reached my arms up to Nefrigar. He pulled me against him so quickly even I failed to see it, and folded us away.

The End